Praise for *Women Are Like Chickens:*
All E...

"Reading *Women* ... watering plate ... guacamole, salsa ... albondiga soup, ... novel's heart is a Mexican restaurant in the Mission Barrio of San Francisco. Around the café revolve four young women, whom I found to be some of the most interesting, well-drawn characters in contemporary Chicana literature. This rite of passage story explores the lives of these women as each grows into young womanhood. I recommend it highly. I am sure it will garner many awards. It shines."

—Rudolfo Anaya, author, *Bless Me, Ultima*

"Annette Sandoval's wise and whimsical novel is the tale of two sisters, their family restaurant, and their circle of friends, set largely in San Francisco's traditionally Latino Mission district. Latino readers will immediately respond to her artfully drawn portraits of familiar characters, not to mention her mouth-watering descriptions of foods we all love, but her story of female friendship and empowerment strikes universal chords that will resonate with all readers. I hope her delightful book finds the wide and appreciative audience it deserves."

—Michael Nava, author of *The City of Palaces*

"The yarn Sandoval spins of their lives…would make an HBO show-runner proud. Death, love, and food are never too far from each other; episodes of powerful yearning, comical justice, and occasional violence replace each other at a cinematic pace. At the center of the novel are three friends. Alejandra Cernuda inherits the family restaurant very suddenly in chapter three, and must support the dedicated but somewhat cloistered crew that works there, in addition to keeping the business afloat. She is all of sixteen. Her sister Leah, fifteen, is yet to discover her secret talents (I won't spoil it for you). Their friends Dulce and Tessa will defy expectations by attending Stanford and back-packing across Southeast Asia respectively. The sheer number of things women accomplish in the novel's 327 pages—writing books, solving mysteries, rescuing babies, rescuing each other, falling in and out of love, and, finally, accepting posthumous donations of other people's tattooed skins—is head-spinning. The plot lines are fresh, inventive, and cohere into a satisfying resolution."

—*Compulsive Reader*

Women Are Like Chickens: All Eggs, Breast and Thighs

Annette Sandoval

Harvard Square Editions
New York
2019

Women Are Like Chickens: All Eggs, Breast and Thighs
by Annette Sandoval

ISBN 978-1-941861-65-3
Printed in the United States of America

Published in the United States by
Harvard Square Editions
www.harvardsquareeditions.org

*This book is a work of fiction. References to real
people, events, establishments, organizations, or
locales are intended only to provide a sense
of authenticity, and are used fictitiously. All other
characters, and all incidents and dialogue, are
drawn from the author's imagination and are not to
be construed as real.*

Dedication

This book is dedicated to Linda Romine and Ric Gagliardi. With friends like you we'll need bail money. ;)

❧

For my sister Martha Alicia Sandoval for shaping some of the characters in this novel.

❧

For Philip 'Pip' Thorson. Thank you for bringing Moose into my life. And laughter.

❧

For all of the publishers who did not feel this novel was a good fit for their list, and the literary agents who thought the market was too narrow for representation. Here's me waving at you!

❧

Para mis comadres: Tía Pachita, Tía Teresita, Tía Irene, Tía Clara y Tía (Nina) Tecla. For teaching me to hear with my eyes.

"True friends stab you in the front."
-Oscar Wilde

PART 1

Chapter 1
MR. CERNUDA DECIDES TO KILL HIMSELF

MR. CARLOS CERNUDA DECIDED to end his own life during a rerun of *I Love Lucy*. He was sitting next to his wife on the living room's plastic slipcovered couch. Their two teenage daughters watched TV from the recently raked shag carpet. One of the girls would occasionally get up to adjust the reception by rotating the coat hanger antenna.

With the not-so-agonizing decision finally made, he tuned back into the show. It was the episode where Lucy places a bet with Ricky. She was going to keep from buying a hat for longer than he could keep from losing his temper. Mr. Cernuda caught himself before he said aloud, "Why a hat? A Cohiba cigar I could understand, but a *pinche* hat?"

As if picking up the vibrations of the question through her jaw, Mrs. Cernuda nodded once. "I *hate* Lucy." Her tone was so full of loathing that Mr. Cernuda resisted the urge to gape at his wife. The daughters knew better than to look back at their mother. In the wilderness they called home, eye contact was an act of aggression.

Mrs. Cernuda spoke again. In his periphery vision, she looked just like a beanbag with a russet potato for a head. "Lucy is so spoiled. She can't cook and never bothers to clean their apartment. She's always spending her husband's money and doing things she shouldn't be doing behind his back. Now what kind of a wife is that?"

Mr. Cernuda was thinking how familiar that sounded when the potato spoke again. "And what kind of a name is 'Ricky Ricardo' anyway? Did his parents really name him 'Ricardo Ricardo?' You see. That's what happens when *los otros* write about us. They always get it all wrong!"

Alejandra cautiously spoke to the *chancla* dangling from her mother's big toe, aware that she could wield the house sandal with the precision of a ninja throwing star. "Enrique. His name is Enrique Ricardo. Not Ricardo Ricardo."

"Oh." Annoyed by the correction, Mrs. Cernuda sunk deeper into the cushions, causing the plastic slipcovers to pass synthetic wind. "Poor Ricky. If he married a good Mexican woman instead of that...he would have been much better off."

Alejandra drew in a deep breath before saying through clenched teeth, "He's Cuban, Mother." She braced for the flying *chancla*.

"I know that," Mrs. Cernuda said, offended by her eldest daughter's oppositional tone. "He's Catholic and he speaks Spanish. If that's good enough for God, it's good enough for me."

On the screen, Enrique bent Lucy over his knee and started to spank her. Mrs. Cernuda perked up. "Harder! Hit her harder!"

Mr. Cernuda watched as his spouse cheered on the domestic abuser. He felt his earlier fatigue return as his vision blurred with tears. This was too awful. Then, at the end of the day, this. As he listened to the laugh track he wondered how many members of the audience were dead.

The newly conceived plan to skip out on the rest of his life filled Mr. Cernuda with giddy laughter. But logistics tugged him back to where his soul hid. How am I going to do it? It should look like an accident.

Mr. Cernuda suddenly became serene as an idea formed. I own a restaurant. Accidents are always happening there.

Chapter 2

MRS. CERNUDA MOVES AWAY

AFTER MR. CERNUDA'S UNEXPECTED DEATH, most of the regular customers stopped patronizing Cacahuates Restaurante. It was not that the people of the Mission District didn't feel sad for the Cernuda women, now without a husband and a father. It was just that everyone knew his widow was running the restaurant, and no one wanted to spend *good* money on a bad meal.

On the Monday after the funeral, Mrs. Cernuda buttoned the top button of the lightweight black *suéter* she wore over her simple black polyester-blend dress. She paused to stare at herself in the full-length mirror. Her lifelong fear of living without the assurance of a man—first her father and then her husband—had come to pass. Why women crave total emancipation was beyond her.

Sighing, she picked up her husband's hefty ring of keys, which now reminded her of the ring jailers carried. With the prison image in mind, she lumbered down the backstairs for her first shift as *la jefa*. With the girls at school, Mrs. Cernuda decided to linger around the kitchen until she received condolences from all of the arriving employees. Gathering up her courage, and a couple of *concha* pastries, she headed to her husband's closet-sized office to start working. When she saw the mound of phone messages, stacks of invoices and mail on the tiny desk, she was instantly overwhelmed.

Mrs. Cernuda cried hoarse, wracking sobs as she trudged up the back stairs to her apartment. She spent the next several days in bed. She only got up to go to the bathroom or to switch channels back and forth between the two Spanish stations on UHF.

The employees were sympathetic. They brought her meals up on trays and took the dirty dishes away. If she did not feel like 'real food,' they ordered whatever she wanted, usually sweet and sour pork from the Chinese takeout near the Civic Center. But they stopped being nice to her when she couldn't bring herself to figure out how to do payroll. Most got jobs at rival restaurants and left without bothering to tell her.

When Quico, the cook and one of the few remaining loyalists, tentatively mentioned that the perishables were threatening to go bad, she snapped like a wishbone. "You see! Even the food is against me!"

Mrs. Cernuda caught the next bus to Watsonville in the Salinas Valley, where she would care for an elderly aunt who did not sent for her. After putting their mother in a cab to the downtown bus depot, the bewildered daughters watched as the taxi vanished behind a corner building. Turning back, they stared at the restaurant's torn awning their father had repaired with duct tape. Leah experienced orphan grief, while Alex savored her first moment of total emancipation.

Chapter 3

ALEX TAKES CHARGE

ALEJANDRA, OR ALEX, age sixteen and Leah, fifteen, stood in the nearly empty dining room of their sinking ship. Lunch rush consisted of a table of National Dollar store employees splitting an order of guacamole and requesting extra bowls of free salsa and tortilla chips.

Leah began to shiver, and Alex gave her a hard look. Her little sister was as thin and dark as their father had been. The linen summer dress she wore, combined with the spirals of black hair coiling to her waist, made Alex think of virgins and volcanoes.

"Why are you shaking like that? It's over 70 degrees in here!" Alex's concern sounded more like a rebuke.

Leah's liquid brown eyes were raw and red with worry. As Alex watched her sister's teeth make white marks on her quivering bottom lip, she awoke from her stupor. This helplessness isn't working, she thought. What the hell are we waiting for? No one is going to show up and pull us out of this mess.

Alex had seen *Gone with the Wind* a bunch of times and thought back to the scene where Scarlett takes charge of Tara—also by default. Alex held up an imaginary fist to the orange glow of the Metro-Goldwyn-Mayer sky. With God as my witness, she thought, I will not be licked, and I will save Cacahuates!

After the customers left, Alex said to her sister, "Come on." At the corner hardware store, Alex bought a thick steel chain and the biggest padlock they carried. Back at the restaurant, Leah held the lock while Alex threaded the chain through the two front door handles. Leah switched the lock from hand to hand, taking pleasure in the cool feel of steel on her warm palms. She was pretending the metal was made of melting Sierra snow beaten solid under the force of a waterfall, when she realized Alex was staring at her.

"You done?" Alex said, snapping her fingers.

Leah's cheeks tinged purple as she handed over the padlock. Alex fastened the hinged shackle through the chain and clamped it shut. She tugged on it twice to ensure it worked. "This will get everyone's attention," she said with a certainty that confused Leah yet somehow made her less afraid. The Cernuda sisters had taken action, no matter how counterintuitive it was to running a business.

Chapter 4
1974
FLASHBACK TO ALEX'S ACTUAL
FIRST DAY AS THE BOSS

THE SERVICE at any family-owned restaurant varies throughout the day, but the absolute worst service occurs between shifts. Hungry customers entering Cacahuates during that nebulous hour separating lunch from dinner are overseen by the day staff preparing to clock out. They are equally shunned by the dinner staff gossiping while setting up.

Twelve-year-old Alex sat at the bar, eating her after-school snack of soup, followed by either a couple of fish tacos, pork *carnitas torta*, or a skirt steak quesadilla. She stopped chewing as she watched yet another hungry customer give up and leave. The loss of business was blatantly obvious to Alex. When she complained to her father, the bartender, he shrugged a what-are-you-gonna-do shrug. He refilled her Pepsi, which was actually a generic cola.

Well, Alex was gonna do something about it. She started doing her homework on the corner stool of the bar, where she could keep an eye on the entrance. As the neglected customers entered the restaurant, a smiling chubby girl in a parochial school uniform approached. With menus in hand, she sat them at the best table by the window, and then stared down the wait staff. A quick game of *piedra, papel, o tijera* (rock, paper, scissors) ensued to see who would wait on the table.

Alex was returning from seating a businessman when she

glanced up at the TV over the bar. It was showing local news, though the sound was off. A picture of Patricia Campbell Hearst, granddaughter of the legendary William Randolph Hearst of "Citizen Kane" infamy, was on the grainy screen. It was the now ubiquitous image where she is wearing a beret and holding an M1 carbine.

Someone seated at the bar said, "The Siamese Liberation Army captured her."

"Why?" Mr. Cernuda said, leaning in a prawn-like posture against the back bar.

"Because they want to destroy the state capitals."

Alex thought, Capitalist state, but said nothing. Correcting adults was just showing off. She knew 'Siamese' wasn't right either, but she could not come up with the actual name.

On her barstool, Alex flipped to the back of her notebook. She started a tally chart to keep track of the customers she seated. As Alex placed the first mark, she thought, Someone has to watch these people. It was the first of many marks.

1978

People may dream of owning a restaurant, but no one dreams of owning a flop. The morning after their mother's exodus to Watsonville, the restaurant's front windows were soaped. A "Grand Reopening Soon!" banner was hung over the dingy awning.

Alex directed the dishwashers to haul away the junk in the attic and all of the restaurant's bulky old furnishings. They complied, but only after select items like the promotional beer posters of busty women in tiny bikinis were taken home. Everything else ended up at Sal's and Will's, Alex's nicknames for the Salvation Army and Goodwill.

When the paint was scraped from the upper windows of the main dining room, the space instantly brightened and felt airy. With the restaurant free from decades of clutter, Alex redecorated sparsely. Palms in rough terra-cotta pots were used to break up the room and create pockets for intimacy. Small sea paintings were hung on freshly whitewashed walls. The effect, as Alex had intended, was of dining at her favorite childhood vacation restaurant by the Sea of Cortes.

The uniforms were next. The puffy white off-the-shoulder Mexican peasant blouses worn by the waitresses were history. But not because they were sexist, like she told everyone. The sight of thick elastic bra straps harnessing honey-brown shoulders ruined the whole effect! Hadn't they ever heard of strapless bras? The uniforms would now be the same for everyone on the floor: black and whites with a pastel tie in the same sea glass colors as the paintings.

As Alex redecorated the restaurant, Quico and Leah concentrated their efforts on expanding the menu. Though standard dishes were retained for traditionalists, regional cuisine from all parts of Mexico were added: savory concoctions like duck with *mole* from Puebla, chicken breast with Cointreau and tequila from Jalisco, and clams with saffron rice from Campeche.

When someone (unhelpfully) mentioned that only one out of ten restaurants would make it to their first anniversary, Alex began to have second thoughts. By mid-summer, she had maxed out both the company and their personal credit cards. Trapped in a gambler's panic and only halfway through the remodeling, she borrowed money from the family's savings account. In order to keep the renovations moving forward, she dipped into it daily.

No longer able to sleep at night, Alex wondered what she had been thinking? Where were all of the overbearing adults when she was making the biggest mistake of her young life? She worried herself sick over the possibility of a failed restaurant and a further splintered family. She pictured herself in some sort of Dickensian debtor's prison, while Leah moved from one set of sadistic foster parents to the next. Her mother would be fine. She had already landed on someone else's feet.

With three weeks left until opening day, a crop of new problems arose. The plumbing, which Alex never thought about since it never gave them any problems, needed to be brought up to code. As soon as the plumbing was up to code, the toilets began backing up. Alex felt like Greek mythology's Sisyphus, condemned to push a boulder up a hill only to watch it roll back down, except for her it was a big turd.

Thank God school was out for the summer, allowing Alex to work around the clock. She was anxious every waking moment, but worrying was never a waste of time for her. Each disturbing thought was invested into a cosmic bank account, which she would later be able to collect upon.

Two weeks before the opening, potential employees didn't show up for interviews, and not a single table was booked. The family's nest egg was not only empty; it now had a $1,000.00 gaping hole through it.

On the day of the restaurant's opening, Alex dressed as if

preparing for the gallows and headed straight for the reservation book. She attempted to create a sense of community by inviting everyone in the Mission District. There were some reservations, but she did not recognize a single name. She swallowed a sob in the back of her throat.

At eleven o'clock Alex flipped the 'Closed' sign to 'Open' She unlocked the foyer door and stared in disbelief at the throng of patrons waiting outside. Not accustomed to making reservations, people in the Mission just showed up, with small children and *abuelitas* in tow. For these same people an RSVP stood for "Remember, Send Valuable Presents" and had nothing to do with responding to the host. At that moment, Alex knew her cosmic investment was paying off big time!

Alex moved through her first day as if in a beautiful lucid dream. The busy kitchen never backed up and the wait staff fizzed with energy and smiles. The unpredictable public did nothing to crush Alex's perfect day. No one sent food back, choked, complained, or demanded to speak to the manager. A parent quickly escorted out every child that went into an ear-piercing meltdown. Some mercifully never returned.

Alex did not know that a press release had been sent to the Bay Area newspapers, along with a sample menu. Many of the reservations in her book on opening day were made by these same food critics. Intrigued by the stellar reviews the 'recycled' restaurant was soon to receive, the place would be packed for weeks in advance.

After the doors closed on opening day, the staff celebrated the restaurant's successful comeback. Around midnight, Alex slipped away to her office. She needed a moment to reflect.

For the first time since her father's passing, Alex

unclenched her muscles and allowed her body to mourn. As music bellowed from the sound system, grief and anxiety gave way to tears of relief. The day's exhaustion was now pulling at her. She placed her arms, and then her forehead, on the desk. She needed to rest her eyes for a second. As her heart rate slowed Alex plummeted into the deepest of dreamless sleeps.

Chapter 5

May 17, 1980

ALEX BLOWS IT

ALEX PUSHED THE SWINGING DOOR with her shoulder and set a zigzag course through the kitchen chaos during the dinner rush. She stopped a safe distance from the cook and the eight-burner stove, where oily sauces splattered from shimmering pans before bursting into confetti flames.

While she waited for Quico to look up, she read the chalkboard used by the employees. Somebody, probably Dulce, had started a list.

Customers' Stupid Questions:

1. When is Cinco de Mayo?

2. Why'd Margarita's parents name her after a cocktail?

3. Do you work here?

"I just heard that the dishwasher isn't working," Alex said to Quico's backside.

Quico nodded.

"Well, which one? Pedro or the machine?" Alex demanded.

Quico dropped a handful of taquitos into a vat of heated oil and the rolled tortillas hissed in protest. "Both. The machine died. Pedro looked at the dirty dishes *en* clocked out. He has pneumonia." Quico's face expressed skepticism.

"Why didn't you tell me about this sooner?"

Quico shrugged at the obvious. "Because *es su* birthday."

Before Alex could ask who was available on such short notice, Quico switched back to Spanish. "It's all been taken care of. Gilbert just got here, and I called the number on the wall. They said a repairman will be here within an hour." He considered telling her when the hour would be up, but thought better of it. If the repairman was running late, he did not want to be held accountable.

Quico shifted to his right and flipped quesadillas on the griddle. He was a slight, effeminate man with thick black hair and sad Indian eyes. He liked to think of his work aprons as wrap-around skirts. Butterflies in flight were embroidered across the one he was wearing.

"Oh, I told Pedro to call you before his next shift. In case he doesn't have a next shift. Now go enjoy your party and stop working."

Alex considered telling Quico she could not run the restaurant without him, but employees tend to confuse praise with a raise. "You're coming to the party soon, right?" she said, while absentmindedly stacking the oven mitts next to the tortilla steamer. Quico nodded without looking up.

❧

Alex had been working at the restaurant since the week after her father's fatal freak accident. He was electrocuted while attempting to unplug a faulty electric bean masher. It was actually an industrial electric potato masher, only they used it for beans. To this day, no one can explain why he was mashing the beans in the first place. Even more puzzling were the waterlogged shoes he was wearing at the time.

Now that Alex was eighteen, Cacahuates Restaurante was

finally legally hers. With graduation a mere two weeks away, she could not wait to throw her complete attention into running the restaurant. Boys were never a problem, which was the biggest problem she now faced. In her eighteen years, Alex had never been kissed, intentionally bumped into, or even pinched by a boy for not wearing green on St. Patrick's Day.

She recently overheard her mother's end of an irate phone conversation. "God did not burden my Alejandra with beauty."

Alex had said nothing, but inwardly she cried. She studied her reflection in the bathroom mirror until her features lost all human characteristics. Alex's round face looked just like a plate of food prepared in a hurry and with the portions all-wrong. There was too much space for her jaw, as if her features had shifted toward her forehead during her parents' rush to conceive a boy. Her eyes were set too close and her lips tended to curve downward, just like the catch of the day.

Alex made her way toward the banquet room, stopping to check with staff members to ensure all was running smoothly. The thought of separating business and birthday had not yet occurred to her.

When Alex reached the party, her jaw dropped. The banquet room, with a capacity of 40, had nearly twice that number of people struggling to mingle. Alex was calculating the fire code violation fine when she spotted her sister. Leah was sitting between two men smoking cigarettes and making wide gestures.

Alex could tell she was trapped by the way she was leaning far back in her chair, as if trying to break free from the full ashtray's gravitational pull. Alex took a sick pleasure in her sister's discomfort, the way older siblings sometimes do.

Leaning across the table, Alex stared into Leah's perfectly symmetrical face glowing warmly in the tea lights. Her wide eyes were outlined with a shimmery copper pencil, and her full lips were painted the color of plums. Alex thought, It's hard to believe we're made from the same recipe and with the same ingredients. "Are Tessa and Dulce here yet?" she said.

Leah did not know. "Please sit down and stop working."

"You want me to sit with you and ignore my guests?" Alex said, making an "are you crazy?" face. Alex turned on her sensible heels and disappeared. To Leah it looked as if the gathering swallowed her sister whole.

Alex was pulled into a tight circle of elderly women wearing similar black dresses over almost identical bulbous bodies. She was thanking her guests (two invitees and two party crashers) for coming when she spotted Tessa and Dulce. The birthday girl's eyes followed her friends through the cocktail crowd, losing them by the gift table.

Tessa was making sure that the card was securely taped on to her present, when Dulce said in a low and level voice, "*¡Híjole!* Check out the cake."

Tessa glanced up. She froze. The birthday cake was actually a three-tiered white wedding cake heavily decorated with clumps of bright red roses. Thickly piped green leaves clung to vines creeping over the cake.

"It looks like somebody ate a clown, then threw up all over the cake!" Dulce said. She poked a sugar flower and half-expected it to squirt water. "Somebody needs to pull that bakery's license."

"It's not from the bakery. It's one of *la señora que hace*

los cakes scary creations," Tessa half-whispered, in case the cake lady was around. "Oh, poor Alex!"

"I'm gonna flick her off the cake," Dulce said, reaching up.

"Wait!" Tessa caught her by the arm. "You can't do that. It's too late!"

"What do you mean it's too late?" Dulce shrugged free. "Nothing's happened yet." She looked around to prove her point.

"Because, everyone has already seen *la novia*. If she's not up there, people will notice."

"So, you're saying that if I flick *la novia* off she'll be more noticeable than if she stays up there, squatting on that ugly cake?" Dulce grinned up at Tessa. She was a diminutive five feet in height, with hair like a thick black curtain. She bought most of her clothes in the boys' department of Kmart, claiming they have the most durable socks. She was now sporting 501 jeans, a 49ers jersey cropped to reveal a stubby navel and the elastic band of plaid boxer shorts.

"Something like that," Tessa mumbled, not really sure how to explain that the damage was already done. She glimpsed at the bride. Her eyes lingered there. "Does she look pink to you?"

Dulce leaned into the decoration. "She's been dipped in food coloring, just like an Easter egg. Why'd *la señora* go and dunk the doll like that?"

"To make her look less like a bride, I guess."

"Dang! She didn't even bother keeping her face out of the dye. Hey!" Dulce's big brown eyes sparkled. "A blushing bride." They both laughed like Elmer Fudd.

"There you are," Alex said, shouldering her way to them.

Catching the irritation in her tone, Tessa said, "Sorry we're late. We drove around for 20 minutes looking for parking."

"We ended up driving back to Tessa's house and walking over," Dulce said, scanning the room for a drink.

"Why didn't you just say a Hail Mary?" Alex said.

"You're kidding, right?" Tessa said, even though she could see that she wasn't.

Alex began to pray while rotating a wrist. "'Hail Mary full of grace, help me find a parking space.' It works every time."

"You see," Dulce said. "That's why I don't bother with *that* God. His mother was a really nice lady, and he put her to work parking cars after she died."

Alex was in work mode and did not hear Dulce blaspheme. She watched as the wait staff carried in oblong trays stacked with salads. "Food's here. Good, I'm starving," she said. When she turned back they were gone.

As if trying to make a connecting flight, Tessa and Dulce dashed through the crowd. They sat hard across the banquet table from one another, and then watched as the stampede of guests (and the uninvited) scrambled for seats. Jerking her head in the direction of a thin man and a stocky man fighting over the final chair, Dulce said, "My *feria* is on the skinny one. He's all gristle."

The impromptu game of musical chairs ended with a thud. Dulce smiled sideways at Tessa as the stocky man headed to the second banquet room set up for the overflow.

Alex took her place at the head of the horseshoe-shaped table, in between her mother and sister. Leah and Quico had selected all of Alex's favorite dishes for her birthday. The first course, a lime-marinated beef salad, was "cooked" overnight in fresh lime juice with a marinade of garlic, peppers, and cilantro before being seared on the grill.

While the tangy flavors lingered on their palates, the empty plates were exchanged with bowls of *sopa de flor de calabaza*, a cheesy pumpkin blossom soup. Leah had planted a pumpkin patch in the community garden to ensure that they would have enough blossoms for this occasion. The main course was lobster crepes with *chile pasilla* sauce, zucchini stuffed with rice, fried sweet plantains, and drunken frijoles.

After the final course, some of the men fought the urge to loosen their belts and nod off. Dulce, so full she could barely breathe, considered a sleepy Tessa. With her creamy-white skin and sulky green eyes, she looked like a young Lauren Bacall.

The dishes were cleared, replaced by brandy in snifters and coffee in white ceramic cups. The overhead lights were dimmed as two busboys trundled in the cake, their faces serious with concentration.

Dulce turned back from the cake to Tessa. "Unless Alex has a blow dryer back there, she's not gonna be able to put out that towering inferno with one breath."

Alex lit up as if by footlights, smiled as the guests sang "Happy Birthday" in a chorus of accents. Closing her eyes, she fervently made the same three-fold wish, for popularity, beauty, and a boyfriend, that never came true. Only this time, she replaced "boyfriend" with "husband."

Alex focused like a swimmer getting ready to compete. She drew in a deep breath and began to blow a fine stream of air mere inches from the lower glinting flames. Her head banked back and easily blew past the second tier. As she reached the final tier, a dead candle, right smack in the middle of the cake, flickered back to life.

On Alex's second breath, the one that rendered her wish completely worthless, she stared through the smoke and into the sloppy dot eyes of the jilted bride. She was suddenly struck cold by the irony of her wish.

As Alex made the first slice into the cake, for good luck, Leah stared into her untouched coffee cup. She had been making her own wishes on Alex's cakes for as long as she could remember. Each wish coming true seemed normal, and held about as much expected awe as a sunrise.

On the overcrowded streets of San Francisco, she attempted to inhabit the spaces in-between others' lives, but strangers zeroed in on her. Panhandlers yelled at her and religious zealots followed her for blocks. Leah took a sip of the bitter liquid as she mourned the missed candle and her unfulfilled wish to become invisible.

Chapter 6

LEAH WALKS INTO A NIGHTMARE

THE DAY AFTER ALEX'S BIRTHDAY PARTY, Leah caught the bus for her Sunday outing to Golden Gate Park. As she stepped onto the soft, yet sharp grass she experienced a sad euphoria. People referred to this as spring fever, but for Leah the yearning was just as insensible during the other seasons. Sometimes for opposing reasons.

For instance, she loved the way the winter rains deepened the green hues of the park and made everything smell of earth and clay. When it was raining she could hike all the way to the Pacific Ocean without running into another person. The few people she saw appeared with their dogs between showers, and then disappeared as soon as it began to rain again. They were usually so far off that she sometimes wondered if she imagined them.

On this late-May morning, the dry breeze was scented with maturing flowers and fresh-cut grass. Leah's eyes swept across the people roaming the park and thought of grazing cattle.

The warm seasons may have limited her solitude, but during the spring and summer months, Leah got to do what she loved best: forage for herbs. She reached into her burlap bag for the list Quico had handed her as she was leaving. Seeing each plant as a destination point, she mapped out a course through the park in her mind. Leah liked having a quest.

First stop, lavender. Quico had mentioned how he wanted

to make a bottle of children's cough syrup for the single mother of six living in the apartment next to his. He would do this by simmering real maple syrup. After removing the saucepan from the burner, he would add a handful of lavender petals, and then cover it tightly with a lid. When the liquid cooled, Quico would strain the decoction into the blue glass bottles she remembered from her childhood.

Leah entered the Garden of Shakespeare's Flowers through the open wrought iron gate and followed the brick path around the sundial. This was one of many gardens throughout the world that grows the plants mentioned in Shakespeare's works. She marveled at all of the connections that one person—and a man, no less!—had made between plants and feelings. She wondered if this place would have felt familiar to him.

Leaning over the lavender plants, she clipped a handful of the least noticeable velvety spikes. The fragrance mingled with her thoughts of Quico and the shiny blue bottles. She was unexpectedly taken back to Alex's first day of school. Leah woke up coughing and was to remain behind with their new cook while her mother took Alex to school. When they left, Leah thought they were never coming back. She crawled under one of the kitchen's industrial tables and began to wail like a coyote pup.

Walking by, Quico handed her a clean towel still warm from the dryer. Leah burrowed her wet face into the terry cloth until her skin had drawn out all of the warmth hiding in the folds of the fabric. She was coughing into the towel when a spoonful of the dark liquid appeared from a hovering hand. Leah obediently opened her mouth. She felt quick comfort as the liquid coated her raw throat. It had the lingering flavor of hard candy.

Leah watched Quico screw the cap back on the blue bottle. He placed it on a shelf out of her reach. She looked around at her refuge, possibly her new home. The table was much bigger from the inside than when she was standing next to it. The pleasant smell of turkeys simmering in giant pots (the actual ingredient for the chicken filling) and the humming dishwasher were making her feel drowsy.

Clutching the towel, she lay down and was falling asleep when a checkered pair of pants walked by. To Leah's sleepy eyes they looked just like two giraffes out for a stroll. More giraffes showed up. Some were checkered, and some were in mourning and wore black. Quico's giraffes sauntered around the kitchen. Right before lunchtime they started salsa dancing.

The phone rang. Quico set a half bag of dry beans next to the table and picked up the receiver. When Leah heard him tell the story years later, Quico would say how he was never sure how long he had left the bag there. At some point, he turned back to find that the large metal bowl, usually stacked on the shelf under the table, was filled with sifted beans. The pebbles and mutant beans had been collected in the smallest bowl of the set.

The next day, Quico placed a box of tomatillos, still in their papery pods, where he had absentmindedly left the bag of beans the day before. He wanted to see what would happen. The moment after the boss's wife and daughter left for school, a dark little form in pajamas with feet crawled under the table. When Quico's little experiment was the furthest thing from his mind, he almost slipped on a shucking that had strayed from the brittle pile of husks stacked next to the box of neatly piled waxy green tomatoes.

Leah's mother found daily excuses for leaving her behind. Quico did not mind. He was on the clock. He turned the girl into a kitchen experiment and tried different ways of coaxing her out of her hiding place. By November, Leah had made it across the kitchen to a miniature workstation constructed for her out of orange crates.

On the morning of *El Día de Nuestra Señora de Guadalupe*, or December 12, Leah and Quico were preparing *buñuelos* for the evening fiesta, following a special mass. She glanced out the window over the sink and saw her mother returning early from school. Leah experienced the relief of familial rescue. Instead of coming into the kitchen, her mother ascended the exterior steps and slipped into their apartment.

At that moment Leah understood everything. All this time she thought that her mother was at school with Alex, when she was upstairs, avoiding her. From that day on Leah started off each school day feeling twice abandoned. Quico had also seen the girl's mother sneak by. He watched in disbelief as she tiptoed up the stairs, the way teenagers do when late for curfew. As Leah turned away from the window, he thought, Poor little thing feels about as wanted as a tossed bottle. But even an empty bottle has value if you redeem it.

Quico asked the wait staff to make up little jobs to keep the girl busy. They readily agreed, since most of the day shift were mothers who appreciated having a child around to remind them of how much they missed their own. Leah thrived on having a purpose. She did a dozen little tasks that no one wanted to do in the first place, like collecting the salt and pepper shakers.

As she grew older and more attentive, Quico passed along the native blends of spices and folk wisdom he learned from his grandmother back in his pueblo south of Mexico City.

Quico and Leah were shucking corn when he told her this story:

"Quetzalcoatl had just created the human race. He was trying to figure out how he was going to feed us, when he noticed a red ant carrying a corn kernel out of Mount Popo. So, he turned himself into a black ant and followed the red ant into the mountain. Guess what he found? He found the greedy little ants' stash of corn. It was almost as big as the mountain itself!

Quetzalcoatl filled his serape with the corn and took it back home. The gods ate until they were full and when they were done, Quetzalcoatl put some of the corn into our mouths. And that was our first taste of food. It was the best taste of food, ever."

Leah smiled at the memory. She rolled a single lavender spike back and forth between her hands. With eyes closed, the clean scent on her fingers smelled faintly of rosemary. At that same moment her mind made a connection. Come September, she would be the one going to school, while Alex stayed behind with Quico at the restaurant. A sense of impending doom bloomed sharply in her stomach.

What started out as a clear and sunny day near Stanyan Street was ending at the Great Highway in fog so dense that she could not tell the ocean from the sand. Around noon, Leah realized she was near the white sage bush and quickly changed course. It was not on the list, but she knew this type of sage was Quico's favorite.

As Leah walked, she breathed in the bag's cuttings. The fragrance of this particular batch of herbs was spicy with a lingering hint of licorice. She experienced a profound sensation that she was not passing through the world. The world was passing through her. Lost in the thought, Leah tripped.

Catching herself, she peered back at the gnarled tree roots, reminding her of fossilized snakes. From her periphery vision she spotted a splash of bright color. The sage and other bushes obscured most of the view, but Leah could make out the corner of a yellow beach towel and a woman's hand resting, palm-up.

Leah stopped. She chewed on a cuticle to help her think. Well, sage is not on the list and Quico is not expecting it.

As she made up her mind not to invade the woman's sunbathing, she pictured Quico jumping up and down as he discovered the fuzzy leaves in the bag. Leah knew Quico would burn the dried sage in an abalone shell, to purify and protect his home. It suddenly felt important to give him that moment.

Leah surveyed the ground ahead and stepped slowly to avoid snapping twigs or crunching dry leaves. She was so engrossed in not making any noise she walked right into the sage bush. Leah heard what sounded like grunting. For a split second, she wondered if there were wild boars in the park. In that same split second, it seemed possible. Buffalo live here; why not boars?

Leah stared at the pinkish palm and curled fingers and thought of a crab on its back. The woman was close, yet the shrubbery was still blocking the rest of her. Leah's mind was having trouble working out why she had not moved, when it dawned on her that no one sunbathes in the fog.

It's funny how the mind can fill in what's not actually there. Leah was staring at the hand when she realized that the red acrylic nails on the index and middle fingers were missing. Of all of the horrifying images about to assault her eyes, this would be the one she carried with her to sleep for years to come.

Consumed with a mixture of fear and curiosity, she took the first step, and then the next in an arch around the bushes. On her third step, she noticed scattered bits of yellow and green beach towel. On her fourth step, she realized it was shredded clothing. On her fifth step, the gang rape of the woman gripped her eyes.

For several seconds Leah did not need air, or even remember how to breathe. Time no longer moved forward. It folded in on itself, which may have explained why the world was tilting slightly and throwing her off balance. Leah stared at the bald man on top of the woman, and then at the other two men sitting, one on each side of her. What seemed most disconcerting was how the woman appeared to be sleeping peacefully through the brutal assault.

The bald man was making the grunting sounds she had heard. Although he was wearing a long shabby coat that covered most of the woman's full figure, Leah could see a sliver of pale skin along the line of the grass and knew that, aside from one chartreuse sock, the woman was completely naked.

As the man began convulsing, the two spectators leaned

forward with expectant smiles, the way one does when watching a famous comedian on TV while awaiting a familiar punch line. The bald man began to spit obscenities into the woman's tranquil face as the other two clapped and laughed. Fearing the woman would be startled into consciousness, Leah fervently wished her dead.

The bald man spasmed a few more times. He collapsed, like someone said "Bang!" and he was playing along. He rolled off her, breathing heavily. Leah could not help but notice the contrast between the woman's pale skin and that of her attackers. The three men's faces and hands were so grimed with dirt she could not tell their race. It's funny the things you think about when you're in shock.

Leah stared at the woman's raw nudity, her pale skin, and the blue veins running through her breast, and thought of a toppled marble statue. From under a tangle of brown hair, Leah could just make out her features. It was a face from another time, like the Victorian lady on the Coca Cola tray, only bruised.

As the woman's leg shifted slightly, Leah was filled with unexpected joy by the movement. She immediately felt ashamed of herself for having wanted to protect this woman by wishing her dead. The woman's head began to languidly move, motioning "no." Her eyes fluttered open. The man to her left grabbed a bottle from the pocket of the faded varsity letter jacket he wore. Unscrewing the cap, he roughly turned her head and tried to get her to drink.

Harshly coming to, she reflexively pressed her lips together. She turned her head and Leah caught sight of more bruising around her neck. Letter jacket forced the woman's mouth open by squeezing her cheeks with his dirty fingers. He poured again. Leah heard gurgling as the woman's entire body tensed. Like a geyser, she spewed up brown liquid followed by some milky vomit.

The three men made sounds of disgust. Letter jacket said, "That was very, very, wasteful." Raising his elbow far back, he brought his fist down hard onto the woman's face. Her head flopped to the side, like a flower with a broken stem.

Letter jacket said, "My turn next. C'mon, help me roll 'er over."

Leah was so weak with dread she did not feel the burlap bag slide noiselessly out of her hand, nor did she notice it bounce a little when it landed on the grass. She did see all three of the men's heads whip toward her at the sudden movement.

Letter jacket stood up slowly, the way one does when on a boat in rough seas. He was thin and wiry, and Leah could see the muscles working under the skin of his bare legs. His penis, stained with dried blood, was erect and pointing straight at her, almost accusingly.

The other two men were now standing, experiencing the same choppy waters as the first. They spread out and started taking cautious steps toward her—the horse they were trying not to spook. Trapped within their eyes, she could see the consequence of last night's missed candle.

Leah did not attempt to flee. Giving them permission to take her next.

Chapter 7

MRS. CERNUDA BECOMES THE FIRST
WORK RELATED ACCIDENT

ON THE MORNING AFTER HER PARTY, Alex attended mass alone, like she did every Sunday. In God's clean and clutter-free house that smelled of Murphy oil soap, paraffin wax, and what she guessed to be myrrh, she could be as relaxed as her waking life allowed. The moment the priest began the sermon Alex tuned him out. Leaning back into the polished pew, she worked on a to-do list in her head.

Mass ended late, thanks to the dozens of church announcements Padre Lucas threw in before the blessing. As Alex did a quasi-genuflection, she caught the time on her wristwatch. Dashing out the back door, she managed to stay ahead of parishioner foot traffic and the inevitable gridlock on the sparkly cement steps.

Alex reached the front doors of the restaurant in record time. Huffing toward the kitchen, she heard the familiar sounds of the day shift preparing for Sunday brunch. Having been raised upstairs from the family business, Alex and her sister spoke a mixed dialect of Spanish infused with the slang from a dozen Latin American countries. The idiomatic expressions mutated with changes in staffing, creating a sub-language foreign to anyone outside of the restaurant. New employees thought their coworkers were either drunk or Castilian.

Dulce was giving someone an English lesson. "A bathroom

is the one at home. A restroom is a public bathroom. Think 'restaurant,' 'restroom.' That's the way I 'member the difference."

Listening to Dulce's disembodied voice, Alex briefly wondered how someone who doesn't speak real Spanish could sound so much like Cheech Marin? She burst into the kitchen where Quico was arranging fruit on a platter for the buffet. Dulce was sitting on a galvanized table, her legs swinging as she explained the many English uses for the word "up."

Quico thought a moment. "What *et* mean *en* 7-Up?"

Seeing Alex, Dulce did a quick jerk back of the head. "*¿Qué onda Jefa?* Great party. What time did *la chota* leave?" Dulce's way of asking when the cops left.

Alex was too busy checking out Dulce's wrinkled busboy clothes to reply. The pastel tie was balled up in her shirt pocket. One black sock was obviously washed in a load with bleach and was now that ambiguous shade impossible to pair.

Alex had the sudden urge to nag, but that never worked. It was like being on a seesaw with that girl! The more her anger rose, the less Dulce seemed to take her seriously. Still, the impulse to lash out was strong, and she knew how to get around Dulce's playful indifference.

Without preamble, Alex said, "What if something happens to you in the Orient? I mean what if you get sick?" On the day after graduation, Dulce was going to backpack through Southeast Asia—alone. For months, the trip supplied Alex with plenty of ammo to nag her foolish little friend.

Dulce made a clicking sound with her tongue. "This again? If I get sick, I go see a doctor, or a *yerbera*. Like I do here."

"Did you know they have cobras there? And I'm not

talking about at the zoo..." As Alex went on about all of the things that could go wrong in such a pagan corner of the world, Dulce hopped off the table. Taking the pre-tied tie out of her pocket, she pulled it over her head. When Dulce knew that Quico and the guys were watching, she pretended to hang herself with it.

"Ja, ja, Cantinflas," Alex said without humor. Her eyebrows met. "Grow up already, you can't be Pilar Pan forever!"

"That was Tin-Tan, not Cantinflas." Dulce tucked the tie under her collar and slid the knot up with her thumb and index finger.

Alex stared at the crooked knot and knew Dulce had intentionally left it that way. Her nostrils flared, a signal to Dulce that Alex's pissed-off battery was now fully charged.

"It's eleven o'clock. I need to flip the sign over," Dulce said, attempting a diversion. She pushed the swinging door and held it for Alex, saying, "Hustle!"

Alex could not help but laugh at the inside joke at their third-grade teacher's expense. The Anglo nun with virtually no eyelashes or eyebrows tried to urge Alex, Leah, Dulce and Tessa back from recess by shouting, "Hustle!" This only caused the girls to stop and look at one another, to see if anyone knew what "hustle" meant. Dulce said it sounded a lot like a dog sneezing.

Misinterpreting their hesitation as an act of student defiance, Sister Philip placed them in detention. Confused by the severe punishment, Tessa looked the word up in the dictionary. When she whispered to Alex, Leah and Dulce that it meant *"apúrate,"* they laughed, and have been laughing about it ever since.

❧

As brunch began, Mrs. Cernuda came down from the apartment to help with the restaurant's Sunday buffet. Her self-appointed task was to ensure that the staff and guests did not abuse the limit of one complementary glass of cheap champagne offered to customers ordering an entrée.

Mrs. Cernuda was reunited with her daughters the week before Alex's eighteenth birthday. Upon entering the restaurant, Mrs. Cernuda was taken aback by the crowded foyer. She wondered what everyone was waiting for. She became confused when she did not recognize a single employee. Her eyes flitted around nervously until she spotted Alex talking to a customer.

Relieved, Mrs. Cernuda ventured further into the dining room unnoticed. As she stood in the middle of the restaurant, the remodeling struck her like a bee sting. Almost more shocking was that few of the faces peering over the clean dinner menus had the broad features common in her people. Mrs. Cernuda gasped.

Instinctively recognizing her mother's quick intake of breath, Alex felt her throat clench tight. Her eyes scanned the dining room and zeroed in on a woman standing between tables 22 and 23. She was wearing the familiar black clothing and clouded look of disapproval on her jowly face.

"Amá!" Alex said, throwing her arms around her mother. When Mrs. Cernuda did not hug back, Alex felt a little stupid, and then hurt. Self-consciously, she dropped her arms to her sides. "What a surprise! Why didn't you call? I would have picked you up."

Mrs. Cernuda glared. "Why are you doing business with *los*

otros?" she said, in lieu of a greeting.

Alex smiled sourly. "Please keep your voice down," she warned as she grabbed her mother by the elbow and led her toward the server's galley in the back. "I can't believe you just said that in front of everyone!" Alex placed a hand on her curvy hip. "Whatever happened to saying, 'hello'?" She almost added, "Or calling us to see how we were doing!'" But Alex had made the executive decision to keep the remodeling a secret. The weekly cash allowance she sent in the mail was all of the assurance Mrs. Cernuda needed to assume that the restaurant was running smoothly.

"Ay, mija, I forget how young you are sometimes. They don't hear us. They only see us when they want us to do something for them," Mrs. Cernuda said, as if Alex was four years old and just asked why their neighbor's Chihuahua was having puppies when she was not married. "You don't know them like I do. Their wallets do not have one picture of their children. Well, maybe one, but it's really old."

"So?" Alex said, not hiding her impatience.

"Their wallets are filled with the business cards of lawyers ready to sue. They'll sue you if they get indigestion, or if they don't like the service. They'll even sue you if they get hit by a bus out front."

Alex stared at her mother and blinked once, the way a doll does. OK, so the missing you part was a lie, but I would have picked you up, she thought. Alex no longer wondered why her mother was back. She did not have the time. She checked the foyer where customers were glaring at their ready tables, and then at her.

"You should over salt their food and maybe they won't

come back," Mrs. Cernuda said.

Alex seized the opportunity her mother was unintentionally providing. "That's an idea." A bad idea, Alex thought, but said, "Why don't you go into the kitchen and say hello to your other daughter? Leah really missed you. Hey, maybe you should talk to her and Quico about the whole salting thing. *¡Ándale pues!*" Alex said, while gently shoving her mother through the kitchen door.

❧

From the corner barstool, Mrs. Cernuda sipped coffee laced with brandy while folding cloth napkins and keeping an eye on the buffet. Throughout the morning, the familiar Sunday patrons of the old days dropped by to lament the restaurant's changes while eating menudo served in lead-glazed ceramic cups Mrs. Cernuda bought on her last trip to Mexico.

As they garnished the spicy soup of hominy and tripe with minced onions, pinches of dried oregano, *chiles* and squeezes of *limones,* Mrs. Cernuda gave them the latest installment of her daughter's maltreatment.

"Oh, it was nothing this time. I caught Alejandra throwing out all of my music, that's all. I said, '*Ay, mija,* what are you doing with that?' and she said, '*Amá,* this is the eighties. Nobody listens to 8-tracks anymore. You should move up to cassettes. Look at how small they are!' How small they are, ha! Do we look like we're running out of room?" Mrs. Cernuda waved her hand, dismissively. "Oh, I could see Cuco Sanchez's face sticking out of the box and I thought, 'Your father spent his whole life collecting this music for the restaurant.'" Her voice began to quiver.

"What did you do?" someone said.

"What could I do? I took the boxes upstairs and put them in my closet." She tilted her head while looking down. It was a pose she once saw in some old religious painting. Unbeknownst to her, only sinners look down. Saints are painted looking up. "That's OK. If God wants to punish me."

The patrons closest to Mrs. Cernuda touched her shoulders. "Don't worry, *Doña Carmen,* you've seen how fast businesses close around here, even when they're run by men. You own the building, right?"

The building with the three apartments above—including the one they lived in—and business were under her husband's name. He left everything to the girls, but Mrs. Cernuda did not want to get into that. She nodded.

"So," the same person said, "when this place goes out of business you can lease everything and retire with a nice income."

"Alex will have the time she needs to find a husband. Leah too," someone else said.

Put like that, Mrs. Cernuda thought how the business's failure might be for the best. She looked around at the calm, beautiful space, and the full dining room. She sighed. *"Ojalá que sí."*

The phone near Mrs. Cernuda's elbow rang and she stared at it. She did not like answering the phone because it was never for her. Plus, she would more than likely have to jot information down, and that usually led to disaster. Alex would accuse her of forgetting something, like the number of people in their party.

Later, she would get yelled at again for writing down the wrong phone number. Mrs. Cernuda could not understand why her daughter got so upset; all of her questions would be answered when they showed up. And besides, if Alex did not make her so nervous, she would not make so many mistakes. So, in a way, it was all her fault.

The phone rang, again. Mrs. Cernuda looked around for her daughter, but did not see her. It rang again. She willed someone to pick it up. The wait staff was darting around like hummingbirds near a hibiscus hedge. It rang again. "I guess I have to do everything around here myself," she said tiredly, as she reached for the phone.

"Caca...Alejandra's," she said, smacking her head for what felt like the millionth time. By changing the restaurant's name from "Cacahuates" to "Alejandra's," she was condemned to begin each phone conversation with a mistake. Again, Alex's fault.

There was a confused silence before a gruff male voice said, "This is Detective Jordan with the San Francisco Police Department. I'm trying to reach Mrs. Cernuda?"

Mrs. Cernuda was not fazed by the call from the police. She assumed it had something to do with raffle tickets. "Yes, this is Mrs. Cernuda, but are you looking for my daughter, Miss Alejandra Cernuda?" This happened all of the time.

"Actually, I'm trying to reach Mrs. Carmen Cernuda."

"Oh, oh, yes." Panicking at the sound of her name, she stood up. "I am me."

"I'm calling about your daughter, Leah. There's been an incident at Golden Gate Park..."

As Mrs. Cernuda listened, she became as still as a mannequin. After a moment, the phone slid out of her hand. It fell into the tall garbage can where it sank to the bottom. Only a few people saw Mrs. Cernuda lose consciousness, but many of the customers heard the gong-like sound her head made when it struck the hollow brass rail at the foot of the bar.

Chapter 8

ALEX'S TURN TO FALL INTO A DEAD FAINT

"OH MY GOD, OH MY GOD, oh my God!" Alex repeated the words like a frantic mantra. She was following the ambulance in her father's old Ford truck, dubbed Pepe Le Pew, on account of its black camper shell with a white stripe on each side. She was driving so close to the emergency vehicle that it looked like an invisible chain was towing her.

At the restaurant, the paramedic said that the gash on her mother's forehead was the result of a fall, but could not say what caused the fall itself. Alex's mind was swarming with questions. What if it's a heart attack? What does a heart attack look like? Does it look any different than an aneurysm? What's the fine for driving within 300 feet of an ambulance? Could I go to traffic school? If not, how will the ticket affect my insurance? Alex began to sob. Although they had never truly had a healthy mother-daughter relationship, she was the only parent left.

Alex parked behind the ambulance and ran alongside the gurney into the hospital. Someone in pajamas stopped her. Not pajamas, scrubs. She was saying something to Alex as a security guard approached. They were both talking to her at once. It finally registered. The nurse was saying, "I'm sorry, but you cannot go beyond this point."

While the security guard said, "You are going to have to move your truck, ma'am."

❧

"Hail Mary, full of grace, where the hell is my parking space?" Alex's prayers were getting uglier by the block. *La Virgen* must have been on break, or visiting her son, because the hospital's parking structure was closed for retrofitting.

Alex drove around for half an hour in search of a space big enough to parallel park her elephant-sized truck. My elephuck, she thought, giving into the insanity of going in circles, no, squares. She ended up parking a quarter of a mile away, in an iffy space next to a curb that had once been painted red.

By the time she returned to the nurse's desk, Alex was sweating. After being handed a clipboard with forms, she was told that there was no new information about her mother. The waiting room was packed. She wondered what all these people were doing here on such a nice Sunday afternoon. Alex was about to sit on an upholstered chair. She hesitated. She stared at the dirty seat cushion worn shiny by thousands of butts and thought, Fart trap! She chose to sit on a molded plastic chair.

After filling out the forms, Alex handed the clipboard back to the nurse. She was staring up at the fish-eyed mirror in the corner of the room for clues about her mother when she noticed the stained acoustic ceiling. Her eyes moved to a dark mass of dead flies at the bottom of a winking fluorescent light fixture. She made a face. If this was a restaurant I wouldn't eat here.

Alex could not shake the feeling she was forgetting something. She started rifling through the contents of her purse, hoping to jog her memory. Nothing came to mind, but she found a stick of gum. She glanced at her watch. Brunch was over and Leah should be home.

"Leah!" she said out loud. Alex flung her hefty purse over her shoulder. She was suddenly annoyed with her sister for frolicking through Golden Gate Park. Leah should be here with me, worried half to death about our mother!

Standing at a row of pay phones, Alex felt around the lining of her purse for the quarter she knew was there. She dropped the coin into the slot and dialed the number to the restaurant. The line was busy. Alex hung up and waited a moment. She dialed again. Still busy. Who's making personal calls and tying up the line? When she hung up the second time, the phone ate her quarter.

"Oh, that's just perfect!" Alex was seriously considering yanking the phone from the wall, shucking it like an oyster, and retrieving her precious quarter, when a man with a stethoscope around his neck approached. He was black and lean, like a long-distance runner. He introduced himself, but Alex did not catch his name.

"How is she?" Alex asked desperately.

"Your mother's going to be fine. We're still waiting for test results." He smiled.

"Are you sure?" Alex said, worried by the good news.

"Her heart's strong and there is a slight concussion. But that's to be expected after the nasty spill she took. We'll be releasing her soon. Would you like to see her?"

"Yes, please."

Passing through the double doors, she was suddenly jarred by the unexpected stench of an alley dumpster. Alex heard moaning, before seeing three semiconscious homeless men on gurneys. The white gauze dressing was a stark contrast to their brown weathered faces and arms. It made her think of new patches on old quilts.

A police officer was keeping an eye on them, while talking to a man in a suit. Curious, Alex was about to ask what had happened to them, when she spotted the side of her mother's head. There was a modified turban around her hairline, but Alex recognized the dark curly hair sticking out in frizzy clumps. She ran to her mother and squeezed her hand.

"Everything is all right, *Amá*. You bumped your head, that's all. You must have slipped on something. Do you remember what it was? Was it a piece of bar fruit, or something from the buffet?" Alex was trying to figure out exactly whose head was going to roll.

"I don't remember anything." Her mother's voice was a rough whisper.

"That's all right. I get to take you home soon. Isn't that great?" Her mother began to sob, and then to snore.

Feeling the spike of adrenaline drop, Alex walked back to the nurse's station. She was pulling a dollar bill from her wallet when the nurse said, "We don't make change. You'll have to go to the cafeteria." Alex opened her mouth, but before she could ask, the nurse said, "Second floor. The elevator is at the end of the hall."

Alex hoped the nurse heard the sarcasm in her voice when she thanked her. The businesslike tap of her Esprit shoes down the corridor put Alex into work mode. She automatically started taking inventory of the patients in the rooms: Two old ladies, old man and empty bed, fat lady and old lady, young lady and empty bed.

Hey, Alex thought, that looks just like...Alex stopped fast.

She backed up. Her hand roughly covered her open mouth. "Oh my God!" she breathed through her fingers.

At the foot of the bed, Alex stared down at her sister. Leah's eyes were closed, but was she unconscious, or asleep? Alex was trying to piece it all together when the nurse without phone change marched in, like a mean majorette.

Positioning herself between the patient and the intruder, she said, "You can't just come in here and use the phone. The nerve!" Noting the half-crazed look in Alex's eyes, the nurse told someone by the door to get security.

Alex was mute with shock. She pointed to her sister, in the direction of her mother, and back to her sister. A security guard appeared and firmly grabbed hold of Alex's arm. He was pulling her away from Leah, when she found her voice. "That's my sister!"

Squinting at Alex, the nurse said, "Are you sure?"

"Of course I'm sure! Don't you think I know my own sister?" An angry Alex fumbled in her purse for her license. "My name is Alejandra Cernuda and she's Leah Cernuda! Check the name on that thingamajig around her wrist!"

"I remember your name." The nurse checked the chart at the foot of the bed. She nodded and the security guard released his grip.

"Leah, Leah!" Alex rushed to her side. Turning back to the nurse, she stammered, "Is she OK? What happened to her?"

"She's not hurt," the nurse said. Her words faltered.

That did not make sense to Alex. "If she's not hurt, why is she here?"

Before the nurse could answer, someone said, "Excuse me. Move!" The doctor, followed by a man in a dark suit, cut through the crowd of hospital personnel congregating in the doorway.

"Ms. Cernuda, my name is Detective Jordan," said the man in the dark suit. "I need to ask you a few questions. Could you tell me what Leah was doing at Golden Gate Park earlier today?"

Alex recognized the detective as the man she had seen talking to the uniformed cop in the emergency room. All of her muscles tightened at the sound of her sister's name being spoken by the authority figure, triggering the innate fear that most Mexicans have of law enforcement agents. Her eyes bounced from the detective to the doctor. "I don't understand. What's going on here?"

The doctor said, "Ms. Cernuda, we've been trying to contact you for hours. Let's step into my office so we can talk?"

"The phone must be off the hook," Alex said, more to herself. "I don't know what's going on here, but I'm not leaving my sister. Why is she here? Did someone hurt her?" Alex's voice strained to contain her terror.

"Physically, Leah's fine," the doctor said. "She is suffering from an acute stress response as the result of witnessing a traumatic event."

Alex looked stricken. It sounded a lot like *susto*. Most of the older people in the Mission District still believe that if a person witnesses a terrifying event, like a car accident, or a murder, their soul jumps out of their body. "What did she see?"

Detective Jordan spoke up. "Your sister witnessed the gang rape of a woman in the park, then the mauling of the three alleged rapists by two off-leash dogs..."

As he explained the events of that morning, Alex felt her legs give out from under her. It was during the moment of free fall that her ebbing mind made the connection between the three smelly transients in the emergency room, Leah, the phone off the hook, and her mother's fall.

PART 2

Chapter 1
THE FIRST OF ALEX'S BIRTHDAY
WISHES COMES TRUE
OR
LOLA FALANA AND CHARO
MAKE AN APPEARANCE

IT WAS A TYPICAL WORKDAY for Alex as she sat in her tiny office balancing the books. Generally, food costs made up around one-third of the restaurant's spending. Another third went to labor and location. As the co-owner of the location with Leah, Alex was pleased with the bottom line. She closed the books and tried to stretch, but her arms and legs hit closet walls.

Alex was at the podium checking the reservation book when something absolutely incredible happened. The divas from Saint Joan of Arc High School, also known as St. Juanita's, though most people called it St. Juan's, sashayed into the restaurant.

Alex had spent her high school years watching as Katrina, Marissa, Danielle, and Mia congregated under the statue of the teenage virgin who saved France. She used to fantasize that she was leaning against the saint's bare foot, while they all decided what to do on the upcoming weekend.

The prettiest one, Katrina, was wearing big hoop earrings, a skimpy white T-shirt, a denim mini skirt, and red high-top shoes. "We thought we'd stop by and say hi, so hi," she said. Alex gaped at her.

Katrina was used to this, and went on. "We just picked up our graduation pictures. We're going to sit in the lounge and go through them if that's OK?" she said, holding up a half dozen photo packets. Still unable to speak, Alex nodded and gestured for them to go ahead.

There were no tables available in the lounge, so the divas plopped down on barstools, chattering and laughing much louder than their fellow patrons. "This music sucks," Katrina said. "Do you have the *Fame* soundtrack?"

"Sorry." Alex's shoulders slumped a little, as her high school inferiority was redirected toward her business's sucky ambient music. She went behind the bar and served a round of Diet Pepsi—on the house.

Katrina was breaking the seal on the first packet of photos, when Marissa said, "Oh yeah, how's your sister?"

"She's doing better," Alex said, a little tired of the question.

"I heard that those gross bums got her pregnant and she's going to keep the baby. Is that true?" Mia said.

"No," Alex said, trying to keep her voice neutral, but showing a little irritation. "They never even touched her."

"Then why'd she drop out of school?" Marissa said.

"She didn't drop out of school. She finished the semester from home, that's all." Alex was about to mention her fear that Leah was still suffering from *susto*. She glanced up in time at their gossip-hungry faces to change her mind.

Placing a palm on the bar, Alex said, "Here's what happened. Leah witnessed a woman being raped in Golden Gate Park by three homeless men. Some guy, not too far away, was tossing a Frisbee with his two dogs and the dogs attacked the bums."

"How did the dogs know there was danger?" Marissa said.

Alex shrugged. Leah still had not spoken to anyone, including the police, about what transpired during those last moments.

"I heard that the dogs were going to be put down. It's some sort of law, but the owner broke them out of doggy jail," Mia said.

This was true and Alex nodded somberly. When the owner went to animal control to retrieve his hero dogs, he was informed that Lola Falana and Charo were considered vicious and were scheduled for termination. The owner returned to the shelter that night and freed not only his dogs; he took all the animals scheduled for euthanasia.

"What about the woman?" Danielle said.

"She had a concussion and alcohol poisoning, but she's going to make a complete recovery. The doctors said that she would have died if she'd gotten to the emergency room any later."

"No, I mean what was she doing at the park?" Danielle clarified.

Alex shook her head. "The night before, she'd been celebrating her divorce becoming final at a pub across the street from the park. She left at closing time, around two in the morning, and was walking home. She needed to pee, so she crossed the street to go behind some bushes and doesn't remember anything else."

"Oh, so she kind of asked for it then, huh?" Marissa said. Alex was stunned by the cruelty of the comment.

"*¡Guácala!* I'll bet she caught leprosy in her papaya," Katrina said and they all laughed. Alex pretended to appreciate the humor by nodding.

"How's your mom? Is it true she tried to kill herself when she found out about Leah?" Mia said.

Alex stared at Mia and sighed inwardly. "No, she slipped on a piece of fruit and bumped her head. She's fine now. Thanks for asking."

Alex picked up a stack of photos, hoping to change the subject. She started shuffling through the mostly fuzzy images of the graduation party she missed. Katrina straightened for a better view. "Too bad you had to stay home and take care of everybody, and missed graduation and well, everything," she said.

Frowning, Alex said, "No biggy."

"Hey Alex, is it true you buy tequila by the truckload?" Danielle said. Katrina nudged her, indicating the question was rude. They all stared at Alex expectantly.

Sensing that a lot was hinging on her reply, Alex said, "Well yeah, for the restaurant."

The divas smiled approvingly. The conversation became more animated and jumped around until they went through the last stack of prints. Katrina was now studying Alex. She said, "Do you like your hair that way?" The question stopped the girl's chatter. They stared at Alex with interest.

"Uh." Alex grabbed a pinch of the long strands from her ponytail. The dry tips looked exactly like frayed rope. Why was she noticing this now, and in front of them?

"We should go to my mom's salon sometime. She can make anyone look good," Katrina said. The other girls nodded their endorsements.

They want to hang out with me? Yes! Alex thought, while filtering out the insult. She made a silent vow never to move out of the way when a good time was approaching. From this moment on, she would hail fun, like a cab, and hop in.

After gobbling several complementary bowls of chips and salsa and finishing pints of soda, the divas began to stretch. Recognizing the gestures of people preparing to leave, Alex excused herself. She stuck her head in the kitchen and said, "Cover me," to the busboy.

When she returned, her former classmates were no longer in the lounge. Alex caught up with them halfway through the restaurant. "OK, let's go make me look good," she said, taking the lead.

Chapter 2

ALEX GETS HER SECOND WISH

AT *LA CASA DE CABELLO,* Katrina's mother, also named Katrina, worked on Alex for close to two hours. When a full foot of her very own hair fell to the floor, Alex barely noticed. The women around her were talking openly about matters that were so private, she doubted they ever reached Padre Lucas's ear. Yet, somehow it was fine to yell intimate details over the drone of blow dryers.

While Alex's hair was being deep conditioned, they tried to top each other's miseries. Mrs. Mendez won easily. She told a story of when she was sitting on her front stoop feeding the pigeons birdseed. A passing *gabacho* slipped on the sidewalk. He was now suing her for more than she owned.

"*¡Sinvergüenzo!* This is the only country in the world where a person can become rich by being either stupid, lazy, or clumsy," Mrs. Mendez said, shaking her head as the other women nodded thoughtfully.

Alex's hair, now shoulder length, was moussed, blown dry, curled in steaming rollers, and then touched up with a hot curling iron. When Katrina Sr. finished, Alex was slowly swiveled 180-degrees, until she caught sight of the back of her own head. It was short and really fluffy, like a dark meringue with maroon highlights. As everyone went on about how nice Alex's hair looked, she began to see what they saw. "It looks great! Will I have any trouble styling it?"

With the correct hair products and styling tools, she was told, she would not have any problem maintaining her beautiful new look. Katrina Sr. smiled. "We sell everything here."

As Alex filled out the check, doing her best not to act shocked by the bill, she could not remember ever spending that much money on herself. She experienced the blunt weight of guilt, followed by the unexpected buoyancy of naughty pleasure. It was like sinning, only she could not come up with the broken Commandment.

"Guess who's missing?" All of the heads in the salon swiveled to the open front door, where Mrs. Orejon was standing.

"Come in and talk louder!" a woman under a dryer called out.

Mrs. Orejon swiped each shoe on the doormat before taking a few steps in. She lightly placed a hand over her diaphragm, as if she was about to break into song. Raising her voice, she said, "China is missing! The police say she was kidnapped."

There was a collected gasp from the women in the shop. The row of beige domes were tossed back in unison, reminding Alex of hungry baby birds.

"Are you sure?" a woman getting a pedicure said.

"*¡Claro que sí!* China went to church to light candles for the hostages in Iran and no one has seen her since!"

As the women in the salon spoke in quick bursts, Alex pictured China in her mind. China—Spanish slang for "curly"—was born with stick-straight hair. She was given the nickname at the age of five. That was when her mother shaved the girl's head, believing her hair would grow back curly.

Alex remembered China at Tessa's birthday party that year. She was the bald kid in the pink party dress. If that was not memorable enough her mother had taped a matching satin bow onto her nubby-head. The tape was not sticking on one side, so the bow kept flip-flopping, like a bad toupee.

Alex was recalling, with guilt, how she relished finally having someone to snub when the pedicurist said, "Maybe it was a serial killer?"

It was suddenly very quiet in the shop. They were all aware that California was the serial murder capital of the world. In Alex's youth, the Zodiac Killer stalked the City, while more recently the Hillside Strangler and Freeway Killers hunted for victims in Southern California. Alex felt a sudden surge of fear for China.

Noticing Alex for the first time, Mrs. Orejon touched her arm. "Alex! I didn't recognize you. *¡Ay, qué bella!*"

All thoughts of China were put on hold. "Thanks," Alex said, reaching up much higher than usual to touch her hair.

Katrina Jr. had a thought. Turning to Alex she said, "Isn't China one of Dulce's friends?"

Alex nodded. "They have been coloring together since kindergarten. They both worked on that mural last summer. You know, the one near the Castro of Benito Juarez and Cesar Chavez holding hands?"

"Oh good! Let's call her and give her the bad news!" Katrina Jr. picked up the phone and punched an outside line.

"I can't. She's in Asia," Alex said.

"*¿Asia? Otra vaga,*" Mrs. Orejon said, confirming a suspicion. "What is it with you girls these days? Can't you act more like young ladies and less like wild gypsies?"

Why, Alex wondered, are the good girls always being scolded for the bad girls' behavior?

Alex's new friends orbited around her like satellites and one got the door. After saying goodbye several times, the new Alex Cernuda stepped out of the salon with her burgundy head, minus most of her hair and eyebrows, held high.

Katrina, Marissa, Danielle, and Mia, from that moment on known as "the posse," took Alex to the trendy little shops in the Marina District. To Alex, Union Street was an unfinished version of the Mission. The buildings were made up of similar two- and three-story framed flats with bay windows and storefronts on the street level. But all she could see were the differences.

Everything and everyone appeared to have been sprayed with a watery primer, but never painted. Where were the colorful signs over the doorways? Or the blue-faded posters in the windows that the shopkeepers positioned to block the sun from shining in their eyes—with no regard to symmetry? And why was it so quiet? Alex felt uneasy, but no one else seemed to notice.

In one of the shops that smelled like a new car, Alex waited for the others to become distracted before grabbing similar outfits from the double-digit sizes. She selected a wide belt that would be cinched close to her waist, because Marissa said that the look was very appealing on Latina women. And that's what Alex now was—a very popular, and attractive woman. Smiling, she thought back to her birthday wish. *Two down and one husband to go.*

Chapter 3

Orale from Jakarta!

This place is a trip. I'm not even short here. I can see over a bunch of sweaty heads!

I'm sitting in a Chinese restaurant, in Indonesia. Can you dig that? When Indonesian people go out for Chinese food, is it the same as us going to an Italian restaurant, or *gabachos* coming to Alejandra's?

Chow mein,
Dulce

✉

Chapter 4

CHINA'S PARENTS HAVE TO REPORT HER MISSING

CHINA WAS NOT KIDNAPPED. Her parents not only knew about her move to New York; it was a point of contention in the Nieves household for weeks before she left. She was gone only a few days when Mrs. Orejon, the Nieves' nosy neighbor, began asking about her.

Mr. Nieves was watering the roses in his narrow backyard when Mrs. Orejon let herself in through the side gate. She was carrying a plate covered with wrinkled aluminum foil. "I made *empanadas de piña* and I know they're China's favorite. Is she in the basement? I mean, her art studio." Mrs. Orejon smiled as she corrected herself.

Startled by the neighbor's sudden appearance, and profoundly ashamed of his daughter's choice to move to New York—practically as far away as she could get without a passport—Mr. Nieves lied. "She's babysitting?"

❧

A few days later, Mrs. Orejon stopped by the house with a grocery bag filled with fabric remnants. "I was wondering if China could use these for one of her art projects, or if nothing else, as rags for cleaning her brushes."

Mr. Nieves panicked. "China is, she went to church to light candles for the hostages in Iran."

"*Ay, qué* sweet. I'll just leave the bag here."

The next morning, Mrs. Orejon dropped by, again. She

wanted to know what China had decided. "I just ran into Martha. She's making a quilt for Yolanda's baby and she wants to see the fabric. But only if China doesn't want it. You know how much I hate to waste things."

Realizing he could not come up with daily excuses for much longer, Mr. Nieves considered telling her the embarrassing truth. Instead, he blurted out, "China never came home from church. We are worried sick. We haven't slept all night!"

Mrs. Orejon looked stricken. "Have you called the police?"

He nodded. "We called last night, but they said we would have to wait 24 hours before filing a missing person report." Mr. Nieves learned this tidbit from watching TV and liked the way it slid into his story.

❧

With Mrs. Orejon's help, the tragic news of China's disappearance spread through the *barrio* like a cold through a preschool. Late that afternoon, the Nieves' home was filled with weeping relatives and concerned neighbors. A full 24 hours after Mr. Nieves claimed that Christina went to church, he picked up the phone's receiver. His eyes scanned the houseguests before landing on his fretting wife. Shrugging, he dialed. "Hello. I *have* to report a missing person."

Being a slow news day, the media jumped on the story of the Catholic high school graduate's disappearance while lighting candles for the hostages in Iran. By nightfall, the Nieves' home was swarming with reporters and camera crews. On TV, the reluctant couple came across as worried parents, which they were, but not for the reasons thought.

❧

Once they found themselves in the center of the media blitz, Mr. and Mrs. Nieves became curiously captivated by the attention. Their newfound celebrity status was reaping many advantages. Mr. Nieves was promoted to usher at Saint Juan's church. Mrs. Nieves, a whiny woman usually ignored, could no longer walk down the street without receiving food, flowers, and sympathy.

They bought a VCR, learned how to work it, and then began taping their television appearances. As they watched the interviews they scrutinized themselves. Mrs. Nieves looked really good in red and not so good in plaid. Noticing the oily sheen on his nose and forehead, Mr. Nieves planned to ask the next make-up artists to be a little more generous with the pancake.

It was not until they were watching themselves being interviewed on *Good Morning America* that the couple realized that they had gotten a little carried away. In front of David Hartman—who looks less like a moose in real life—and the rest of the nation, they brought into existence the Latino Parents of Missing Children's Network, or LPMCN for short.

Chapter 5
DULCE GOES TO JAIL

Greetings from *el bote*.

You read right. I'm in jail. Before any of you start calling embassies, you should know that I could pay the fine anytime. But, it's pretty nice and clean in here. I've got a great sea-view and my cell is bigger than any of the other places I've stayed at.

You're probably asking yourself how I ended up here? It all started when I jumped on the wrong bus in Singapore. A half-a-day later I was the last one on. It stopped in this little town and the driver shooed me off the bus, locked it up, then walked away.

The only place open was a teahouse. I ran out of water hours ago and was so hot and thirsty my tongue felt like a role of paper towels. I walked in and everyone got real quiet. I ordered a Pepsi. The man behind the counter pointed outside and told me to go! I figured he was pushing their product, so I said, "All right, already. I'll have some tea, with a side of ice." He slapped the counter and told me to go, again. I said, "You tripp'n?" Seeing how I was outnumbered by a bunch of sleepy men, I left.

It was Africa hot, so I walked across the street to the shade. I was trying to figure out how to get out of Dodge, but this place wasn't on my map. I heard the ocean behind me and made my way through some jungle plants. I was on the most *suave* beach I've ever seen.

I had my bathing suit on under my sweaty clothes and decided to go for a nice cool swim. My toes were barely in the water when some fishermen working on their nets charged over, screaming, like I was on fire or something!

They dragged me to their jail. It was smaller than the one on Mayberry and it was on stilts. The Sheriff started talking to me in Malay. His voice got louder, like he thought I was ignoring his questions. I remembered that I was in caning country, so I said real calm, "Hi, I'm Dulce Racelis. Is there a problem, sir?"

I guess I can pass for Malaysian because they all looked at each other. His deputy brought in my backpack and clothes. Before I forget, thanks again for the backpack, you guys. It was the best graduation present, ever. If it wasn't for you three I would be carrying all my stuff around in my mom's baby-shit green Samsonite luggage and her little matching train case.

Anyway, they found my US passport. The sheriff started talking to me in broken English. He told me I broke Islamic laws by exposing myself in public. Ain't that always the way with religions thought up by men? I said, "What can I say, I'm just another dumb tourist."

Seeing how I wasn't going to be caned, stoned for adultery, or amputated for stealing, the fisherman got bored and left. I could tell that *la chota* didn't know what to do with me. They didn't want any trouble from my embassy, but they needed to make me some sort of an example. The sheriff fined me $30.00.

I had just put my clothes back on and was opening my wallet to pay the extortion fee when the sheriff's wife came in with their lunch. She was carrying a tray with a bunch of little plates of food on it. It smelled really good and I was starving.

The wife didn't know what to make of me, either. She just stared at me talking in English. My stomach picked that second to growl like a bunch of zoo animals. Zaheera (the sheriff's wife) handed me something wrapped in a banana leaf. I unwrapped it and took a bite. It was so good my eyes rolled back in my head. Zaheera looked flattered. I guess that proves that food is the best language out there.

She pulled up a chair for me to sit down and join them. I didn't want to piss the sheriff off, but I was hungry and tired. I figured I might as well get something out of the $30.00 fine. His wife made a face at him and he let me sit down.

I watched as they scooped the stuff from the plates on top of their round pile of rice. I copied their make-your-own-snow-cone way of eating. It was one of the best meals of my life. Next to Leah's cooking.

Their two kids came by to check me out. I gave them souvenir Disneyland pens, the ones with the Monorail that looks like it's gliding when you hold it up or down. The kids got all excited and wanted to know all about Disneyland.

What could I say? It's the crappiest place on earth. The only real good ride is Monsanto's Adventure Thru Inner Space: the one where you shrink and shrink, until the people can see you through the telescope where you are suddenly white and have really lame hair. Then, you're under the microscope and that fake blue eye is looking down around you, but never right at you. That ride should be an E ticket, but it's free!

I spent the rest of the day playing checkers with the locals. They use pearly-white and purple seashells for the checkers. I let the sheriff win, but nobody else.

It's late now and I'm in bed writing to you. I'm planning on staying for breakfast. Maybe lunch. Then, I will go. When you get this that means I was released, went to the post office and mailed this letter. I'm on my way to Thailand, or already there.

Sihat selalu!
Dulce

P.S. Here's a little tip for you. If you take off your Keds in Malaysia, always give them a good shake before putting them back on, because scorpions like to take naps in them.

✉

Chapter 6

ALEX MEETS HER THIRD WISH

AT CLOSE TO TEN, Alex padded into the kitchen with a raging hangover and a scowl on her pimple-speckled face. She mumbled something that may have been good morning to Leah, while reaching painfully for a mug. Leah was cutting through stacks of old tortillas for making chips. "Good morning," she said. Her words yelding to a yawn.

After the nightclubs closed, Alex, the posse, and some cute guys they rounded up at the Palladium staggered back to Alejandra's for an after-hours party. Leah was startled awake from a disturbing dream by the sudden jolt of brass instruments blaring out of the bar's sound system. She did not fall back to sleep until the party broke up at dawn.

"We got another letter from Dulce! She's on her way to Thailand," Leah said, pointing to the envelope on the corkboard with her chin.

"Great," Alex grumbled. "I hear the prison food is rated much higher there."

A delivery was being rolled in from the alley as Alex poured a cup of coffee. Judging by the holes in the boxes, it was produce. Alex's trained eye instantly spotted the soggy bottoms on some of the cardboard boxes, which risked spoiling the produce, not to mention problems with the Department of Health, should they happen to conduct a spot-inspection.

Alex already decided not to accept the shipment, when she realized it was not her regular deliveryman. The man behind the hand truck wore a white T-shirt with sleeves rolled up, revealing the contours of biceps and a smeared tattoo. What really struck Alex were his eyes. They were warm and bright, like jars of honey on a window ledge.

A sweet ache gripped Alex as her chest tightened. A warm liquid filled her cheeks, causing a rare blush. Her skin was suddenly alert as perspiration misted her forehead and recently bleached upper lip. At that moment, Alex married him with her eyes.

Behind him was Nene, her regular deliveryman. "Hey Alex!" he said, with forced enthusiasm. "This is my cousin, Jaime. We just fished him out of the bay. Nah, seriously, he just got here from Manzanillo and I got him a job working with me."

Nene switched to English. His accented voice suddenly intimate and urgent. "I know your order *es* all messed up, but if you send *et* back, we're gonna lose our jobs. I'll have to go back to working at the Sebeneleben and I hate that place. I was robbed twice *en* one week by the same *vato!*"

With an effort, Alex pulled her eyes from Jaime to Nene, briefly wondering what he was yammering on about. Assuming her silence meant refusal, Nene began to whine, "If you sign this I promise I'll name my next kid after you. Pleeeze?"

"Boy or girl?" Alex said, taking the clipboard from Nene, she signed off on the order.

"Oh yeah, that's right!" Nene said, brightening. "The next set of twins will be named after you. Both of them."

Leah followed Alex's ethereal gaze to the short man

standing next to Nene. She almost cut her thumb off when she saw her grandfather's young face in the old framed photo on her mother's nightstand.

Chapter 7

THE GODS MUST BE CRAZY

IT WAS MID-MORNING on a Wednesday. Mission Street was hot, dense, and alive with crowds in motion. Tinny dance music blared from the open doors of the shops and echoed from the nearly empty bars. The cars waiting for the light to change were tuned to the same radio station. With the bass up high, Tessa could feel the collective beat of the street in her chest.

As she passed a newsstand, the pages of a newspaper ruffling in the breeze caught her attention. "A Dingo Took My Baby!" Not exactly sure what a dingo was, Tessa bought a copy and began to read. She was trying to picture a little wild dog carrying off a ten-pound baby into Australia's outback, when she had the unmistakable feeling she was being checked out.

She tuned in to the two men standing next to her. In Spanish, they were openly debating the color of her nipples. One guessed they were small and pink, like the noses on kittens. The other agreed they were pink, but insisted they were the size of sand dollars.

Tessa rolled her eyes. Experience taught her that there was no default reaction to take. If she shot back an insult in Spanish, they would realize she was not a *gringa* but a *güera,* which would open up all lines of communication. Shifting her stance away from them, she thought of one of her *abuelita's* favorite adages. "To men, women are like chickens—all eggs, breast and thighs." Resisting the urge to cluck, she returned to the article.

"Ay mamí! Deja ver tus tetas," one of the men said, staring directly at her chest.

The other made kissy sounds. In a thick accent, he said, "Hey sexy. Planet on *mi* face."

Tessa fumed as the men laughed. This, right here, was exactly what she was not going to miss at Stanford. She was sick of the constant harassment by Latino baboons drenched in Old Spice, and their blatant disrespect of women—and even worse, pubescent girls.

The rational part of her brain knew that the macho act had surprisingly little to do with her. These two men were bonding by showing the other that they were not gay. How ironic was that? Another, and much larger part of her brain, the one that controlled her hands, wanted to knock their heads together.

She folded her newspaper and was about to walk away, when she realized one of the men looked familiar. She had recently seen the "Planet on *mi* face" guy with his wife at a friend's baby shower. They chatted for a while. What was her name? She remembered.

Looking him square in the eye—which was the last thing he expected—she said in Spanish, "Hi. How is Marisol?" Before he could answer, she continued, "Are you going to *Miguel Ángel's* party?" Marisol mentioned something about her great-great-uncle turning 109 and was having a party, or more accurately, the gathering of friends and family were invited over to chug beer while watching him nap on a cushioned chair.

At first, the two men's reactions were identical: surprise followed by shame. Planet's expression morphed into concern when he realized she was acquainted with the missus. His nod was grim.

Tessa walked away with a bounce in her step. She thought, all those years of putting up with that shit, and I figure out the solution one week before I move. Isn't that always the way?

Her thoughts were interrupted by a group of kids in front of Walgreen's. She was wondering if they were on some sort of field trip, when she noticed the doll in their teacher's hand. He was taunting one of the boys by holding it out of reach.

The image reshaped as Tessa drew closer. The crowd of kids was actually adults surrounding a giant. Up close, she could see that he was over seven feet tall and had the physical characteristics of Down syndrome.

The Cabbage Patch Kid he was clutching was the girl doll with two ponytails of shaggy red hair. A "$19.99" tag was dangling from either her pale blue dress or white pinafore. The store's manager was the one reaching for the doll. Curious, Tessa stopped to watch this silly little war play out.

That was when she noticed a diminutive woman she guessed to be the giant's grandmother. The woman tried to intervene, which only angered the giant. Tessa did not like where this was heading.

Remembering the graduation money her own grandparents had given her, she decided to pay for the damn doll. Tessa paused in mid-step. If I pay for this now will I be making things worse? What's going to happen the next time he's in a store and wants something? Changing her mind, she turned to leave.

At that moment, two police cars pulled up from different directions. The tension quickly escalated as four officers got out of the cars. Panicking, the elderly woman grabbed hold of the doll's little shoes and tried to tug her free from her grandson's bear hug. The giant raised a huge hand. In one gesture, he swatted his grandmother and wiped the amused expression off the face of the crowd.

The old woman landed on her back with a thud. As Tessa and others went to her, the giant made unintelligible sounds. Two of the policemen beat the back of his legs with their nightsticks until he was on his knees. The third moved behind to choke him with his nightstick. The giant was felled like a tree. It was only after he was rendered unconscious, and the shouting died down, could they hear his grandmother's heartbreaking sobs.

Tessa stared at the resigned crowd, the weeping woman, and the dog pile of cops on the misunderstood giant. The Cabbage Patch doll lay face down in gutter water. Tessa was near tears as she thought, No one was saved.

❧

Tessa was trying to shrug off the SFPD's latest arrest when she realized the street music had followed her into the restaurant's bustling kitchen. Leah was pulling trays of Anaheim chilies out of the oven. The heat from the pilot light softened the pale skins overnight. She was reaching for the final tray when Tessa spotted her.

"Hey, aren't you ready yet?" Tessa said. She was not about to tell Leah what she had just witnessed. Leah would absorb the pain and make it her own.

Leah stared blankly at her.

"The Gods Must Be Crazy, remember?" Tessa urged. "I scored two tickets to a special preview for being the fourth caller. We made these plans last week."

"Oh, I am so sorry. It completely slipped my mind," Leah said, without looking at Tessa. She was such a bad liar.

"That's all right. I'm early. Go get ready."

Leah shook her head at the misunderstanding. "I can't go today. Maybe in a couple of weeks."

Crushed, Tessa said, "The tickets are for today." Her anger flared. "Plus, I won't be here in a couple of weeks. I'll be living in Stanford, remember? This was supposed to be our last chance to hang out. Just the two of us."

Leah rubbed her forehead, suddenly hot. "I'm sorry, but we're short-staffed. Quico's in Mexico and Alex hasn't been around much lately. I need to fill in everywhere. I will pay you back for the tickets."

Tessa did not mean to be pushy. She was aware that Leah was covering some of Quico's shifts while he was away, but she also knew they had a well-trained kitchen staff. And yes, Alex's newfound popularity was making her scarce at the restaurant, but she was there every morning to update and print the menus, make register change, solve any staffing problems and get the place running.

Still, Tessa had the nagging feeling that Leah was using their absences as an excuse to become a recluse. "It's only for a few hours, Leah."

Leah did not answer.

"You look so pale. I'm worried about you."

Leah's eyes were downcast.

"I'll tell you what. We'll do anything you want on your next free night. So long as it's before I move. Maybe we can pull Alex away from the brown Barbies. How does that sound?" Tessa said.

Leah tried to smile. The moment she agreed, she began to worry about the hostile forces lying in wait for her. Who would she encounter when she next stepped onto the cracked sidewalk straining to hold the mercurial city together?

Chapter 8

LETTER FROM DULCE

Greetings from Bangkok ;)

I just got here, so I guess I should pick up where my last letter left off. After I served my time in jail, Maget, Zaheera, and their two *criaturas* took me to the nearest train station and saw me off. As an ex-con and a woman, I knew if I stayed in Malaysia I was gonna be fined for dropping *pedos*, or something, so I was glad for the police escort. For a *recuerdo*, I gave Zaheera and Maget a booklet filled with sketches I had made of all of them. Zaheera cried when she flipped through it. I could tell they were good tears by the way she traced the lines with her fingers.

It was raining switchblades when I jumped on the train. I was watching Malaysia go by all blurry when a couple of Tasmanian backpackers sat down behind me. They were pretty spooked. We got to talking and they told me they had seen *la chota* shoot and kill four guys sitting in a car because they were planning on robbing a bank.

Malcolm and Campbell (that's their names) saw the whole thing. They saw the "suspects" eating in their car right before the shooting. We all figured that bank robbers don't take a lunch break in front of a place they're about to hit.

The Tasmanians just dropped out of some kind of Buddhist labor camp, 'cause Campbell was sick of eating rice, meditating, and sweating his *culo* off in the fields.

Malcolm looks like he's from a small town, sort of gullible, but really nice. Campbell is funny and goofy. The *chistes* that come out of his mouth are milk-up-your-nose funny. I miss real milk. Can somebody please tell me what kind of messed-up animal soymilk comes from?

We got to Bangkok in the middle of the day. Man, was it hot. Bangkok is one smelly town! Even the traffic cops wear masks. It smells like petrol fumes, the sewer, and fresh cut fruit. So your mouth waters the way it does right before you throw up, and it waters for the sweet fruit—all at the same time.

We went straight to the port to meet up with Malcolm's brother, Gavin (they have the fakest sounding names in New Zealand). He's sailing through Southeast Asia on a schooner and was cleaning it when we showed up.

I'll write more after we check this place out.

✉

¿Qué pasa, kielbasa?

What can I say? Bangkok is like Las Vegas. The more you do, the more the amnesia kicks in. I will only remember this place in pictures. A lot of pictures that would be illegal for me to mail through the US Postal Service. ;)

It's time to move on, so Malcolm and Gavin are headed to Australia, and then home. They invited me to go with them, but I've already seen enough drunk Aussies and don't need to go there and see a million more.

We dropped Campbell off on an island off the coast of Thailand and that's kind of my fault. I heard about the full moon party from other backpackers and that everyone eats psychedelic mushrooms. It's the best-kept secret in Asia. Not anymore.

I'd told the Tasmanians about the island before I knew anything about the mess Campbell's in. It turns out that goofy Campbell is an outlaw. Back home, he's wanted for a pharmaceutical scam that worked like this:

Campbell would call a pharmacy and say he was with the police department. He'd tell the pharmacist they were on the trail of some guy filling fake prescriptions. The pharmacist's business was next on his hit list. He'd say that they were setting up a sting operation and all that the pharmacist had to do was fill the prescriptions. They'd be waiting outside to "catch him in the act."

Campbell said that all of the pharmacists smiled when they handed over the bags of pills. He paid with some expired credit card he'd found, and then just walked out the door. Campbell would be on his dirt bike and halfway home before the pharmacist figured out he'd been duped.

It gets better, I mean worse. Campbell was pulling his scam at a pharmacy in Christ Church (that's the capital of New Zealand) when he bumped into his mother's bridge partner. He'd already handed the fake prescriptions over, so, like they say, the jig was up. Just like that, *la chota* had Campbell's name and his old lady's address.

After hearing about the psychedelic island, Campbell said that it was the place for him. He said that meeting me was kismet. Malcolm and Gavin started calling it "Campbell's

Mushroom Island."

Before we left Campbell there we checked the island out. It was daytime, so all of the Gilligan and the Mary Ann tourists looked *crudo,* kind of dirty, and for some reason, really bruised. By the time we set sail Campbell had a cheap place to stay, a baggy of mushrooms and a big smile on his face. Who knows? It might be a decent place for him to hang out, until things cool down back home.

Mao mâak,
Dulce

Chapter 9

LEAH LOSES HER SOUL, AGAIN

ON THE MORNING after Alex's eighteenth birthday, Quico, the cook, received news that his mother was dying. He caught the next flight to Mexico City, where a nephew picked him up and drove the rough roads south to their cobblestoned pueblo. Quico spent the next three-and-a-half months saying goodbye to his mother, another three days after her death attending her Rosario, and before he was completely prepared to say goodbye, she was put to rest under a blanket of rich earth.

❧

When Quico returned from Mexico, Alex picked him up at the airport. As they drove along the dark stretch of freeway back to the city, she filled him in on the incident at the park. Relieved at finally having someone to unburden her folk illness fears, she told him that she thought Leah was suffering from *susto*.

When Quico first saw Leah, he noted the weight loss, dark circles under her eyes, listlessness, and despondency, and knew Alex was correct. But since Leah was not treated right away, he worried that she may be suffering from *espanto*, a more severe and potentially fatal form of *susto*.

Quico immediately phoned Doña Luz, a local *curandera*, to make an appointment. She was pretty booked, but had just had a cancellation for the following evening. Quico thanked her. He breathed a sigh of relief. Tomorrow at sunset, Doña Luz would perform a *limpia,* or ritual cleansing, to lure Leah's frightened soul back into her body.

ઠ❧

Doña Luz was standing on the porch of her stucco home when Quico and Leah pulled up. As they got out of the car Doña Luz's eyes surveyed Leah with interest. Her round wrinkled face reminded Leah of a baked apple doll. "When was the last time you were outside?" the *curandera* said.

Leah's stomach clenched, as she said, "Over three months ago." She felt Quico's worried eyes on her.

The *curandera* led them to the side door of the detached garage, where an altar was set up. A *mantilla,* bread, glasses of water, and bundles of flowers were carefully arranged near a statue of *La Virgen de Guadalupe.* On the cement floor, several white candles were positioned around a painted silver cross.

Once settled in a wicker chair, Leah reluctantly recounted the details of that horrible day in Golden Gate Park. She felt embarrassed by Quico's presence. In attempting not to look at him, her eyes kept blinking back to his, where she caught glimpses of fear and pain. As much as Leah regretted not sparing Quico the ugly details, talking was making her feel better. She wondered if pain ever really went away, or if it simply shifts around like desert sand.

When the sky turned pumpkin-meat orange, Doña Luz lit the candles. She instructed Leah to lie down on the floor for the *barrida,* or ritual sweeping. Leah positioned her legs and arms directly on the cold cross. Lying flat on her back, Leah's curved skull felt as fragile as a raw egg.

With the palm of her hand, Doña Luz gently closed Leah's eyes. Starting with the crown of her head, the *curandera* brushed

Leah briskly with an herbal broom with twine tied around the stems. During the *barrida,* Leah listened to a multitude of voices chanting and briefly wondered who had joined them. The air carried the exact same fragrance of the herbs she collected on that horrible day. Leah began to weep.

It was dark outside as the tears eventually subsided; when the chanting ceased, Leah felt serene. She heard the rustling of Doña Luz's floral print skirt as she stood up. The old woman jumped over Leah, luring her frightened soul back into her body.

One of the *curandera's* bare feet inadvertently kicked a candle on to its side, and sent it sliding across the cement floor. The flame touched a pile of oily rags which instantly combusted. Leah sat up with alarm. The three watched as the flames danced up the mantilla and ignited the dry flowers on the altar. Within the blaze, the statue of *La Virgen* continued to look sleepy, polite, and slightly bored.

The fire quickly spread to the ceiling and was eating the walls when Quico hoisted Leah to her feet. Pushing the two women through the side door, he steered them to the safety of the driveway. They stood there rooted to the spot. Leah heard the shriek of sirens as bright flames and black smoke devoured the *curandera's* garage. She felt the briefest of tugs from her body as the night inhaled her soul.

Chapter 10
MOTHER MARGARET SINS

MOTHER MARGARET STARED ABSENTMINDEDLY at the cross on the wall opposite her desk before noticing it. She realized that it was not a crucifix, but a plain wooden cross. She remembered inquiring about it once years ago, when she became the principal of Saint Joan of Arc High School, but sadly, no one knew it's providence.

She went to the symbol of God's love through his begotten son and gently lifted the cross off of the nail. She examined it up close while turning it over. The grain of wood was dark and heavily lined. The back looked no different than the dusty front. She wished she knew more about the type of tree it was carved out of.

Sighing resolutely, she gently kissed the cross where Christ's heart would be, if it was a crucifix. She was placing it back on the hook, when something stopped her in mid-reach. On the old wallpaper, a clean, visible outline of the cross was imprinted. Taking a step back, Mother Margaret stared at what was not there and felt the weight of her conscience grow heavier.

✟

There was a synergy in the Mission after China's disappearance. Mother Margaret was grateful to see so much religious and financial good come from the tragedy. What was even more miraculous was how the attendance by early 20-

somethings, the smallest demographic group, nearly doubled.

For the first time in over a decade, a student from St. Juan's received her vocation. This blessed calling from God occurred at the same church where China was last seen by dozens of her fellow parishioners, moments before her abduction. Several girls in the junior high and elementary levels also expressed interest in becoming nuns, even though some found the thought of marrying Jesus "kind of gross."

It was divine intervention when Mother Margaret ran into Eddie the mailman on the front steps of school that morning. Holding her hand out, she said, "I'll take that and save you the last few steps."

An envelope from the admissions office from a film school in New York caught her attention. "Who applied to a school out there?" she happily said to herself as she tore the envelope open and unfolded the single sheet. "Christina Nieves" popped out from the paragraphs. Mother Margaret clutched the letter close to her chest as she hurried to the office.

After locking her door, she reread the letter requesting Christina Nieves's high school transcripts. "China," she said, "alive!"

Mother Margaret leaned back against the wall, directly under the cross, and sunk with relief. But the negative impact the good news would have on the parish brought her back to full alertness. Needing some time to think, she shoved the folded letter into her concealed pocket.

After a sleepless night of weighing the truth against the cover-up, Mother Margaret got to school early. She sent China's transcripts to New York before tearing the admission's office letter into confetti. She flushed the bits down the four toilets in the girl's restroom, and then washed her hands.

Mother Margaret hung the cross back on the hook. She stared out the window. It was windy outside and the olive tree branches seemed to be waving at her, as though God was trying to get her attention. She stood there for a long time thinking about how one never really sees the wind, only what it catches.

Chapter 11

LETTER FROM DULCE

¡Quihubo from Borneo!

I stuck my watch in my backpack, so I don't know what day it is.

The Tasmanians dropped me off in Borneo a while ago. I'm staying at an artists' community I'd heard good things about. Artists from around the world are here to learn stone carving. I'm working on two pieces.

I started by making drawings of my ideas. I found two pieces of sandstone that fit the designs. I made the drawings on the stones and am carving them out. It's a real good way to spend the day.

I'm going to hang around here for a while. I'll be back in *San Pancho* in October. I'll call the restaurant when I book my ticket.

Stay gold, Pony Boy,
Dulce

✉

Chapter 12

LEAH'S FIRST DAY OF HER SENIOR YEAR

LEAH WAS THINKING how she liked the way the floor heaters made her first class of the new school year smell of ironed linen when the bell rang. The sudden noise sounded like shattering glass in her head. Taking a few calming breaths, she stood up and collected her books.

Leah made her way through campus as if inside a bubble, noticing how different teenage girls act when they think they're being watched. They all seemed to turn into concentrated versions of themselves. Those with a sense of humor become comedians, smart girls were always nerds, and an angry few reigned as bullies. Not able to find traces of herself in anyone, she wondered who she was to them.

As the lunch bell rang, Leah was aware that Alex, Tessa, and Dulce would not be in the cafeteria saving her a seat. But, when she saw strangers sitting at their spot, Leah wanted to run back to the restaurant and hide under the table in the kitchen. Instead, she passed through the lunch crowd and kept going until she reached the outdoor water heater.

On the chilled cement steps, Leah silently ate the lunch Quico packed for her. By the time she finished the tuna stuffed avocado and the bag of chips, her butt was completely numb. Standing up, she dusted the crumbs off of her pleated skirt. She still had 19 minutes to go. Tomorrow, I will bring a book with me.

❧

The first day of school ended uneventfully, thank God. Leah stood on the corner waiting for the light to change. The crossing button felt stuck and never seemed to alter the direction of traffic. It was something to do, so she pushed it again.

All day long, a noisy group of classmates with mean laughter seemed to be walking behind her. This particular group stopped for the light. Fear flushed acid through Leah's veins when she heard a booming voice among them. It was Becca, campus bully and the most Samoan-looking Mexican she had ever seen. Noticing Leah, big Becca began to sing the Star Wars anthem with new lyrics made up on the spot:

"Le-ah, Pri-n-cess Le-ah,

Why can't ya be-a,

Bit less fucked up."

The group erupted with laughter. Even Becca was happily surprised by what came out of her mouth. The lyrics and the laughter struck Leah like two hard slaps. As the students standing next to her slid away to avoid deflected attacks, Leah saw herself through their eyes. She was placed in the grim category of "target."

❧

The next morning, Leah woke with cramps and nervous diarrhea, as she would every school day for the rest of her senior year. During religion class, a far too enthusiastic classmate turned in her chair and said in a whisper, loud enough for everyone to hear, "Someone wrote about you in the second stall of the restroom. They also made a cartoon of you and, well you should just go see it for yourself."

Like identifying a body at the morgue, Leah dreaded going, yet she needed to see for herself. She waited outside the restroom until the coast was clear, and then ducked into the second stall. Leah gasped. It was much worse than she imagined.

"Bum-fucking Leah!!!" was carved into, not written on, the metal door. Above the quote were four stick figures. The three had cigar-shaped penises and the fourth was in a triangle skirt, bent at the waist. A smiling face decal normally associated with having a nice day was on her emaciated shoulders. The jaundice representation of Leah appeared to be smiling blankly, while doing it doggy-style with all three partners.

Chapter 13

MOTHER MARGARET SPILLS THE BEANS

DURING CONFESSION, Mother Margaret dutifully spilled the beans of her cover-up to Padre Lucas. Grasping the significance of the lie and the ramifications of the truth, the priest doled out a hefty Act of Contrition. Expecting to hear something about making restitution, she was shocked when Padre Lucas slowly slid the tiny window closed.

Feeling partially absolved from her sin, Mother Margaret went back to the business of school and religion.

A few days later, the honorable Archbishop Wong phoned Mother Margaret to say that he needed to discuss Christina Nieves with her and Padre Lucas, in person. Mother Margaret was in a state of near-hysteria as she spruced up the school for the visit. They toured the grounds before retiring to her office for some coffee and grasshopper pie.

The Archbishop immediately raised the subject of China. "I am very impressed with the way our community has pulled together during this time of spiritual crisis."

Mother Margaret solemnly nodded. If he keeps talking, I won't have to, she thought.

"Some of Christina's advocates are petitioning for her beatification. Believe it or not, I don't think the idea is so far-fetched. I'm not sure if you are aware of it, but our beloved Pope has already canonized more saints than all of his predecessors combined. Christina could very well become the first Mexican-American saint in Roman Catholic history while serving as succor for the Americas."

"But, your Grace," Mother Margaret stammered, "how can that be? There is no proof that China was actually abducted or killed." She hoped she sounded more like the voice of reason than an accessory after the fact.

"Yes, a very good point," Archbishop Wong said. "We are all praying for Christina's safe return, but one must prepare for all possible outcomes."

"It is in God's hands," Padre Lucas said, because he felt obligated to say something. As Mother Margaret nodded, she wondered how one prepares for the most inevitable, not to mention the most disgraceful outcome that was sure to be theirs.

Chapter 14

DULCE RETURNS TO THE MISH

DULCE'S PLANE LANDED nearly an hour ago and there was still no sign of her. Alex was getting antsy. She went to the airline counter, where the woman in crisp polyester clicked on the keyboard, but retrieved no new information. The plane landed on time, and no, she did not have access to the passenger list.

Alex and Leah were arguing over what to do next when the sliding glass doors finally parted for Dulce. With her brown face screwed up like that, she reminded Leah of a catcher's mitt.

"Where were you?" Alex demanded as she hugged her.

"I was officially detained," Dulce said, spitting out the hot words. Her eyes fixed on Alex. "Hey, where'd your hair and eyebrows go?"

"Complete makeover," Alex said. Her face exhibited expressions new to Dulce.

"Leah!" Dulce said, hugging Leah around the butt and lifting her slightly off the floor. A startled Leah squealed with laughter. She blushed at her outburst as Dulce placed her back down.

"Why were you detained?" Alex began to walk. She needed to get back to the restaurant.

"I guess they've never seen a Mexican entering the country legally before. They needed to make sure my passport wasn't fake," she said.

Leah watched as the pissed-off Dulce was left behind, like shed skin. She wished she could shrug off confrontations so easily. Instead, she tended to carry misery in a locket in her mind. People can be so loyal to the wrong moments of their past.

"So, what's new around here, besides Alex's head?" Dulce said.

Alex held out her large hand and something glimmered on one of her splayed fingers. "I'm getting married, Dulce. Can you believe it?" Alex could barely contain her excitement.

Dulce gave her a cool stare. "Who's the father?"

Alex slapped her arm playfully. "I'm not pregnant, silly! My fiancé is named Jaime Pedrosa and he's marrying me because he wants to, not because he has to."

"What?" Dulce said. "No maternity dress for the bride? Do they even make them that way?" They both laughed.

The three were approaching the airport's exit when Leah said, "Here's your jacket. You do know summer is over, don't you?"

"Oh yeah. Thanks." Dulce stared at the Raiders jacket in her hands. "Did you stop by my house to pick this up?"

Alex and Leah glanced at one another. Alex was elected to speak. She began slowly. "Well, no. Dulce, your parents came by last month and dropped off your stuff."

A stunned Dulce walked two steps ahead as she took in the unexpected news of returning home to discover she was homeless. She was wondering if her parents had changed the locks, when Leah caught up with her and placed an arm over her shoulder.

In a warm whisper, Leah said, "Let's go home."

Dulce frowned and shrugged dramatically. "I can't ask one of you guys to sleep on your own couch."

"You're not moving in with us, *tonta!*" Alex cringed at the thought of living with Dulce. "We're sticking you in the attic."

❧

Back in the Mission, the three-flight walk-up led to a small landing and a freshly painted open door. Alex was breathing heavily through her mouth as she got the lights. Dulce whistled. "This place is enormous! I remember when we tried to play in here when we were kids, but there was no room," she said. The ceiling came to a point, making the room a long triangle. At the far end was a bay window facing the street.

"Well, the length is the same as the restaurant, but as you can see, the ceiling points so the walls slant in," Alex said.

"This is your kitchen." Dulce turned in the direction of Leah's voice. She was standing in front of a portable bamboo bar.

Dulce recognized it as the service station bar from way back, when Mr. Cernuda had ventured into catering. The new business went belly-up after an employee drove off for a wedding with the fully stocked van. He kept going until he reached Santa Ana, where he threw a party for his son's third birthday. The stripped-down van eventually turned up in a chop shop in San Diego.

Dulce was rendered speechless by all of this unconditional love and loyalty. She blinked back tears as she held her arms out and hugged them both. Alex smelled different, like drugstore cologne—Jean Nate or Charlie. Leah still carried the fresh scent of cut grass.

After Dulce christened her tiny bathroom, they sat and talked while her numbness wore off. "Dulce, we have something else to tell you and it's not good," Alex said, picking her words carefully.

Dulce's tired expression shifted. "Dang! I was only gone for four months. What the fuck else happened?"

"It's China. She's missing." Alex said.

"She disappeared after you left. The police think she was kidnapped," Leah said, from her seat on an old trunk.

Dulce stared down at a loose thread in the fabric of the chair and began to tug at it. Alex's eyes flared at Dulce. Turning to Leah, she said, "Dulce knows something." Then back to Dulce. "You know where she is, don't you?"

"China's parents are so worried," Leah pleaded.

"Huh," Dulce laughed a humorless laugh. "I may know something, but before I tell you, I have to swear you to secrecy."

The sisters exchanged glances. They eagerly nodded.

"I saw China the day before I left. She stopped by to say goodbye 'cause she wasn't going to be here when I got back."

"Are you saying that she ran away?" Alex said.

"*Naranjas.*" Dulce said, shaking her head. "China's eighteen. She moved, that's all."

"Why didn't she tell her parents?" Leah said.

"She didn't?" Dulce looked puzzled. "I'll tell you what; I'll call her tomorrow and find out the details."

"You have her phone number?" Alex said, incredulous.

"And her address. I sent her a postcard from Borneo," Dulce said.

Alex sighed audibly. "We're giving you until noon, then

we'll call her parents ourselves."

"Fair enough," Dulce said, while rummaging around in her backpack for several scrolls. "Here you go. It was either this or T-shirts."

Leah's breath caught in her throat as she unrolled her scroll. It was a series of exotic fruit, some she did not recognize. Alex's scroll depicted a six-paneled narrative of what appeared to be Dulce's adventures: Dulce at the market, visiting a temple, pitching pennies with a group of boys. "Did you teach them how to gamble?"

Shaking her head, Dulce said, "Do you really think that I'd corrupt decent people like that?" Alex noted she dodged the question.

"Speaking of teaching, I met this couple at the artist community in Borneo. They teach art in Amsterdam. Check this out, they want me to go to their school. They're taking my sculptures with them when they go home. Then they're gonna send me an application and submit it with my work."

Alex considered Dulce as a student and how she always wanted to learn, yet hated being instructed. She chose not to mention this for fear of quashing Dulce's motivation. Anything was better than the Kerouac lifestyle she seemed drawn to. She remembered something. "Wait a sec. Isn't that the place where drugs, prostitution, and God-knows-what-else is legal?"

Dulce smirked. She opened her mouth. But before she could say something Alex would regret, Leah spoke up, "Dulce must be tired from her flight. We should let her get some rest."

꩜

After Alex and Leah left, it took Dulce some time to still

her roiling mind. As she untied her braid and shook out a foot and a half of jet-black hair, she thought back to the time her brother stabbed her. She had been reaching for the final slice of pizza, when he picked up a knife and plunged it all the way through her hand. Dulce was 12, Ray 17.

In a panic, their mother wrapped a dirty dishtowel around Dulce's hand. "There you go again! You should know better than to make your brother mad!" she said. A shocked Dulce watched as the psychopath smirked as he ate the last slice of pizza. A smudge of her blood was on the crust.

As Dulce touched the "stigmata" scar on her left hand, she tried to remember if he actually ate all of the crust. Ray, now 23, was unemployed and still living at home. She thought how broken parents always prefer their broken children. She couldn't help but wonder if they would ever miss her, or she them.

The smell of fresh paint was getting to her. Dulce was struggling to open the window, when she noticed something scratched in the putty. The recent paint job had coated the letters smooth. She leaned close to read the one word: "Velvet."

Chapter 15

MRS. CERNUDA MOVES TO MEXICO

THE MORNING SKY hung heavy with steel wool clouds as Alex sat in the kitchen, sipping coffee and reading the Sunday paper. Leah heated water in the kettle for her morning tea. It was the same kettle their mother had bought years before that never whistled. For most of her young life, the water evaporating from the hot kettle was a point of contention between her parents.

Leah plucked the tiny chamomile petals in a "he loves me, he loves me not" gesture. When the steam billowed, she moved the kettle from the burner. Keeping her hand on the wooden handle, Leah felt the low rumble settle and thought of distant thunderstorms. She poured the still water into the teapot and smiled as the steam caressed her face. The kitchen soon smelled clean and slightly medicinal.

"Girls, I need to talk to you," Mrs. Cernuda said, hurrying into the kitchen. She appeared shaken. Alex quickly closed the pink pages of the entertainment section. Leah sat down slowly, bracing herself for bad news. Their mother began to speak. When she realized she was competing with the radio, she briskly shut it off.

"I have spent the best years of my life raising you two girls," she blurted out. The look that passed between the sisters was not lost on their mother. She glared at Alex before continuing. "God has answered my prayers and sent you a husband."

I cannot believe you're taking credit for Jaime, Alex thought, but said nothing. She wanted to see where her mother was going with this.

"I've done my duty as a wife, and a mother. And now, I need to retire..." Alex wanted to interrupt her right there, and say, "Retire from what? You are only 43 years old!"

"Now that you are getting married, your husband will take care of you and you can take care of your little sister. So, tomorrow I'm moving back to Mexico."

Alex and Leah's eyes grew as wide and round as saucers. Realizing she had just stunned her daughters into silence made her feel better. Smiling, Mrs. Cernuda recited her itinerary.

Mrs. Cernuda spent the evening on the phone saying good-bye to relatives and friends. The sisters listened to their mother's end of the conversations, which varied with each telling. By the final call, the first and last accounts of her decision to move had as much in common as a paper and linen napkin.

❧

The next morning, Mrs. Cernuda's bewildered daughters took her to the airport. By nightfall, Carmen Cernuda would become Jalisco's newest resident. For the rest of the week, Alex swung back and forth between ripples of relief and pangs of guilt for her relief, while Leah experienced the raw pain of childhood rejection.

Chapter 16
LEAH SINGS

IT WAS LATE OCTOBER when Leah, according to school gossip, went from being a nymphomaniac to a lesbian. Her new insatiable appetite for sexual conquest was already legendary at St. Joe's, the all-boys' high school nearby. At the Cow Palace drive-in, Leah was jumping from the backseat of one car to the next, when it occurred to her that she never climaxed. She realized that the problem was not with the boys' lack of experience, but the fact that they were male.

An unnamed source placed Leah at the movies with a woman who was a good ten years older than her. They were at the Lumière Theater off of Polk Street, the one that shows foreign films. They were spotted holding hands while standing in line for a French film. The older woman pretended to whisper into Leah's ear, but was actually nibbling on her earlobe.

❧

As the tide ebbs before a tsunami, there was a vacuum of silence at school. Leah could feel eyes burning holes in her. When she forced herself to look in their direction, the stares turned away. Near the statue of Joan of Arc, she overheard a conversation about Becca jumping *la Trampa* after school. With a start, Leah realized they were talking about her.

When the last bell of the day rang, Leah was certain Becca would be waiting on the other side of any door she chose. She ducked into the library to hide. Expecting Becca's large head to peer in, Leah flinched each time the door opened. She pulled an extra credit assignment for her American Government class out of her folder. It read, "What is protected by the First Amendment?" Leah wrote, "Not me." As she erased her words, she wished she could fade away as easily.

After the library closed, Leah stood on the front steps of St. Juan's. Becca was leaning against a parked Impala, wearing black corduroy pants and a Giants sweatshirt. It suddenly dawned on Leah that she was waiting on campus for Becca to go home and change into her fighting clothes. Leah wondered how many girls had been pummeled before this brutal pattern emerged.

Becca's homegirls were leaning their butts on the front fender, chewing gum slowly. The onlookers, mostly classmates, stood around chatting in a small cluster. Becca's head was bobbing to the song on the car's radio, content to soak in the atmosphere she roused. Her predator's eyes instinctively narrowed when she spotted Leah. "Hey, *Trampa!* Did you get lost in there?"

Leah wanted desperately to turn and run back into school. Instead, she took a step, and then each step slower. As Becca approached Leah, her homegirls fanned out and blocked all escape routes. The spectators formed a perfect semicircle out of striking distance. It seemed so well choreographed, Leah briefly wondered if they had been rehearsing.

Becca was suddenly so close to Leah all she could see was a face shaped like a thumb. Becca had that crusty white stuff on the corners of her mouth, and her breath smelled of peanut butter. "I hear you went from dicks to chicks!" she said.

Tense laughter erupted from the crowd.

The laughter was suddenly far away as some force began to tug Leah's consciousness out of her body. She was both in and out of the bubble at the same time.

A smiling Dulce meandered through the crowd and toward Becca. The laughter dried up. Dulce checked on Leah, who was looking down. Dulce read both fear and resignation on her face.

"*¡Orale!*" Dulce said. Leah's eyes were on her in an instant, but Dulce did not seem to notice. Singling Becca out, Dulce gave a quick jerk back of her head. "*¿Qué onda Becca?*" she said.

There was a look of recognition on Becca's face. "Hi," she said, and immediately regretted it.

"Looks like I almost missed all the fun," Dulce said, walking well into Becca's personal space.

The circle tightened, but now Becca's backup stood beyond the spectators. "I hear you been spouting off stories about my *ruca*. I also hear you're really bad at it. A lesbian, a nymphomaniac? What's next, a lesbimaniac?" There was a ripple of laughter. "I think someone needs to 'splain women to you, Becca." This time the crowd laughed openly. Dulce became serious. "You think 'cause I graduated, I evaporated?" Becca glared at Leah. "No, she didn't tell me. You of all people should know how fast news travels around here. 'Specially when you go around spreading it."

Dulce leaned forward and lowered her voice to a mean whisper. "Whatever happens to Leah will happen to you. It doesn't matter who says something to her, or touches her. You're the one who's gonna have to pay. *¿Entiendes?*"

Becca nodded cautiously, before resting her chin close to

her chest.

"All right then." Dulce took a step back and like a flock of birds in flight, the crowd behind her moved in sync. "Would anybody else care for a free consultation?" Dulce glanced around. "Let's go."

Leah walked close behind in the trail Dulce cut. It was silent for a second. Then all of the students began to chatter at once, with the exception of Becca.

Dulce and Leah slowed when they were a block away from school. Dulce said nothing. She wanted to hear what Leah had to say. It took another block. "How did you know?" Leah mumbled at a red light.

"How did I know? A better question would be what took me so long to find out?" The light changed and they began to cross. "Poor Becca," Dulce said. Before Leah could react, Dulce continued, "She gets an ass-whooping almost every day when she gets home. If it ain't her old man, it's one of her blockhead brothers." Dulce nodded greetings to an elderly couple passing. "The next day she goes to school and tortures some kid. She'll push 'til they push back." Dulce peered obliquely at Leah. "You never pushed back."

Leah looked stricken. "If she knows what it feels like to be picked on, why is she so mean?"

Dulce raised her shoulders and let them drop. "Pecking order."

Leah suddenly burst into tears. Dulce pulled her from the stream of walking traffic and into the doorway of a vacant store. "Leah, it's OK! She's never gonna bother you again, I promise!" Dulce's voice was so tender that it made Leah cry harder.

After a series of sobs, Leah barked sounds before language formed. Needing to complete the purge, she told Dulce her other troubles. She was followed home from school by slow-moving cars. Strange men would insist that she get in. "One had his you-know-what in his hand," Leah said, blanching.

Dulce thought for a moment. Putting an arm around Leah's shoulder, she led her back to the foot traffic of the sidewalk. "I'll tell you what—when we get home I'll teach you my don't-fuck-with-me walk."

"You walk like an ex-con," Leah said.

Dulce smiled at the compliment. "Oh yeah, well you walk like you're one of those little brown birds with a broken wing."

Leah wiped her tears with the sleeve of her sweater. "I can't ever go back there," referring to high school.

Dulce stopped. She put her hands on Leah's shoulders and stared into her eyes. "If you don't go back there, *there* will never leave you," she said. "I mean, do you really want Becca shadowing you for the rest of your life, doing the Becca butt boogie?" Dulce started singing their favorite childhood song, altering the name. She forced Leah to march in step.

"The party was jumping
When Becca got off of her stump
The whistles were blowing
And everybody did the bump
But all the time Becca
Had been working on a goodie
Now folks call it the Becca Butt Boogie
When Becca Butt did her goodie
She started the Becca Butt Boogieeeeee
No question…"

Dulce nudged Leah, who awkwardly joined the chorus, "Bump, bump, bubbadump. Bah bump bump bump, bubbadump."

Dulce threw her head back and laughed. It was such a wonderful laugh. Dulce began the next verse. Leah joined in. "When Becca got moving…"

❧

On Monday, Leah trudged into school as if wading through deep water. At lunch, she sat in her usual spot on the cement steps in front of the water heater. She quietly picked at her shrimp quesadilla, while rereading the same page of *The Bell Jar*. She half expected Becca to trap her there, and then bludgeon her with one of the loose stones under the statue of St. Joan.

It was late in the school day when she first saw Becca. Leah halted. Her heart started beating in her ears and she could see little stars in her vision. But Leah had the impression Becca had spotted her seconds before, and intentionally turned away. As Becca hurried in the opposite direction, the beat in Leah's ears took on the tempo of the *Bertha Butt* song.

❧

Quico was illegally parked outside of St. Juan's. When Leah saw him, she was sure Dulce betrayed her confidence. It became clear on the drive home that Quico knew nothing about Becca. It just occurred to him that he drove by Leah's school every day, around the same time that she got out. The short trip would give them a chance to talk shop, or in Quico's case, complain.

"I can't work the line with Sapo anymore. He keeps handing me wet oven mitts. And he smells like asparagus pee and he never washes his clothes. I'm not kidding. I got one of those Chiquita banana stickers and put it on his back pocket last month, and it's still there."

Relieved, Leah made concerned sounds, while nodding sympathetically. She rolled down the window and breathed in the Mission. The breeze, scented with roasted coffee, barbeque, incense, churros, Suavitel, exhaust, cigarettes, and a marinade of melancholy, nipped at her scalp and caused her long curls to lift and dance.

Chapter 17

THANKSGIVING AND THE GIRLS' REUNION

AROUND 60 of the Anayas's friends and family were expected for Thanksgiving dinner this year. Even though it was a potluck, Mrs. Anaya started saving for the feast in September and had spent the last several days preparing the traditional Mexican-American banquet of turkey with two kinds of stuffing, tamales, a rich *mole poblano* to be poured over either the turkey or the tamales, buttery mashed potatoes and gravy, yams buried under layers of sweet guavas and marshmallows, green beans drowned in cream of mushroom soup, Brussels sprouts con chorizo, *rajas, guacamole, arroz, nopales,* salsa, canned cranberry sauce, and four desserts.

Tessa was home for her first visit since going off to college. When Alex, Leah, and Dulce arrived at the Anayas' house, they squealed as they group-hugged Tessa. Mr. Anaya cut the reunion short by rounding up all the kids for the annual holiday photo. Through the lens he could see that his generation produced mostly girls. Out of the dozens of related children in the fidgeting huddle, only about a third were male, and less than half of those carried the Anaya name.

Mr. Anaya sighed resolutely. He said, "OK, say *chispas!*" The camera clicked late and the photo caught the group with gaping mouths. After the flash, everyone except Dulce dispersed. She stood there a moment longer, watching the fireflies born from the flash.

"So? How is Stanford? Are the parties great?" Alex said, giving Tessa a wink and a nudge.

Tessa was still trying to get used to Alex in all of that make-up. The lavender and purple shades applied to her lids looked like painful bruises. And the white rayon blouse with shoulder pads as big as maxi pads was such an unfortunate choice for Alex's full figure.

"They are pretty much what you would expect." Tessa didn't attend parties. She was awarded much less financial aid than she was expecting. To cover her expenses, she worked part-time at Kinko's, which made her first semester in college all the more stressful.

Changing the subject, she said, "So, what's been going on around here?"

"The other day I ran out of postage stamps and still had a letter to send to China," Dulce said, sidling up to them. "You know what I did? I switched the addresses. So, when the letter was returned, 'cause of insufficient postage, it was mailed to her."

"What if the post office doesn't catch it?" Leah said.

"Then the letter comes back to me. You see, it's a foolproof plan," Dulce said.

"Yeah, it's proof that you're a fool." Alex snorted. "*Babosa,* don't you realize you're defrauding the government!"

Finding humor in Alex's reproach, Dulce said, "You say it like it's a bad thing."

"How is China these days?" Tessa whispered. Since Dulce, Alex, and Leah agreed to let Tessa in on the secret, they gave her the occasional, incredible update.

As soon as the Nieveses heard the rumors of possible sainthood, they erected a shrine in their daughter's bedroom. It quickly became a site of pilgrimage for the handful of believers, and the scores of the curious.

"Ha! Tessa," Dulce laughed, while tugging at her arm, as if Tessa was distracted. "Alex is throwing a fundraiser for China at the restaurant, and she donated a huge check to *la causa!*"

"You have got to be kidding!" Tessa half-smiled. She looked at Alex, whose mouth was curving downward, like an upside-down pinto bean.

"It's a tax write-off." Alex's eyes got thin. "You're one to talk. You made the 'Where is China?' posters."

Tessa shifted her surprise to Dulce, whose head cocked. "You got me there! But I was paid for my work. Hey, when you stop and think about it, you sort of paid me. Thanks, Caca Alejandra!" Dulce said, using Mrs. Cernuda's restaurant phone greeting.

Alex was about to pinch Dulce again when someone caught her eye. "He's here, he's here!" she sang, hurrying to the open front door. She threw her arms around a man a good three inches shorter than her. Dulce chuckled as Alex's enthusiasm almost knocked him over.

"Did you really send the letter to China without postage?" Tessa said to Dulce, suddenly struck by how familiar Jaime looked.

"*Chale*, that only works if both addresses are in the same city. I just like messing with her," Dulce said.

As they approached, Alex waved an arm dramatically. "This, is Jaime," she said, like she was unveiling a game show boat.

His eyes mesmerized Tessa. They were the color of a sunset when viewed through brown stained glass.

"Hi, Jaime," Dulce said, mock-yawning.

After some small talk, Jaime said to Alex in Spanish, "Would you like something to drink?"

Alex smiled, caught unprepared, the wallflower asked to dance for the first time. "The sodas are in the backyard. Here, I'll show you," she said, grabbing Jaime's hand. She mouthed, "Isn't he great?" to Tessa, who smiled and nodded.

Alex led Jaime through the living room, wanting everyone to see that they were a couple. Three strangers strolled through the open front door. Jaime released his hand from Alex's grip and waved for them to follow.

Leah became uneasy. "I guess Jaime invited some of his friends. I hope that's not a problem?" she said, hesitantly.

"Of course it isn't. You know my mom. She thinks she coined the phrase 'The more the merrier.'"

"A little English is a dangerous thing," Dulce said.

Jaime and his buddies were back in the living room, balancing a plastic cup of beer in each hand. Tessa watched Alex trail behind. Realizing who Jaime reminded her of, Tessa stared at Leah. "Is it just me, or does he look like your grandfather?"

Leah seemed not to hear Tessa. They watched as one of Jaime's friends, dressed in a black cowboy hat and a black Wrangler shirt with silver arrows over the pockets, intentionally brushed up against Tessa's aunt. He whispered something into Jaime's ear, before following her into the kitchen. Jaime's laugh was like that of a boy at a really good booger joke.

Chapter 18

THE DAY AFTER THANKSGIVING

TESSA, ALEX, LEAH, AND DULCE nearly ate their weight in leftovers before filing into Dulce's flat. Most of her furnishings were sold or given away and replaced with an odd, yet functional, collection of city property. A park bench with cast iron rod ends acted as the couch. A large wooden cable spool resting on its side served as the coffee table. A little further was Dulce's bed—a picnic table with the lower legs cut off. A futon pad, saffron-colored sheets, and a small pillow covered the wooden tabletop. The bench seat on one side served as a bookshelf.

Tessa drifted through the room slowly, the way one does in a museum. "It's..." she paused. It suddenly became really important to use the right word. "You!"

"Isn't it?" Dulce agreed, arms crossed and nodding.

Paintings from thrift stores and dumpster-diving expeditions were tightly arranged on the now deep indigo slanted walls. Even though Dulce saw some of the pieces more as space fillers, the effect was moving. "You see, I have got this theory," Dulce explained, with wide hand gestures. "If you combine a lot of odd things together, it kinda evens out."

It dawned on Tessa that she was referring to the four of them. She smiled thoughtfully. "It really does."

Once the tour was complete, Alex put the group to work. Their assignment was to make the paper flowers that would be strung across the cars of the wedding party. The fake carnations could almost pass for real ones from the moving vehicles. Almost.

All four were adept at the flower-making task since the responsibility usually fell to the young girls in the bride's family. Each had enough relatives to have mastered the craft by the age of eight. Alex understood that flowers made with the care of her friends would be more meaningful, not to mention turn out much, much better.

Alex and Tessa were sitting on the park bench, while Dulce and Leah sat cross-legged on a commercial mat with a Sambo's Restaurant logo woven in. As Alex went on about all of the wedding preparations she was working on, the squares of tissue were stacked like pancakes, and tied in the center with thick thread. Starting with the top tissue, each layer was gingerly separated, tugged, and shaped.

They were filling bag number three. Alex was explaining how to keep the romance in a relationship alive when Dulce stopped her. "Romance? Do you hear yourself when you yammer on like that? If you could see the male brain on TV, it would look exactly like Pong." Tessa and Leah laughed and tossed pink and white paper florets at Dulce. Alex growled as she picked up and carefully reshaped each one.

"I'm serious. Latino men are even worse. They're only wired to see women one of two ways." Dulce's head began to move back and forth as if watching Pong. "Virgin, whore, virgin, whore," she repeated.

Alex glared at Dulce. "What makes you an authority on the male psyche? I mean, you've never even been on a date." She laughed harshly.

"The same authority that makes you Venus de Chimayó," Dulce said. She stared at Alex's forehead, as if she could see inside. "Your brain would look like Pac-Man. Big mouth and all."

"Ooh, ooh, wait!" Alex said, springing to her feet. White tissues fluttered from her lap like frightened doves. She turned up the volume on the radio. "Here's our wedding song! Jaime picked it. Isn't it perfect?" Billy Joel sang, "Don't go chang'n to try and please me..." The rest worked in silence as Alex remained by the stereo, as if locked in conversation.

Leah felt a heavy sadness settle over her. Within the walls of their safe and predictable world, Alex altered their lives. In that brief instance in the restaurant's kitchen, Leah was replaced by Jaime, and unceremoniously dismissed. The sudden realization that she was now an "I" left her slightly winded.

When the song was over, Dulce spoke up. "I hate to have to tell you this, but someone has to. Alex, you can't marry Jaime."

Tessa's hands faltered. She was suddenly fearful that Dulce would vocalize her baseless misgivings about Alex's fiancé.

"What do you mean?" Alex's face grew long with worry.

With all of that eyeliner and red lipstick Alex was wearing, she reminded Dulce of one of those sad clown paintings. "You're going the wrong way on the color chart. You're supposed to marry lighter."

Alex huffed. "Shut up Dulce! That's not even funny!"

Dulce was now grinning. "The successful person always marries lighter. Everybody knows that. You're the one bringing home the *jamón*, and..." she said, squinting "you're more of a caramel beige; Jaime is more of an olive brown."

Alex chucked a flower at Dulce, overhand.

"What! I don't make the rules." Dulce turned to Tessa and Leah for support. "Help me out here. Am I right, or am I right?"

Chapter 19

ALEX GETS MARRIED!

ALEX AND JAIME'S WEDDING was perfect. It took place two days after Christmas at Saint Juanita's church. There was standing room only once the guests filled the bride's side, and then overflowed into the groom's side.

Aware that the Nativity scene would still be displayed under the marble altar of the church, Alex dressed the Three Kings, Mary, Joseph and Gabriel in the wedding colors. Even Baby Jesus was diapered in a remnant of bridal satin, for luck—not that they would need any.

One week before the wedding, Alex rushed into Dulce's studio, unannounced. Dulce tried to protest, but when she saw that glint of matrimonial madness in Alex's eyes, she got the hell out of the way. After scrubbing the floors and stacking the art supplies in the shopping carts at the far end of the room, Alex brought up her wedding gown. Behind her Leah carried the bridesmaids' dresses, her eyes telling Dulce to behave.

Alex, assisted by Leah, dressed first. She practiced turning in tight circles, salsa, followed by freestyle dancing in the $3,000 gown. Dulce kept trying to catch Leah's eye to make her laugh, but she knew better. Leah blurred her vision and maintained her composure, even when the unfocused Alex attempted to curtsy. She broke her forward fall with the palms of her hands.

Dulce and even Leah laughed themselves to tears the first time Alex took a break. She just said, "OK, OK, take five!" like they were on Broadway. She plopped down on the bench. The hoops flung straight up, offering the two bridesmaids a clear shot of Alex's thick thighs and grandma *chonies*.

Alex experienced the satisfaction of watching the tables turn when Dulce tried on her pink taffeta dress. Dulce shot Alex a dirty look. "Getting married doesn't give you the right to make me wear this Pepto Bismol parachute."

Ignoring her, Alex handed Dulce a folding fan. "Here. Take it already," she said, quickly stepping back, as if she just lit a firecracker.

With a flick of the wrist, Dulce opened the fan. She glared at the cheap lace, and then at Alex. "What the fuck is this?"

"It's the frame for the bridesmaids' bouquets. Oh, wait until you see it when it's done. It's going to have a cluster of pink rosebuds, baby's breath, and long satin curly ribbons." Alex sighed at the mere thought of their beauty.

Dulce's kewpie doll lips opened, spewing out a litany of vulgarities toward the Southern belle. While they argued, Leah squeezed into her garment. Although her dress was made from the same luminous pink fabric as Dulce's, the maid of honor's dress was long, snug, and strapless. Both Alex and Dulce stopped arguing to gaze at her.

"What?" Leah said, startled. She searched for stains or a tear in the seam.

"You look great, Leah. Just like a torch singer!" Dulce said. Alex nodded grimly.

❧

On the morning of Alex's wedding, the bridesmaids met

at *La Casa de Cabello* Salon. Leah was dabbing a little liquid foundation onto the back of her hand as Alex watched. It was too light and made her skin look muddy, but Alex said the color was perfect. To further downplay her sister's beauty, Alex talked Leah into wearing her hair in a style that did not suit her, or anyone under the age of 70.

Tessa was a rock. She never argued and never did anything but show support to Alex. Unlike Dulce the barbarian, who kept referring to the "posse" as the "pussies," Tessa was amiable to the rest of the bridesmaids: Katrina, Marissa, Danielle, and Mia.

Dulce did manage to redeem herself a little at the reception. When the guests were inebriated to the point of mistaking a 20-dollar bill for something smaller, Dulce dimmed the lights. She got the band to start up with the dollar dance, a tradition where the guests line up to dance with the bride or groom and pin money to their clothing. Before Alex knew it, her gown was completely sheathed with bills. When she spun in the candlelit room, the fabric transformed into military camouflage.

❦

In April, Alex discovered she was pregnant and much to her surprise, Jaime was as excited as she was. He kept referring to the baby as his son or Jaime Junior. Alex thought it was cute, until the baby's gender lit the fuse to their first fight.

They were watching *fútbol* on TV, when Jaime pointed to the set and said, "My son will be out there someday."

"You know," Alex said, tracing his ear with her fingertip, "it could be a girl."

Swatting her hand away, Jaime brought his face close to

hers. "My son will be a boy!" he shouted.

Before storming off, Jaime chucked his full beer bottle across the room. Alex sat numb until a goal was scored. She stared in disbelief at the liquid dripping from several wedding photos hanging in silver frames, she thought, But what if it's a girl?

Chapter 20
TESSA AND THE COOKIE STANDOFF

TESSA WAS WALKING on Palm Drive toward Stanford's campus with a box of cookies in hand. She was due for her shift manning the Valentine's Day bake sale booth five minutes ago and picked up her pace. She joined several campus organizations, including the *Hermanas Unidas Raza Latina*, or HURL, for short, a Latina organization committed to supporting students of color—preferably brown.

On Valentine's Day, all HURL members were asked to bake cookies to sell at their booth stationed by the campus bookstore. Since Tessa's dorm room did not have a kitchen, much less an oven, she walked to the bakery in town and bought a dozen chocolate chip cookies. It did not really make much sense to buy cookies to sell for such a slight profit, but she could see no way around it.

Tessa was now ten minutes late, which was the norm since her schedule usually overlapped. Free time no longer existed in her life as she managed five pre-med classes, a job, extracurricular activities, and studying. The lack of room for error made her anxious. Something would have to give and she decided to quit HURL. She would let the president know the next time she saw her.

As Tessa approached the table, she could not believe her bad luck. She groaned to herself when she saw that Guille Góngora, president of HURL, was manning the booth. She was wearing overalls and her short, slicked-back hair was either wet or gelled. "You're late and we didn't see you at the demonstration, Dr. Kildare," Guille said. She had taken an instant dislike to Tessa at the first meeting, as had some of the other members.

"Study group," Tessa said, without inflection. She was trying to establish a let's-not-talk tone for the next two hours.

"Studying what? How to line your pockets with the savings of your sick and dying patients?"

"No, that's an upper division course," Tessa said deadpan, while scanning the table. Noting that everyone else brought cookies shaped like hearts, she thought, Duh! Making room between a box of sprinkled hearts and powdered hearts, she placed her round and blotchy cookies on the table.

The scent of Irish Spring soap began to mingle with the smell of baked goods. Tessa turned her nose to find the source. A tall man with a backpack was staring down at the assortment of hearts. Tessa moved to stand behind the table, where Guille checked her out from head to white L.A. Gear shoes. She chuckled at the tri-color laces.

The student selected a chocolate chip cookie. He dug in his jeans for 75 cents. Guille put her hand out, palm up, but he waited. For a moment Tessa was nonplussed. Taking the coins, she thanked him. When he smiled, the sky reflected in his blue eyes.

Tessa fought the urge to watch him walk away. She could feel Guille's eyes on her as she dropped the coins into the coffee can. Before Guille could express an opinion about the transaction, her attire, or anything else, Tessa asked, "Whose idea was the bake sale?"

Guille shrugged, knowing it had been her own, but smelling a trap.

"Let's try pooling all the money we spend buying these chunks of cholesterol and drop it straight into this can. Taking the eaten profits into account," she nodded her head toward the bit of broken heart in Guille's hand, "we'll make about the same amount. And instead of standing around for two ineffectual hours, we could be doing something constructive, like visiting schools in the barrio and recruiting students."

Guille shot Tessa a dirty look. "You know, there are two types of minorities on campus, Teresa Anaya. Those who want to be white, and those who stick to their own kind." As Guille lectured her about imperialism, sexism, and racism, Tessa thought, Oh my God. This is worse than the Mission!

When the lecture was over, Guille reached for another cookie. "I thought minority organizations were about supporting each other, not imposing limitations," Tessa said. "Look Guille, I'm taking part in HURL and anything else that piques my interest."

Guille loaded all of her disdain into one word. She aimed it at Tessa.

"Malinche!"

❧

"Sanctuary," Tessa mouthed as she reached her dorm room. Emma glanced up from her book. "How was the bake sale?" she said. Emma Brannan, psychology major from Washington, D.C., had light brown hair and a face sprayed with reddish freckles. She wore tortoiseshell glasses with lenses so thick they made her eyes look huge.

Tessa dropped onto her bed. The lack of a response

caused Emma's eyebrows to furrow. "Do dog years convert into hours?" Tessa told her about the cookie standoff and being called *Malinche*, the Mexican equivalent of Benedict Arnold.

Emma thought a moment. "It sounds like more than a personality conflict. All the doctor potshots she takes at you. You said Guille's a sociology major and will probably become a social worker, right?" Tessa nodded. "It's almost like she is trying to debase your ambition. Maybe she thinks you're showing off by reaching for higher levels of education."

Tessa studied Emma. "You learned all of that in Psych 101?"

Emma shook her head. "Mostly from watching reruns of *¿Qué Pasa, USA?*"

Chapter 21

LEAH HAS A RUN-IN WITH THE LAW

LEAH GRADUATED from high school unscathed. It was the same year that the nuns left St. Juan's—including a relieved Mother Margaret. That night, she experienced her first restful sleep in close to a year. She was awakened only once by Jaime and Alex's lovemaking. They sounded more like a howling monkey and constipated cavemen than anything remotely sweet and romantic. She could not remember ever hearing such sounds from her parents when they shared that same bed.

Leah missed being part of a family. Her father had been dead now for three years. His face was no longer clear in her memories. The flash from his gold-framed front teeth blinded his features, the way the glare from a windshield obscures the car. Leah began to weep.

When Alex and Jaime returned from their Mexican Riviera honeymoon, he went from being guest to being God. He immediately assumed the role of the man of the house, expecting Leah to tend to him when his wife was not around. Leah dutifully made his meals before escaping to her room. She could not stand listening to him eat. It was too much like some of the sounds he made when in bed with her sister.

❧

Jaime's one chore was to take the garbage out. Leah was in the kitchen washing dishes the first time he begrudgingly attempted the task. He stared down at the tall can he overstuffed, and blew out a breath. After tying a plastic knot, he yanked on the bag, lifting the metal can. He braced the can with the sides of his shoes and pulled with steady force until the bag squeezed free.

Leah did not realize she was staring until Jaime shouted in Spanish, "What the fuck are you looking at, you dry old hag?"

Leah felt a sudden pain in her chest. As if her heart could not decide whether to beat faster or to stop. Jaime unexpectedly moved toward the window. Leah adjusted her position slightly and watched as he opened the window with one hand and tossed the garbage bag out with the other.

He turned and was suddenly inches from her face. "There, I've taken the trash out. If you don't like the way I do it, do it yourself!" His breath smelled like cigarettes and dirty feet. "Alex better not catch you, either."

Jaime stomped out of the kitchen. From the living room, he yelled back, "And don't forget the little can by the toilet."

As soon as the front door slammed, she raced to the window and leaned out. The bag of garbage had hit the asphalt and popped open like a piñata. It narrowly missed a policeman on a motorcycle, who was now yelling up at her. He demanded that she come down and pick up the mess, or he would come up and arrest her.

Chapter 22

TESSA AND EMMA GO TO THE MOVIES

TESSA'S ALARM WENT OFF at 5:45 am. After a shower and a quick breakfast of coffee and a toasted bagel, she went to her morning classes. In the afternoons, she would attend the extracurricular activities she signed up for to ensure she made the most of her college experience. From there she would head straight to her shift at Kinko's. At night, she and Emma did homework in their dorm room, occasionally mixing it up by studying at the library.

On this particular evening, Emma closed several thick books. She whined, "Stanford's hard. Hey, there's a film called *Harold and Maude* playing. Do you want to go?"

Tessa thought of the mounting papers that were due and was about to say no when she heard herself say, "I'll get my jacket."

❧

"Don't you see? By driving his car over the cliff to make people think he had died for the umpteenth time, Harold was happier," Tessa said to Emma as they shuffled out of the theater.

"I loved the soundtrack," Emma said.

Tessa nodded. "Did you see Cat Stevens's cameo appearance?"

"No way! When?"

"At the funeral. He was standing in front of Ruth

Gordon."

"I'll have to see it again."

Out in the chilled winter night, Emma's lips took on the shape of a partial smile, the way they do when you think you know a person, but are not really sure. "Atticus?" she said.

Emma and this Atticus person hugged. They each marveled at how grown-up the other was. During their exchange, Tessa figured out that the two were childhood friends. Atticus's watery blue eyes were concentrating on Emma, so Tessa took a moment to admire his features. He was at least six feet tall with hair somehow both blond and dark.

Tessa eased her eyes onto the pleasant angles of his face. His lips were thin with almost no color. Tessa pictured her full lips enveloping his.

"Oh gosh, Tessa!" Emma said, startling Tessa out of her fantasy. "I am so sorry! I haven't seen Atticus in ages."

"I kind of caught that," Tessa said.

"Tessa Anaya, meet Atticus Weston," Emma said.

"We've already met," he said, shaking her hand slowly.

"Are you sure?" Tessa said, enjoying the mystery.

"Very sure. I ate your cookie," he said, straight-faced.

Emma's eyebrows arched. Tessa suddenly placed him as the soapy-scented student. She laughed sheepishly. "Bake sale, Em. He was my first customer."

"And not a very memorable one," Atticus added.

"No, that's not it. I was in the middle of something."

"I heard," he said. Tessa suddenly felt a hot blush burn her cheeks at the realization that he, and others, had witnessed her petty confrontation with Guille.

"Hey, why don't the three of us go and grab a cup of

coffee and discuss whether the film was a dark comedy or a grisly social satire," Emma said.

"Social satire," Tessa said at the same moment that Atticus said, "Dark comedy." Tessa and Atticus stared at each other. They laughed.

But, Tessa did not want to be a third wheel on Valentine's Day. "You have a lot of catching up, and I have a couple of papers due."

"Oh, please, please come with us," Emma said, bouncing, like she needed to pee.

"Next time," Tessa said, taking a step away.

"Tomorrow night, then," Atticus said. "I'll pick you up at seven. I'll probably be coffeed out, so how about dinner instead?"

Tessa smiled, "I have to work tomorrow."

Emma recited Tessa's schedule.

"Well, Wednesday works for me," Atticus said.

Tessa shot her roommate an "are you sure you don't want him?" look before giving in. "Sounds great."

As Tessa headed back to her dorm room, she felt recharged. Piecing together what little she knew about Atticus, she was pretty sure that he never wore a protective charm against the evil eye when he was a kid. He had probably never made kissy sounds at a passing woman in his life. She smiled, certain he had never uttered the words, *"Ay mamí."*

Chapter 23

TESSA GOES ON A DATE

Atticus picked Tessa up a little after seven. They made nervous small talk as they strolled through Palo Alto's business district. The eclectic mix of stores, pubs, and cheap restaurants was done in 1940's architecture, attracting a diverse group of students and locals alike.

They were deciding where to eat by perusing the menus taped to restaurant windows when Atticus grabbed her by the hand. Tessa felt her legs go mushy. "Oh, I know a great place. They serve the best Mexican food around," Atticus said.

At the Green Enchilada, Tessa stared up at the creepiest mural she had ever seen, depicting an Aztec priest performing a ritual human sacrifice. She wanted to ask the East Coaster exactly what made him such an authority on Mexican food, but resisted. Between school and work, she was annoyed by too many inconsequential things.

Smiling, Atticus handed her his unopened menu. "You choose."

Tessa knew he was expecting something a bit exotic, but not too exotic. She scanned the menu. The items were limited to the same tired combination platters, burgers and something called the "¡Ay Caramba! Gut Buster." Tessa wished they could go to Alex's restaurant for 'real food.'

She felt obliged to order in Spanish. She chose two of the

three specials written on a grease-stained paper thumb-tacked to a paneled wall. The waitress, whose name was Alma, did not speak Spanish. "My parents are making me work here," she explained, as if it was a punishment.

"Oh. Is this their restaurant?" Tessa said.

"No," Alma said, sounding offended. "They own Golf World down the street."

Tessa ordered again as she pointed to the paper on the wall. "We'll have the number two with pork and the number three."

When Alma left, Atticus helped himself to a jalapeño from a clear plastic jar. He held it up. "You know, this *gringo* can eat really hot peppers."

"Really?" Tessa said, flatly, finding his attempt at solidarity charming. Pathetic, but charming.

"I mean it, the hotter the better. You don't believe me?"

"No, that's not it. How can I explain this? If you said that in Mexico, people wouldn't know how to react, since *chiles* are a staple of the diet." She thought a moment. "It's like if someone were to say to you, 'You know,'" she said, imitating him. "'I can eat really crunchy granola. No, I mean it, the crunchier the better. You don't believe me?'" They were both laughing before she finished.

"Ouch! I think I get it. Boy, you're not going to cut me any slack, are you?" Atticus said, placing the jalapeño on a paper napkin and licking his fingers.

Tessa stared at him before answering. He had no idea that he was as exotic to her as she must seem to him. "Do you really want me to?"

Atticus bashfully ran a hand through his hair. "No. Never."

Tessa felt her weariness transform into affection.

Over *birria* and *sopes,* Atticus admitted to being named after the levelheaded Atticus Finch in *To Kill a Mockingbird.* He then spoke candidly about his life and being the son of a Senator. "I took to it right away, but it's been a strain on my sister. Melanie's really great, but shy. For her, it must be like being from an athletic family and preferring books to sports..."

Tessa was admiring Atticus's devotion to his sister when he said, "You don't look Mexican."

Tessa blinked at the shift in conversation. "Sure I do."

"No, really you don't. You're tall and could pass for Irish or Italian."

"Have you ever been to Mexico?" Tessa said, straight-faced.

Atticus looked like he was just caught drinking from the milk carton. "No, but everyone knows what Mexicans look like. Just like everyone knows what Africans look like." He hesitated. "I'm on the verge of being labeled as culturally insensitive, so let's start all over. So Tessa, your family's from Mexico?"

Tessa laughed. "A pueblo near Guadalajara. Some of the Spaniards settled in the area after the conquest."

"Are you saying that you're a direct descendant of the Conquistadores?"

"Your guess is as good as mine."

"That's pretty cool," he said, while disentangling her features.

"Not really. I doubt that I'm the descendant of an early interracial marriage; my Indian ancestors were raped by the Spanish men that enslaved them to create a new labor force."

Will you shut up already! She scolded herself. You almost blew it with the whole jalapeño thing!

"Huh, I guess I never looked at it that way."

They both stared out the window during this first lull in conversation. Well, there goes the second date, Tessa thought, feeling a sharp pang of regret.

"Do your parents speak English?" Atticus said.

Tessa was relieved by the question. "Pretty much. My mom still gets 'kitchen' and 'chicken' mixed up and doesn't realize it. So, if I ask where my dad is..."

"He's in the chicken," Atticus finished her sentence. His eyes were smiling into hers when Alma showed up with another table's entrées.

Chapter 24

ALEX MISSES A BIRTHDAY CANDLE, ON PURPOSE

ALEX WOKE UP bright and early, eager for her birthday celebration to commence. Tessa had arrived on a bus late that morning. She, Dulce, and Leah were taking her to the Palace for a lavish, yet leisurely, brunch. When they were done pigging out, they were going to head to the Anayas' house for cake and presents.

Showered and powdered, Alex put on the yellow crepe dress she bought just for the occasion. She smiled at her reflection in the hallway mirror. She loved being pregnant because her hefty shape finally made sense, and there was plenty of maternity clothes to choose from. She was plump and happy, and youth gave her the look of a big-boned cherub. She touched her belly constantly to show she was with child, and then sopped up the attention. People in the Mission love pregnant women.

After Jaime's outburst, Alex worried constantly about the baby's gender. As crazy as it sounded, she was sure he would accuse her of infidelity if she gave birth to a girl. She prayed daily to *La Virgen* and Saint Monica for a son—both women having given birth to healthy and successful males. She received no sign her prayers were answered.

Alex was on the verge of a nervous breakdown when she remembered her birthday wishes from last year. It was no coincidence that all three came true. She was a member of the posse, she looked fabulous, and not only was she married, her husband was *caliente!*

While stuffing her swollen feet into pumps, she thought, This afternoon I'm going to wish for a baby boy, then blow out all, but one of the candles on my cake. Smiling, Alex checked her teeth for lipstick.

ॐ

"Oh my God! What just happened?" Tessa said, breaking the silence in the room filled with the smell of snuffed-out candles.

"Dang," Dulce said. Her tone heavy.

Leah appeared stoic.

They were sitting in the Anayas' living room among the birthday debris of crumbled wrapping paper, triangles of cake, and melting ice cream. Leah had been in a state of shock since Alex left to go to work when Tessa and Dulce's words finally reached her. Leah's eyes went from Dulce to Tessa, not sure if she heard them correctly.

Noticing the look, Dulce scratched her head hard as she chose her words. "You see, me and Tessa have this little tradition. We kinda make our own wishes on Alex's cakes." The two started making their own wishes on Alex's birthday cakes when they were kids. The fact that they came true seemed normal, and held about as much expected awe as flight—birds for Dulce, airplanes for Tessa.

Leah could not believe what she was hearing. She thought, You, too?

Misinterpreting Leah's shock as incredulity, Tessa jumped in. "I know, I know. It sounds a bit crazy but it actually works."

"Not anymore." Dulce snorted. "Whatever Alex wished

for last year must have come true, because she just missed a candle again, only on purpose this time."

"It's possible she's short-winded from her pregnancy," Tessa said.

Dulce was about to say something about how believing in wishes was not very scientific of Tessa when Leah spoke up. "I make wishes on Alex's cakes, too."

Tessa and Dulce's stunned faces fixed on hers.

"*¡No mames!*" Dulce said, wide-eyed.

"Did they come true?" Tessa said.

"Yes," Leah said. "But, last year..." She shook her head.

"What did you wish for last year?" Dulce said.

Leah thought back, but said nothing.

"You better tell me or I'll sic Becca on you," Dulce demanded.

Leah's lashes blinked rapidly. She wasn't 100 percent sure if Dulce was kidding. "To be invisible to strangers," she said, feeling self-conscious.

Dulce jumped to her feet, startling Leah. "It's gotta be the wish. Last year, when Alex missed that one *pinche* candle, the opposite of your wish came true."

Leah suddenly went pale with tension. "Golden Gate Park!" she said.

Dulce nodded somberly. Jerking a thumb toward Tessa, she said, "This one wished for a full scholarship. She got it, then Reagan Hood and his band of scary men stole some of it back to give to the rich. She's working at Kinko's so she can eat."

Leah turned her worried gaze on Tessa. "I am so sorry. Why didn't you tell us? We would have given you the money."

"Thanks, but that's not necessary. I'm fine, really." Tessa sneered at Dulce. "Let's not get off track, here." She gestured to the cake. "What does any of this mean?"

It was quiet as they considered the wishes they just made. They stared at the missed candle.

Leah dropped her head into her hands. She rocked back and forth. "Oh no," she spoke above a whisper.

Dulce studied Leah. "Oh no, what?"

Leah raised her eyes, and then her head. "It's really difficult living with...newlyweds." She decided at the last second not to mention Jaime by name.

"I'll bet," Dulce said. "You couldn't pay me to live with either of them."

Tessa nodded in agreement. "Why don't you move? You need your own space as much as they do."

Leah was considering this when Dulce said, "Then what?"

Leah looked puzzled. "I don't understand."

"You gonna stay here for the rest of your life, standing two feet away from Quico in the kitchen? Pretending like you're invisible?" Dulce said.

"What's wrong with that?" Tessa demanded.

"That's not what she wants. She wants to go to cooking school, don't you?"

Leah was mystified. "How did you know?"

"Your cooking magazines. When you get to the back you always stare at that same ad. The one for the cooking school in Sonoma."

"Napa," Leah shyly corrected Dulce. "The Culinary Institute of California."

Dulce placed her hands on her hips and stared down at

Leah. "So, are you gonna call the school tomorrow and have them mail you an application, or am I?"

Chapter 25

JAIME GETS A PROMOTION

ALEX AND LEAH were sitting in their living room poring over a catalog from a manila envelope. Leah flipped through the glossy pages, pointing to areas of interest. Alex knew her sister was not asking for her opinion about the school; this was her timid way of saying she was leaving.

Jaime's voice entered the room before he did. "You want to go to a school to learn to cook? What the hell have you been doing at the restaurant all this time?"

Leah flinched. They were speaking in English and Alex was quietly impressed that he understood so much of their conversation.

Jaime scratched his beard stubble. "I don't know, it sounds expensive. I need to think about it," he said, walking past them to the kitchen. Alex tried to spring to her feet, but her round belly shoved her deeper into the cushions. It took a few attempts before she could heave herself off of the couch.

Leah heard the chair scrape, and then Alex's *chanclas* flopping on the kitchen's linoleum floor. She turned and watched Jaime slump onto the chair. Alex poured coffee and pecked him on the forehead as she placed the steaming mug on the table. She spun around and was back with his breakfast before he took his first sip.

"I have money," Leah said.

Jaime's eyes asked how much? He nodded once as he

decided to find out later from his wife. It was painfully easy to read the thoughts on his face.

"If you want to learn to cook I'll send you to Chiapas. My mother will teach you real cooking," he said.

Leah glanced at Alex. "I thought you were from Manzanillo?"

Jaime did not clarify. With a gesture of impatience, he rolled a tortilla like a cigar and bit off one end.

Turning to Alex, Leah said, "It's a three-year course and I'll receive a bachelor's degree in Professional Studies."

"No, you won't. You'll be back here by Christmas knocked up, and with no man," Jaime grumbled. His crude response showed once again how most of the things he said mirrored such a primitive mind.

Alex nudged her husband. "Jaime's just worried about you," she said, and attempted to smile. "It sounds really great, Leah."

❦

Can someone please explain to me how I'm supposed to run a family business without a family? Alex was having trouble concentrating on invoices. Leah was leaving at the time when she needed her most. This only proved what Alex had always suspected: Leah has a selfish streak.

Left with no blood relations of working age, Alex started grooming Jaime in restaurant management. She used the "old button" selection strategy to tap into his managerial potential. As in sewing, when one is selecting buttons from a bin, one does not look for similar buttons; one eliminates the buttons that look least alike.

Alex quickly recognized the areas in which Jaime exhibited

little aptitude: decision-making of any kind and working with vendors. What was left was counting money and food tickets. And, much to her relief, greeting customers.

The logistics and operations also fell into place. Alex would handle the administrative side of the business: bills, payroll, schedules, etc. Quico was put in charge of ordering all of the perishables, non-perishables, and bar supplies. Jaime would manage the restaurant in the evenings. Her staff was great and the place ran itself, but she saw no point in mentioning that to her husband.

Alex planned on working at the restaurant until the moment she went into labor. She had even packed some paperwork into the diaper bag. Unfortunately, her swollen feet and legs forced her into an early maternity leave. She was put on strict bedrest until the baby's birth

When she left Jaime in charge for the first time she turned back to wave, but he was already busy greeting customers. He was so handsome in his new wardrobe of bright Miami Vice-style T-shirts and sports jackets, Alex fell in love with him all over again. She sighed deeply before turning, and waddling away.

Chapter 26

LEAH'S FIRST DAY AT THE CULINARY ACADEMY

"MY NAME IS Chef Jacob Lasson and this is Basic Skills. In this class, I will be teaching you fundamental culinary skills or cooking principles, such as knife work, equipment knowledge, kitchen terminology, and kitchen logistics," the instructor said from behind a black marble counter.

He was thin and not too tall, with an amiable face and eyes that twinkled like Christmas lights. The white chef's jacket he wore was so stiff, it could have been patterned from a cake box. On his head was the traditional chef's hat, or toque, with one hundred pleats to represent the one hundred ways a trained chef can prepare an egg.

Leah arrived at the academy the day before, and was still awestruck by the location. The mock castle surrounded by vineyards had been home to several wineries before being purchased by the academy in the 1950's. Within the heavy coolness of the building walls, reminiscent of a cave, were lecture classrooms and kitchen facilities, which included butchery, bakery, *garde manger,* and a professional production kitchen.

The classroom Leah now sat in was a cooking theater with walls the color of white pepper. All levels of seating offered a clear view of the fully equipped demonstration kitchen below. Leah and the other students were dressed in similar attire to their instructor, only their institute-issued white paper hats and chef's jacket were of inferior quality.

"During your last semester, I will again instruct you in professional production. Why am I your first and quite possibly your last instructor at CIC?" He paused and appeared to be expecting a show of hands. "To ensure that down the road when I ask you to score, sear, sweat, or even bake in a bain-marie, you'll do it the right way. My way." Leah smiled.

Tossing a piece of chalk from hand to hand, Chef Lasson said, "What constitutes food? Food nourishes the body, but isn't it more than sustenance? Of course it is or we wouldn't be here. I like to think of food as a form of communication." He paused. "Let's examine food from this perspective, shall we? Let's try to take food in as the language of a culture. An oral history, pardon the pun. When you eat Indian food, for example, your taste buds are learning about the culture. It speaks of the climate, the agriculture and even the religious beliefs.

As in other forms of communication, there are individuals that possess a gift. Unlike other prodigies, great chefs are not set apart from other children. You'll never hear how little Constance was flambéing bananas at the tender age of three."

Chef Lasson's thin mustache and goatee spread into a smile. "Just out of curiosity, does anyone here have a good palate?" Several hands went up, including Eric Peterson, an older student who had been working in the kitchens of Manhattan, and made sure the other students were aware of his vast culinary experience.

"Can you explain to me what a palate is?" The five students with raised hands quickly recoiled them, including Eric. "The palate according to Noah Webster..." Chef Lasson turned to the chalkboard. The chalk squeaked as he wrote:

1. The roof of the mouth

2. Taste

He drew a big u-shape on the chalkboard, representing the tongue. He turned back to the class. "There are 10,000 taste buds on your tongue, and in each of your mouths there are four types of taste buds: sweet, bitter, salty, and sour. Other qualities of taste include smell and touch, but to a limited extent."

He began rifling through drawers. "In order to experience taste the substance must become liquefied by saliva so it can be absorbed through the taste buds. But how do you account for taste itself? People chew cow dung, enjoy Pop Tarts." Giggles rippled through the classroom.

He pulled a small mahogany box from the lower drawer. "Let's try an experiment. I want the five individuals with discriminating palates to step up here. You and you," he said, pointing to the two students hesitating in their seats.

He pulled a handful of black sashes from the box and held them up. "We are going to be conducting a taste testing here in a moment, but before we do, why don't we give our five volunteers a hand." The other students, safe in their seats, applauded enthusiastically.

Chef Lasson blindfolded each of the students with a sash. He asked, "Any food allergies?" Before they could answer, he clapped his hands once and said, "Good! Let's get started."

The students stood in a frowning row. Leah thought of Goya's painting of peasants before a firing squad.

Chef Lasson held up two large chocolate bars in their wrappers for the seated students to see. He placed a square of chocolate on each of the five tongues, the way a priest does with the Eucharist. With a show of hands, he asked the relieved volunteers which ones tasted American chocolate. Eric Peterson was one of two to answer correctly.

"As we just witnessed, sight is also important to the experience of taste." The five students were dismissed to applause. "I want you to consider why you are here. Now is the time to tune into your inner motivation. Incidentally, this will be on your final."

Chapter 27

ALEX BECOMES A KEPT WOMAN

ALEX SHIFTED UNEASILY from working seven days a week to the comparatively leisurely life of a housewife. What on God's green earth do kept women do all day long? Associating daytime TV with luxury, she turned on the set and started flipping through the channels. She was not sure which was worse: the programs or the commercials? Disgusted, she shut the idiot box off.

Leah's move to Napa should have been sad, but the baby now has his own room! Having gone shopping for the basics—crib, bassinet, changing table and rocking chair—Alex got a little carried away and bought furnishings for the entire apartment. She was standing in the entranceway, scrutinizing her new living room set, when the door swung open, smacking her rump.

"Now you're waiting by the door for me?" Jaime said, tersely.

Alex quickly moved out of the way. "How did the interviews go?" She wanted to steer him clear of one of his moods. That, and it was his first time conducting wait staff interviews. She was curious to hear how it had gone.

"Not bad, I guess." Jaime grabbed a beer from the refrigerator.

"How many showed up?"

"I don't know. Eleven, maybe." Not to elaborate seemed

like an admission of guilt, so he added, "It took all morning." Alex almost smiled at the gripe, feeling nostalgic for the restaurant biz.

The interviewing process was not what Jaime had expected. Most of the women were career waitpersons. They made him uncomfortable with their direct stares and specific questions about the restaurant's seating capacity and schedules. After the fourth interview, Jaime developed a test. He asked each of the candidates—he saw them as candidates—if she could tie a cherry stem with her tongue. This thinned the stack of applicants to none by noon.

Jaime was getting ready to go to lunch when a buxom *gabacha* with bleached hair and over-powdered skin showed up. She was the kind of woman worn down by a lifetime of wrong men. She had no resume, no references, and if his wife were interviewing her, no chance. But this was Jaime's business of operation now.

Sitting on the corner of the table in the storage room, Jaime said, in his thick accent, "No bar 'sperience?"

"Well," she said, shrugging her shoulders while bringing her elbows to her side to squeeze her breasts up to accentuate her cleavage. "Not cock-tailing."

Jaime saw this as an invitation. He shut the door and locked it. Before the interview was over, Jaime rubbed his prick between her heavy breasts, and then shoved it in her mouth. When he was about to come, she tried to turn the blowjob into a hand job, but Jaime resisted. He came on her cheek and chin. Bad attitude, he thought.

"Anyone good?" Alex asked.

"Not really. One was OK. Put another ad in the newspaper

and run it for a week. Say something like, 'No experience necessary.' I was thinking maybe I should train her myself."

Chapter 28

LEAH MAKES NEW FRIENDS

"OK, WHAT IS THE DIFFERENCE between stock and broth?" Chef Jacob said. He waited. Leah smiled to herself, but did not offer the answer. "The words are not really interchangeable, you know," he said.

A bored-sounding Eric Peterson spoke up without raising his hand. "A stock is the water extract made by simmering bones."

"That's right." Chef Lasson nodded. "A stock is made primarily from bones and foods slowly cooked in water, and/or wine, and will congeal when cool. A broth, on the other hand, is made from meat, except, of course, for vegetable broth. Broths do not congeal. So, with that distinction made, let's begin."

He stepped over to the demonstration table and stood behind an array of cookery. On the marble counter before him were a stockpot, a food processor, metal and wooden spoons, a colander, a blender, a food mill, sieves, and other items. "By the end of this particular session, you will be familiar with the tools of the stock trade."

Eric Peterson passed Leah a note. He did not try to sneak it like a high school note. He simply handed it to her as if it was a business card. With attention diverted from the lecture, Leah stared at the paper.

"The origin of the word 'stock' derives from the trunk of

a tree..." the chef was saying. The piece of paper remained out of context until Eric shook it, triggering Leah's reflexes. "After some time, the word referred to a family's lineage. We've all heard the expression 'He comes from good stock...'"

Leah took the note. She discreetly pulled the corners of the folded paper apart. "Dinner" was scribed in tight block letters, with no punctuation. The lack of a question mark made Leah feel cornered, like the decision was already made.

The instructor's tone changed and Leah was suddenly aware that he was still talking. "I'm going to let you go early today, but before you leave, you have to contribute any food fact to the class. It does not have to be academic. Just some useless food trivia that you carry around in your noggin will be fine."

"Um. When you eat a McDonald's Big Mac combo, you've consumed enough calories for two days," an attractive woman chirped.

"Very good, Jill," Chef Lasson said, adding, "Almost half of the calories are from icky fat. It also has over eighty grams of cholesterol. You are dismissed, so long as you do not consume one," Chef Lasson said with the slightest of bows in Jill's direction. Smiling, she quickly gathered her books.

Immediately, another voice spoke up. "I'm pretty sure that an ostrich egg has enough yolk to fill 24 hen eggs."

"One hell of an omelet," Chef Lasson said. "See you on Monday, Dylan."

Leah watched as her fellow students departed one by one. She glimpsed at Eric. He was searching for food trivia towards the corner of the room. The momentary stumping of Eric Peterson prompted Leah's mind to come up with her own food trivia, and make a quick exit.

Leah could write a book on all of the little-known food facts she had come across. She would call it *Culinary Tidbits*, or better yet, *Food for Thought*. Before she chose one, she was on her feet, looking like she was about to pledge allegiance to a flag.

Chef Lasson looked up. The students in front of Leah twisted in their seats to face her. Trying not to panic, Leah's thoughts fled to the safety of Quico's kitchen, the stovetop, the cast iron skillet of beans resting on the burner. "Refried beans are not really fried twice," she said. Her voice was as thin as a thread. "In Spanish, they are called *frijoles refritos*, which means well-fried beans."

"So, it's some sort of a Spanglish translation error?" A student behind her asked.

Turning abruptly, Leah said, "I guess so."

"Food for thought," the Chef said. "Thanks, Leah. Have a good weekend."

On Tuesday afternoon, Leah was walking by the European students who gravitated into a group. They casually watched as she was about to pass. Having promised Dulce that she would force herself to be more social, Leah drew in a deep breath. She said a timid, "Hi." Much to her surprise they all said hi back, with one or two saying, "Hi, Leah."

At the start of the next class, the European students invited her to sit with them. Leah studied Eric's backside. In some unexplainable way, she felt miserably bound to him. After a brief, but agonizing moment, she lowered herself onto the offered chair. For the next two hours, Leah winced every time Eric glanced at the empty seat next to his.

From that day on, Leah found herself in the company of friends from Italy, France, and Austria. They spent the warm autumn weekends exploring the restaurants and wineries in Napa and Sonoma counties. Over dinner, they argued with buoyancy over whose native dishes were best. Understanding that Leah was shy, they enjoyed her company as the audience who never took sides. In time, they would respect her culinary adeptness and go to her for cooking advice and emotional support. For the first time in Leah's tumultuous life, her inner sea was calm.

Chapter 29

LEAH HAS A LUNCH DATE

IT WAS EARLY OCTOBER and the quiescent Sunday morning was rapidly warming to an Indian summer day. Most of the students from the academy were heading to the harvest festival in Sonoma. Leah's friends were going and insisted that she come along, but she still craved the solace of long walks on Sundays. Somehow, being invited was just as good as actually going.

The elegance of autumn made Leah swoon as she stepped out into a field of grapevines. The golden light on the turning leaves and the sweet smell of morning air instantly refreshed her soul. She held a green grape up to the light and could see the seeds within.

※

By midday Leah felt the sun heating the part on her scalp. Her warm skin was salty and smelled of toasted sunflower seeds. She spotted movement in the field and raised her hand to shade her eyes. A cluster of men and women were harvesting aged grapes, their faces pinched by the sun.

If I were standing there, between those two girls, she thought, I would blend right in. One of the women waved and Leah waved back. As she resumed her walk, she considered the harsh circumstances of the migrant workers. She experienced the familiar weight of guilt for her good fortune.

Leah ended her walk in St. Helena, a quaint historic town

where dry corn and colorful squash decorated the storefront windows. Hungry, she headed straight to her favorite deli. Fearing holding up the line, Leah carried small bills and change in a little pouch pinned to her waistband.

Still in the habit of looking down as she walked, she noticed arnica growing by the curb. It was next to a pair of white Nike's. As Leah's eyes flashed up she saw the back of hairy hands, and then Eric Peterson's face.

"Hello, stranger," Eric said, spitting out his gum. Leah stared at the wet wad of chewed gum on the sidewalk. It looked like a tiny brain.

"God, Leah! I wanted to grab a bite with you, not get married!" He glanced at his watch. "It's lunchtime. Let's go eat now."

Again, Eric was not asking her; he was ordering her. Leah wanted to tell him to leave her alone but could never be that rude. She was beginning to hyperventilate when she remembered one of Tessa's more generic brush-offs. "I already have plans, but thanks."

Eric's eyes were flint. "All righty. Your loss," he said, impatiently tapping his shoe near the wad of gum. When Leah realized he was waiting for her to cave in, she walked away. Possibly too fast.

❧

Leah turned a corner and ran right into a pair of huaraches. They were on the feet of Chef Jacob Lasson. Her Basic Skills instructor was standing in front of a bistro, reading a menu on an easel, when she blindsided him.

"Leah!" he said, startled. "Is everything all right?"

"Yes, Chef Lasson," Leah managed to get out. She was

thinking, Didn't anyone go to the festival?

"My name curiously changes to Jacob once off school property," he said, smiling easily. Leah stood mute with embarrassment.

"So, how are your other classes going?"

"Fine." Her cheeks were rosy and Jacob mistook the shy blush as a glow from the heat.

"I was about to have lunch. Would you like to join me?"

Leah mumbled, "No." She stepped backward and almost tripped over a weedy crack in the sidewalk. It was a dandelion. Jacob reached out a hand, more as a gesture than to save her from her own clumsiness.

A pudgy man in a black suit came out of the restaurant. "It is always a pleasure to see you, Jacob," he said.

"Hello, Alan! How's business?" The two shook hands and began to speak in French.

Leah turned to leave. She stared at the town's main street, a mere three blocks in length. Running into Eric would be unavoidable. Her mind was working on an alternate route home when she felt the two men's eyes on her. "Are you sure you won't join me?" Jacob said.

Being in a restaurant for an hour should ensure a safe walk back to the academy. "All right," Leah said, in a tone so filled with reluctance, the two men exchanged a look.

"Excellent! This way please," Alan said, grabbing a couple of menus.

"After you," Jacob said, extending an arm.

Jacob's eyes were small and sweet when he smiled, reminding her of raisins. His hair, usually covered with the toque, was thick and the color of cinnamon sticks. It was a little lighter than his trimmed mustache and goatee. He was wearing a soft, faded blue linen shirt that must have been carefully washed hundreds of times, along with khaki pants. He looked different out of his chef's uniform. Much younger and more handsome.

The entrance to the restaurant was dark and cool with terra cotta tiles. For a second, Leah felt like she was entering the foyer of Alejandra's. But the similarities ended there. This dining room was decorated with a French country theme. Above the linen tables were paintings of gardens and vineyards in chunky wooden frames.

Alan walked through the dining room until he was struck by blinding sunlight, as if being visited by an angel. Placing one hand on the back of a chair, he smiled at Leah. She remembered the bistro's outdoor seating, too late. She stared at the table, and then up and into the faces of the passing pedestrians on Main Street.

"I need to wash my hands. Will you excuse me?" Jacob said.

Choking back a whimper, she nodded and sat down. Leah was panic-stricken over Eric's possible reaction to catching her with their instructor—her lunch date. Would he cause a scene? What would the chef think of her if he did? What if Eric reported them back at school? Would Jacob be reprimanded? Could she be expelled? It suddenly felt as if Eric wielded more control over her life than she did.

Jacob returned smiling. A food server approached, saying, "Hi, Jacob."

"Oliver! How are things?" Jacob said. Oliver, pronounced with the French flair, wore a white chef's jacket and black pants. He was almost dressed like a student from the academy. Leah suddenly worried that he was a classmate.

Oliver began to recite a long list of specials and Leah became intrigued by the dishes. Oliver asked Jacob if he had any questions. Jacob raised his eyebrows and looked into Leah's eyes. "Leah?" he said. She inquired about the halibut and, unknowingly, asked the same questions that popped into his head.

After ordering lunch, Jacob opened the wine list. "Do you know much about wine, Leah?"

She almost confessed that she wasn't old enough, but caught herself in time. "I've read more than I've tasted."

Jacob nodded. He studied the list on faux parchment paper. "Do you prefer white or red?"

In her mind's eye, Leah watched the leaves of the Cabernet grape turn red, while the Chardonnay leaves yellowed around the edges. She wanted to tell him that she loved them all. "I really do not mind. It's up to you."

After ordering the wine, Jacob followed Leah's large and luminous eyes to the hills rimming the Napa Valley like a jagged bowl. He startled the silence by saying, "Napa is a lot like the Bordeaux country in France." Leah said nothing. Jacob tried again. "Did you know that the Bible says Noah planted the first vineyard?"

The bottle of pinot noir arrived. As Jacob performed the tasting ritual, assisted by Oliver, she almost broke down and confessed her age. But that would only create more awkward moments.

"I almost forgot the toast," Jacob said, while raising his glass. "He who plants a vine becomes entangled in its branches."

"Idwal Jones," Leah said, carefully clinking his glass.

Jacob's eyes glinted with amusement. "How did you know the author of such an obscure quote?"

"I—I read it on a wine decanter in one of the shops," she admitted.

Jacob chuckled to himself. After a long silence, the first course was served. "So, what sparked your culinary interest, Leah?"

She loved the way he said her name. It sounded like he was melting the vowels on one of the squares of chocolate hidden in his desk. "I was born into it. My sister owns a restaurant."

"Really, where?"

"San Francisco."

"What's the name?"

"Alejandra's. It's in the Mission District," Leah said, dismissively.

Jacob's face brightened. "I've been there many times. It's one of my favorite restaurants!" Leah looked up from her pear salad with caramelized walnuts and crumbled blue cheese, surprised. "The last time I was there I ordered the *guiso de puerco*. I just tried to say 'pork stew,' did I get it right?"

"Yes," Leah said, wiping her mouth on the starchy white napkin. "The dish with pineapples. It's a peasant dish and one of my favorites."

"What did you do at the restaurant?"

"Cooked."

Jacob was clearly impressed. "I've been trying to figure out how it was prepared since then. What type of chili did you use?"

"Chile guero."

"Oh, those skinny yellow chilis?"

"Yes. That's right." Leah's eyes brightened, like black glass. "I can write down the recipe if you want."

"I have a better idea. We have such a culturally diverse class this year; how about if we reserve a kitchen for a cooking demonstration? We can invite your friends. I'll bring the groceries. Just make a list."

Leah smiled at the thought of having friends. She was about to decline the offer, but remembered the food debates she had witnessed. Much to her surprise she liked the idea. She said, "All right. But I better do the shopping."

Jacob could see that she was trying not to offend him, and laughed. "I do know something about selecting fresh produce." The realization that he appeared to read her thoughts turned Leah's cheeks dusky. "How about if we go to the farmer's market together?" Jacob suggested.

They spoke in length about the new cooking style called nouvelle cuisine, and how quickly it was catching on. The challenge was to create recipes based on what the body requires for a healthy balance instead of using heavy sauces and processed food.

Leah was animated as she talked about how California agriculture was inspiring the dishes. "Cooking should follow the seasons." Leah's mind was suddenly ripe with words. Jacob realized instinctively that she was saying things she had never felt comfortable sharing with anyone before. He felt both sad and privileged.

They were lingering over a shared chocolate torte, while sipping the last of the silky wine. Leah wished this meal could go on forever.

Jacob cupped his chin in his hand. "Why are you here, Leah?"

Her face split with a shy grin. "I thought I had the semester to think about it."

"But you already know."

What Leah wanted to explain was so nebulous it was difficult to define. She took her time, searching for the right words. "The first day of class you mentioned how cooking is experienced through all of the senses. Do you realize how rare that is? I mean we usually take the world in through a filter, so we are only aware of two senses, maybe three at any moment. We watch and listen to a movie. We look at a rose, close our eyes to smell it." She gazed thoughtfully at the ruby drop of liquid in her glass before continuing. "I cannot think of any other experience that is so whole, so encompassing. Am I making any sense?" Leah laughed to herself at the unexpected pun.

Across the street Eric was peering into a store window. Once again, Leah felt hunted. She stood with such force she knocked her chair over. Alan and Oliver descended as Jacob stood up. Reflexively, the three men stooped for the chair. Leah heard a confused mixture of French and English. She was almost through the now empty restaurant when Jacob caught up with her.

"Leah! What just happened?" he said, perplexed.

"I am so sorry, I completely forgot that...I have to be somewhere."

"I understand. Do you need a ride?"

"No!" she said, while stepping backwards. She was torn

between running out the door and expressing her appreciation for the best afternoon of her life. "Thank you for lunch," she said.

As she turned to leave Jacob caught her hand and gently shook it in his. "Leah, I really enjoyed talking with you."

Leah's own physical reaction to his touch amazed her. It made her want to cry. She mutely withdrew her trembling fingers and left.

Chapter 30

DULCE MAKES A DECISION

MRS. ALEX PEDROSA did not seem as fond of Dulce as Ms. Alex Cernuda use to be. Early in the pregnancy, Dulce chalked up the hostility to renegade preggo hormones. She made an effort to dismiss the verbal jabs, but the more the strip of elastic stretched around Alex's girth, the more she henpecked.

After lunch shift on a Friday, Dulce caught BART to the downtown galleries near Union Square. It was raining sideways when Dulce surfaced from the subway. She was drenched by the time she reached the Wintle and Kenen gallery's exhibit on Balinese art. She did a quick scan of the stark white room, noting several styles of paintings on display. To her left were several sandstone sculptures on pedestals. The recognition of two of the sculptures altered her breathing.

Rainwater trailed her to the first piece, a minimally defined sculpture of a female torso. As she approached the sculpture of a boy with a large rock breaking smaller rocks into smaller fragments, she remembered how challenging it had been to sand his arms that thin without breaking them.

Under the unfamiliar titles of both works was the name Willem Brinker. Dulce had been back from Borneo for one year and never heard from the Dutch couple she met there. "So that's why," she said to herself. She was seething with anger when an idea blinked, like a neon sign in her head.

Back at her flat, she reached for the old globe that would

have been new when she was in third grade. She had carved a small slit through Greenland, a country she was not planning on visiting. Every day after work, she pushed her tip money through the slot.

Gathering the globe, a knife, a beer, and the travel section of the Sunday paper, Dulce climbed into bed. She carved lateral slits through the Atlantic and Pacific before cutting along the equator. Bending back Colombia, Ecuador and Brazil, she pulled out handfuls of crumpled cash.

Dulce shook open the travel section of the Sunday Chronicle. She scanned the pages until she came across the ad she was looking for:

"Discount last minute fares to Amsterdam!"

❧

Cocktail napkin from Dulce:

Alex,
Be back in a few days, or a few years.
Dulce

Chapter 31

LEAH AND THE FIRST CULINARY COOK-OFF

CHEF LASSON RESERVED a class for the Saturday demonstration on Mexican cooking. The classroom was an open space of chrome, clean surfaces, and white tiled floors. It was equipped with nine work areas. Leah stood for a moment watching the early morning rays of the sun stream into the room. It felt good to be alone in a quiet kitchen.

She chose the station with the best natural light and started setting up. Before nine, people began to amble in. The aroma of coffee, the hissing and popping of *chiles* on the hot *comal*, and then Leah's smiling face greeted them. She was chopping the ingredients for *Pico de gallo* salsa with quick deft strokes. Not liking the way blenders and food processors tended to make the tomatoes frothy, Leah preferred to chop by hand. That, and she loved the scent of fresh salsa on her palms.

"Good morning. Coffee is ready," she greeted each one. "There's also fresh squeezed orange juice."

On the table before her were the utensils Quico had dropped off on a recent visit: a *molcajete* and *tejolote*, a three-legged mortar and pestle made of volcanic stone; a *metate* and *metlalpil*, a slab used for grinding; a *cazuela*, a glazed earthenware casserole dish; a *comal*, or griddle; and a cast iron tortilla press.

Her classmates slowly circled the table, examining the

traditional cookery, as if studying artifacts from an archaeological dig. These pieces were such a stretch from the sleek, modern equipment of today, some wondered if Leah was going to be able to pull it off.

By nine, Chef Lasson and the invited guests were sitting and leaning on tall stools around the demonstration table: Rainier, Maurice, and Émilie from France; Sabine from Vienna; and Enzo and Chiara, both Italian, but from opposite ends of the boot. Leah also invited David and Heather, two introverted students who were at sea on campus.

Leah welcomed the group. She began by saying, "I think the first rule to Mexican cooking is to forget everything you know about Mexican food. Some of the dishes that are considered Mexican are not really Mexican at all, like fajitas and nachos..."

Jacob did not expect such an elaborate demonstration. When he first mentioned the idea to Leah, it was more of an excuse to spend time with her outside of class. Studying Leah, Jacob could see that she had the posture of a chef and moved with an economy of graceful motion. He wondered if the other students, who would soon be cooking for the group, were not feeling a little intimidated.

Leah gathered a half dozen smooth and waxy chile peppers as she spoke. "Mexican food is a fusion of Native American, Spanish, and French culinary traditions. It has also been influenced by the English, Lebanese, Chinese, German, African, and Italian cultures. Although the dishes vary from region to region, they all share common flavors and techniques unique to Mexican cooking."

Stirring a pot, she continued to speak softly, but with

authority. "Since there is so much detail to making these dishes, I have done some of the prep work. Making good food takes time and you will all be hungry soon." The group collectively grinned.

"Excuse me, Chef Leah. That is not one of the crappy set of school-issued knives," Rainier said, pointing to the set of Wüsthof cutlery on the counter.

Leah broke into a reticent smile. "I brought my own set from home." They all laughed. Jacob beamed with pride.

During the cooking demonstration, Leah passed around bowls of prepared ingredients, allowing the group to smell, touch, and taste the finely minced herbs and spices. As she passed around *hoja santa*, an herb with a similar flavor to anise, she told the story of how Cortes's friars considered the native herbs to be the work of the devil. "More than likely, the plant was renamed 'holy leaf' to keep the friars from banishing it. That one clever person preserved the use of this special plant, which continues to influence the dishes of today."

Leah's classmates watched as she transformed dry chile pods into rich sauces and the powdery *masa harina* into tortillas. By noon, the mid-afternoon dinner of several courses, known as *comida*, was ready. Leah presented the dishes simply in earthenware platters and hand-painted bowls.

When the light was slanting in from the west, *the guiso de puerco*, or pork stew (in honor of the chef), *cebollas de la cazuela*, or onion casserole, *arroz verde con uvas* or green rice tossed with grapes (in honor of the vineyard), *frijoles de la olla*, or a pot of pinto beans, *ensalada de achicoria con aderezo de limón*, or chicory salad with lemon dressing, and baked apples drizzled with *cajeta de higo*, or fig caramel, were ready.

As Leah sprinkled minced cilantro onto the casserole, Chef Lasson closed the demonstration by saying, "I want to thank Leah for inviting us along on this incredible immersion into Mexican cuisine. Great job, Leah!" The group applauded and Leah gave the slightest of curtsies. She began to pass plates around.

Rainier, who was documenting the event with his Nikon, ran out of film. He went back to his dorm for another roll, telling the group not to touch a thing. He wanted a pristine shot of "the first cultural cook-off," as it had been dubbed. Nobody waited. As soon as he left, the group served themselves while asking Leah questions.

Studying each bite, some of the Europeans struggled to find English words to describe the flavors. No one could agree. Leah held the glass of iced *Jamaica*, or hibiscus tea, out to Jacob. He brushed his fingers over hers before taking the glass. Leah felt her face grow hot.

"Is this how you follow orders?" Rainier snorted when he returned. With his eye up to the lens he took a quick series of shots as he walked toward the table.

"Oh, Chef Lasson. Your wife is outside. She said she's been waiting for a long time," Rainier said. He smirked at the chef. "I think you are in the shit house, or is it the dog house?" Rainier, who could never keep his idioms straight, looked around for help.

Leah experienced the sensation of plunging into ice-cold water. Wife, she thought.

Jacob's face turned ashen as he glanced at his watch. "I didn't realize it was so late," he said, to no one in particular. "Thanks, Rainier."

Chapter 32

LETTER FROM DULCE IN THE NETHERLANDS

Hallo from the Netherlands!

You read right, the Netherlands. Did you notice the stamps? Nice, huh?

You guys must be wondering what the hell has happened to your Dulcecita? *¿Qué noticia?* The note she left only had a few words and they didn't explain too much.

A few days ago, I walked into this gallery and what did I see but my own sculptures. The ones that are supposed to be in Amsterdam. I kid you not! But, instead of having "Dulce Racelis" as the artist, the Dutch teacher's name was under them!

I knew it was a mistake. So, I decided to go and pay Elly and Willem a visit, just to clear things up. I hopped on a plane and kept going until my passport got stamped a bunch of times. To tell you the truth, I never knew where the Netherlands were, like I'm still not sure which states make up New England.

I went to the school and started walking around. I saw Elly teaching a class and stuck my head in through the door. I made a gun with my hand and pretended to shoot her, but I smiled and winked when I did it.

I asked some guy who was so white he was almost invisible, where Brinker was? He told me the old *pedo* is the

Dean of Students and how to get to his office. I could see him on the phone in his office, cause his door was open. I walked in and kicked back on a really old leather chair. It looked like an imitation of an old chair, but it was the real thing.

No sooner did I get comfortable when Elly jogs in. She didn't knock either. They didn't say much, just made sounds and moved in little jerks, like when you try to drive with the emergency brake still on. I said, *"¿Qué pasa, güey?"* I tossed the program from the gallery on the desk.

They both started talking real fast. They said that they were getting ready to call me with the good news. Not only was I accepted to the Amsterdam Institute of Fine Arts, I qualified for a partial scholarship! I kind of scratched my head, since I never applied. The next thing I know I've filled out the paperwork. I'll be starting school next quarter, which is a few weeks away. So you see, it was all a big mistake.

I'm staying with Willem and Elly until they find "more suitable arrangements" for me. They are such a trip! My temporary phone number and address are on the back of the picture. Feel free to call collect, any time!

Tot ziens (means 'see you later' or 'more Tater Tots' I'm not really sure, yet),

Dulce

✉

Chapter 33
TESSA GOES TO WASHINGTON D.C.

WITH SOPHOMORE YEAR almost over, Tessa was making plans to move home for the summer, but not before flying back East with Atticus for Senator and Mrs. Weston's 20th wedding anniversary party, which conveniently fell on the weekend after the school year ended.

Like all good Latina daughters, Tessa decided to lie to her parents, knowing they needed to believe that she was chaste. Flying 3,000 miles with some strange man to meet his family would only shock and hurt them. She called to say that she was staying on campus the extra week for upper-division orientation.

Her next call was to Alex. The two made arrangements to have Tessa's things stored until she returned.

❧

"Tell me something else about your family. Something new," Tessa said. She and Atticus were at the airport, waiting to board their flight.

"What do you want to know?" Atticus said, stretching his long legs.

"They're Protestant, right? What exactly does that mean?"

Atticus made a face as he thought about it. "It means they attend religious services on Christmas, Easter, and during elections."

Tessa was imagining an attractive family standing on the

church steps for a photo-op, when Atticus said, "My dad is great. He's such a character, a real prankster. When he was in college he threw a huge end of midterms party at his frat house. He made flyers and handed them to everyone, nerds, unattractive girls, he didn't judge. For that night, no one would be turned away." Atticus adjusted his baseball cap. "He charged a few bucks at the door and when the place was packed, he walked over to the neighboring frat house. He called the police and reported that shots had been fired at his address."

Tessa's mouth gaped. "Why did he do that?"

"Money and beer, of course. When the police raided the party, everyone scattered. It was written off as a stupid prank. After the police left his friends came back to the frat house and partied all weekend long."

Tessa pictured the jocks and sorority girls—all giggles— returning to the frat party their subordinates had paid for. She was not impressed.

Seeing the lack of appreciation on her face, he changed his tone.

"Whenever I talk to him he always asks how...you are."

"Really?" Tessa said, wanting to hear exactly what he had told his parents about her. But she caught the pause. "Why do you say it like that?"

"It's nothing. Don't get mad."

"Too late. Tell me!"

"This is so stupid," he said rubbing his eyes. "When I first told my parents I was seeing someone, they wanted to know all about you. One of the things I mentioned was that you are of Mexican heritage." He gave her a look that said, Well, you are. "My dad asked if you have a green card."

Tessa blinked a few times.

"What? Naturally he's concerned about me. I guess he thought you were an illegal alien trying to find a way into this country," he said, momentarily assuming a slightly defensive ire, before becoming uncomfortable.

"So, I snuck into Stanford, as pre-med, to find a husband and get a green card?" Tessa snarled. "I was born in California. You're the foreigner around here!" Tessa said.

"Don't get mad at me, my little mail-order bride." Atticus tried to kiss her, but Tessa raised a hand and blocked his face. "Do you really find your racist father funny?"

Atticus unexpectedly laughed. "I'm sorry, I know this isn't funny. I'm laughing because I'm afraid to tell you the rest. I have to in case he slips." He burst into another fit of laughter, but Tessa caught a flash of fear in his eyes. "Whenever I talk to my dad, he asks, oh God, he asks me, 'How's Maria?'"

Tessa was a little thrown. "Did you tell him my name is Maria?"

"Of course not. He just can't seem to remember 'Tessa.'"

Tessa stared off in a daze. "I cannot believe I'm meeting him, today!"

"It won't be bad."

"It already is. I don't want to go, Atticus!"

"Oh, come on. I knew I shouldn't have told you."

"What do you mean you shouldn't have told me? You should have told me sooner!" Tessa shoved him.

"You're right. I'm so sorry, but that's them." Atticus watched Tessa fume. "Oh, come on. I am not my family, just like you're not yours. Didn't you tell me about how baby's parties go on until three in the morning?"

"So? We know how to celebrate the special moments in life."

"And how your aunt killed a hen to bring someone's fever down. And not for making chicken soup."

"That was my great aunt."

Atticus attempted to keep a straight face as he said, "If you, Teresa Anaya, stared at a dog while it was pooping, you would get a pimple in your eye."

"I was a child!"

Atticus touched her hand. "This is our last chance to be together until fall. Do you really want to be apart for one week longer than we have to?"

Tessa heaved a sigh. "All right, but only because we already have the stupid tickets. And one more thing—we're staying with your cousins."

"Cousins?" he said, smiling and squinting. "My nearest relatives live in Pennsylvania. Besides, my parents would be offended."

"Oh, let's not offend the bigot. I'm out of here." As Tessa rose, she snatched the straps of her bag.

Atticus stood up. He grabbed Tessa's arm as a metallic voice announced the boarding of their flight. "Let's play it by ear and see how it goes. If you're not comfortable, we'll go to a hotel. Does that sound fair?" Atticus kissed her cheek. It was a kiss with a question in it, to see if they were good.

Tessa sighed. "Fine, but before you meet my family you're getting a haircut. And, since you really don't have a religion, you'll say you're Catholic. I'll teach you the basics."

Chapter 34
NAOMI DISCOVERS A SECRET

ON THE NIGHT BEFORE Tessa and Atticus arrived in Washington, D.C., and a few blocks from where they would be staying, Ms. Denise threw an impromptu party. The next morning, Naomi scanned the mess tiredly, assessing her workload. Empty liquor and beer bottles filled several bags piled in the kitchen. The sink had broken glass in it and smelled of vomit. Naomi silently prayed for strength before getting to work.

By the time she finished cleaning, twilight was settling over the house. She rolled her stiff neck and headed to the laundry room, where a stack of old chenille curtains had been placed next to her purse. This was Ms. Denise's way of telling her to store the curtains in the attic before she left. Scooping up the curtains, she trudged up the backstairs.

By the time she reached the attic steps, her arms were weak and her muscles were burning. After several failed attempts at reaching the light switch, she chugged up the steps in the dark. She was about halfway to the wardrobe when the tip of her shoe tapped some sort of box. Shuffling around it, she managed to reach an old card table before her arms gave out.

Naomi carefully made her way back to investigate. Flipping on the light switch, she saw the round hatbox covered with a matching lid. Assuming it contained hats, she went to pick it up, but remained bent by the box's weight. What could be so heavy? Naomi thought as she reached for the lid.

Chapter 35

TESSA MEETS THE WESTONS AND MARIA

THE PLAN WAS for Tessa and Atticus to go to Washington, D.C. to attend his parents' anniversary party. After a week, Tessa would return while Atticus stayed on to spend the summer with his family. What they never anticipated was that Tessa would not only be flying back alone—she would be returning single.

As the plane landed at San Francisco's International airport, Tessa felt like she had reached the destination of her depression. She stared out the window where little had changed. Unbuckling her seat belt, she wanted nothing more than to slip back into the seam of her relatively normal family and scrub the last several days from memory.

☙

A week earlier, Tessa and Atticus arrived in Washington, where a chauffeured sedan drove them out of the airport chaos. Feeling disgusted with herself for coming, she spoke little on the drive. After several attempts at small talk, Atticus announced, "We're here!"

Her eyes flicked out the window, surprised by the two-story brick colonial home with black window shutters and four Grecian columns stretching to the rounded ceiling of the second floor. "You live at the public library?" Tessa said, with a hint of a joke.

Atticus smiled. "Be it ever so humble."

The driver got the door. The heat and humidity were instantly pushing at Tessa from all sides. She watched, surprised, as Atticus rang his own doorbell. She was wondering where his key was when Atticus said, "My parents are going to love you." He kissed her damp temple. Tessa already did not like the Senator, yet held out hope at getting along with the racist's wife.

A grey-haired man with the same watery blue eyes as Atticus opened the door. Smiling, he blinked at Tessa the way Atticus did when surprised. Tessa read, "Where's Maria?" in his expression. Embracing his son, the two smacked each other's backs twice before letting go.

"This is my father. Whatever you do, don't turn your back on him," Atticus jokingly warned.

"It's very nice to meet you..." As expected, the Senator could not remember Tessa's actual name, but he avoided calling her "Maria" by lingering on the last word. He extended his hand and yanked her toward him. Bending her backward, he kissed her like the famous V-J Day photo.

"Come inside before you melt," he said. As they entered the foyer, she turned back to Atticus to see if he had caught the tongue in his father's kiss. Atticus was smiling and turning his face up to catch the cool air.

A petite woman descended the stairs. She had an angular face and champagne-colored hair that was styled like Krystle from *Dynasty*. She smiled questioningly at the woman standing next to her son—also wondering where Maria was, no doubt. Shifting her gaze back to Atticus, Mrs. Weston said, "There's my boy!"

"There's my girl," Atticus said, bear hugging his mother.

"Mom, I'm sure you know who this is."

"Of course I do. Welcome, Tess," she said, placing an air kiss next to her cheek. Tessa thought, At least she got most of my name right.

"It's nice meeting you, Mrs. Weston."

"We are so glad you are here. But you must call me Joyce," she said, taking Tessa by the arm.

"I guess that makes me Bob," the Senator said, as he and his son followed their women into the living room.

"OK, Joyce, Bob. Call me Tessa," she said, wanting to get the names straight up front.

A young woman rose from a beige couch. "Hey Mel!" Atticus said, his face brightening.

Melanie, pale and petite, wore no make-up. Her straight hair was shoulder-length and had been dyed a dark cherry red. A thick band near the part showed blond roots. She wore all black and her long sleeves were stretched out.

As they hugged, Melanie whispered vehemently into Atticus's ear, "It's already happening."

"Melanie is also studying medicine, at Smith," Joyce said.

"Nursing, mother," Melanie shot back. "Why do you say it like I'm going to be a doctor?"

Joyce inspected her daughter. She explained to Tessa, "Melanie is excessively affected by her emotions."

"Stop it!" Melanie said, pulling her long sleeves over her hands. The gesture reminded Tessa of two turtles retreating to safety.

"What have I done?" Joyce said. Tessa realized with a stab of surprise that Joyce intentionally struck that nerve.

"You're apologizing for me and acting like I'm not here!"

Melanie said.

Joyce glanced at Tessa with an expression that said, You see what I mean?

Melanie caught the exchange. "That's it. I'm leaving." She stormed out of the room.

"Excuse me," Atticus said, going after his sister.

"Aw, don't do that son. You're encouraging her to act out," Senator Bob whined.

Tessa stood in the awkward silence with the Westons for what felt like a week. With bags packed and by the front door, she was ready to go home.

Mr. Weston surreptitiously checked out Tessa's curves. He smiled amiably into her eyes as he said, "You know, some of my best friends are Hispanic."

Tessa smiled as she thought, If I had a dollar for every time I've heard that since I left San Francisco, I wouldn't have to work.

❧

Tessa got up early on her first morning in the District, still amazed that she and Atticus were not shown to separate bedrooms. She tried to sleep in, but the thought of being three thousand miles from home had a caffeine-like effect on her system. She showered, dressed, and watched Atticus for signs of stirring as she closed the bedroom door.

She meandered through the house, stopping to study paintings or to look out windows. Tessa was noting Joyce's deep and profound love for the color beige when she heard her voice. Joyce was in the formal dining room speaking to a woman with the patient expression of a maid. Atticus's mother was wearing a shimmery white silk blouse and tan slacks.

She smiled when she saw Tessa. "Good morning, Tess. How did you sleep?"

The way Joyce kept dropping the last letter of Tessa's name was making it difficult to like her. "Just fine, Mrs. Weston," she said, cordially.

"It's Joyce. Call me Joyce."

It's Tess-a, call me Tessa, she wanted to say, but gave up. It's never a good idea to antagonize the hostess so early in the visit.

"Your timing is perfect," Joyce said, while turning slightly toward the rotund woman, barely five feet in height. "This is Cleaning Maria."

Tessa waited for the rest of the introduction, "Maria, meet Tess," or something to that effect. Instead, Joyce said, "Would you mind mentioning to her, in Spanish, that the small area rugs and runners need to be rolled up, taken out, and beaten, and not merely vacuumed."

Tessa translated. Maria's sweat and oil-sheened face filled with comprehension. Nodding, she stared curiously at Tessa.

"I'll bet you're ready for some coffee?" Joyce said, leading Tessa into the kitchen, where a woman in a full apron sliced fresh peaches. Tessa wondered how many servants the Westons employed.

"This is Cooking Maria. Since they're both named Maria, we've added 'Cooking' or 'Cleaning' to their names." Joyce smiled at her own logic.

Tessa was stunned by the generalization. It was as if Joyce was talking about puppies from the same litter.

"Is Atticus still asleep? I have got to make some phone calls. Please make yourself at home. Oh, coffee? Maria, please get Tess some coffee. Why don't you read the paper? Maria, did you bring in the newspapers? If you need anything else, come and find me," she said.

"Thank you," Tessa said to the closing door. She wondered how much coffee the woman had already tossed back.

Tessa suddenly felt out of place. She introduced herself in Spanish. The cook impassively nodded while handing her a cup of coffee on a saucer. Turning, Maria stooped and picked up a fallen yellow piece of paper.

Tessa's eyes scanned the dozens of little yellow squares of paper adhering to the walls and cabinets. The spidery letters labeled the contents of the drawers. One had "Utensils," the other "Plastic Wrap." The "Dishes" and "Cups" were kept in the cupboard, and under the sink were the "Dishwasher Soap & Dish Soap." In the cabinet to the right were the "Cans."

Tessa figured that one of the grandparents with a failing memory visited often, and the notes were kind reminders by a concerned family. She took comfort in this thought. Taking a seat at the breakfast nook, Tessa began to read the paper.

"My name is Remedios," the cook said in Spanish as she poured pancake batter onto a hot griddle.

"Oh, nice meeting you. I thought Mrs. Weston…Joyce said your name was Maria?"

"She did," Remedios said, without elaborating.

"Would you like me to clear up the confusion? I'm sure it would make things a lot easier around here and prevent any mix-ups between you and Maria."

Remedios clucked. "Oh, she knows it. I never recognized my own name when she called me, so I never answered her. But whenever *la señora* called for Maria, I always looked up. She doesn't speak English and I was ready to translate. *La señora* is not a stupid woman. She noticed how I always paid attention when she said 'Maria,' and that was that. The name has stuck to me like chewed gum to my shoe."

Tessa pointed behind her. "How does Maria feel about sharing her name?"

"You mean Amparo? She doesn't mind. She's just glad to have a job without pap..." Remedios looked up from wiping the pancake batter from the lip of a bowl, panicked. Lulled by her native tongue, she let her co-worker's illegal status slip.

Tessa thought about mentioning how Mr. Weston had also referred to her as Maria, but something made her let the moment pass. Instead, she said, "My mother is a 'Maria' in San Francisco. She's been cleaning houses since I started kindergarten. You three should start a club." Tessa said this so deadpan she did not expect a reaction.

Remedios barked out a laugh, surprising her. Tessa knew she was in. The two began to chat as Remedios cracked eggs over a mixing bowl. Tessa absentmindedly moved to the stovetop, picked up the spatula and kept an eye on the pancakes. Glancing around, Tessa's curiosity got the best of her. "What are the yellow notes for?"

In a nearly perfect American accent, Remedios said, "Mrs. Weston is teaching me English. I taught high school English in Colombia for three years." She switched back to Spanish, "But the better the English, the heavier the workload, so I keep to myself."

Tessa was pouring her second cup of coffee when Joyce returned with a sheet of paper in one hand and a silver fountain pen in the other. "Tess, you are a godsend. Would you mind translating this checklist for the gardeners?" Tessa's eye flickered to Remedios's backside, knowing she was grinning at having her point proven so soon.

As Joyce read the list aloud, Tessa's mind relived the night of naughty sex she had had with this woman's son. After turning in early, Tessa and Atticus played out several sexual fantasies he dreamt up while still a pimply kid in the same bedroom. Knowing that his parents were in the house had made Tessa lusty.

Tessa enjoyed being the panty-less cheerleader sneaking into the quarterback's room after the big game. She twirled handfuls of undergarments, like pompoms, and even made up a silly cheer that ended with "Yay, team!" She had attempted to do the splits on Atticus' face, momentarily suffocating him.

"Could you do that for me? I would really appreciate it," Joyce said, jarring Tessa back to the present.

Tessa nodded, dumbly. Having no idea what she just agreed to.

Chapter 36

TESSA GETS CAUGHT BETWEEN A ROCK AND A CRAZY PLACE

FOR THE NEXT SEVERAL DAYS, the Weston men proudly kissed their women goodbye before going to the office. Tessa and Joyce spent their mornings running errands before lunching at a different restaurant, and with an entirely different set of women. Over niçoise salads and ice teas, Tessa watched these women and noted how their perfectly enunciated words carried little volume, emotion, or stress of urgency. Tessa had never felt more Mexican in her life.

She smiled as she thought of her mother and *tías* lunching at home, with voices so melodic, they sounded like songbirds. Even from the next room, Tessa could tell when they were exchanging gossip. After a particularly scandalous morsel was whispered they laughed with their mouths closed, like Wilma and Betty. Tessa regretted not being in their warm and animated company.

At Thursday's luncheon, Joyce, once again, graciously offered Tessa's translation services to the group of women— some of whose husbands were contributors to the Senator's campaign fund. By now, Tessa had figured out it was the favor Joyce had asked for when she was thinking about naughty sex with her son. It serves me right.

Joyce's dearest friend jumped at the offer. "You have to fire my maid," she said. Unlike the other women, demure and subtle, Denise looked and acted like a country singer.

"Why?" Tessa said, suddenly alert by the break in her new routine.

"Because Naomi's been stealing from me, that's why," Denise said. The women at the table became outraged and supportive.

"Is it possible that one of your kids moved some of your things around?" Tessa suggested.

"I don't have any kids. And before you ask, I'm in between husbands right now," Denise said, like she was talking about jobs.

Tessa pictured the middle-aged woman with over-tanned skin firing her housekeeper. She would probably say something stupid, like, "No come backo! Comprende?"

Tessa nodded. "Um, sure." Guille was right all along. She really was *La Malinche*. Tessa could suddenly see how easily manipulated the Indian woman had been by the Spaniards. Her love for Cortes and desire to please him got a little out of control, and changed the course of world history, that's all.

❧

After lunch, Joyce needed to run more errands and dropped Tessa off at the house. Feeling soaked through from the heat, she decided to go for a swim in their ignored pool. She changed into her swimsuit and was passing Melanie's door when she impulsively knocked.

"What now?" a terse voice said.

"It's me, Tessa. I'm going swimming. Do you want to join me?"

There was a pause. "I'll meet you down there."

Having expected Melanie to refuse, Tessa regretted asking

her. But then again, she suspected that Atticus's little sister was not as messed up as her parents seemed to think. They had just convinced her that she was.

Tessa trotted down the stairs and into the kitchen where Remedios was consoling a crying Amparo. "What's wrong?" Tessa said, staring into their troubled faces.

Amparo wiped her nose with a tissue. "My sister, Naomi, is in trouble. She found a box for hats in the attic of the woman she works for. It was filled with jewelry. There was also a gold frame with a picture of the van Vleck twins."

Tessa frowned. "Who are the van Vleck twins?"

"They are a family that lives near here. Last year, their maid was fired for stealing from them. One of the items she was accused of taking was that same pure gold picture frame," Remedios said.

"Hold on." Tessa struggled to understand. "Are you saying that someone in the house that your sister cleans for stole from the van Vlecks?"

"We think it was Ms. Denise," Remedios said.

With a start, Tessa recognized the name. "Ms. Denise," she said, placing the towel on the counter as she ran their lunch conversation through her head. Seeing no way around the truth, she softened her tone. "Amparo, I've been asked to fire your sister." Remedios and Amparo's eyes widened. "I had lunch with Ms. Denise this afternoon. She said that her maid was stealing from her."

"But that's not true! She hasn't done anything wrong!" Amparo said.

"In six months, at least eight maids have been fired for stealing. They were honest and hard-working women. But everyone's heard of the Spring Valley thefts and they couldn't get work," Remedios said.

"What makes you so sure it's Ms. Denise?" Tessa said, showing the palms of her hands. "I'm not saying that it's Naomi. She couldn't have casually walked into all of those houses. But we can't point a finger at Denise."

"Ms. Denise lives alone, so no one else could have left the box in her attic. And, like you yourself just said, the thief was able to enter all of the houses," Remedios said, looking away. "Now that I think about it, all of the robberies happened to friends of Ms. Denise and Mrs. Weston."

"Were the police contacted for any of the robberies?"

"Yes. Every time," Remedios said.

"Were any of the maids questioned by the police?"

"All of them were, but none were arrested. And even though they were cleared of the charges, their employers fired them. Some didn't have papers and were deported," Remedios said, glancing worriedly at Amparo.

Amparo began to weep into her apron. Remedios hugged her and made hushing sounds.

Tessa was at a loss for what to do. She had already agreed to fire the faceless maid, but the situation had changed. Was there a way to maneuver around the housewives without drawing any attention to herself?

She glanced at the clock with the note under it that read, "Clock." Denise mentioned something about heading to Virginia after lunch. "Will Naomi answer the phone if you call Denise's house?"

"No. She doesn't speak English as well as I do," Amparo said.

Tessa had heard her attempts at communicating in English, and tried not to grin. "I need to call a cab and I'll need Denise's address." She thought a moment. "And gloves and a paper bag."

Some sort of shift took place in the room. The three realized they were not alone the moment before a voice spoke up. "I'll take you." Melanie was standing by the doorway. There was an awkward silence as the women in the kitchen stared at her.

Tessa thought how Melanie's Spanish accent was pretty good. She turned to Amparo. "Write your sister a note."

Tessa had Denise's address, transportation and a note for Naomi. Now all she needed was a real plan.

Chapter 37

TESSA BURGLES MS. DENISE'S HOME

As Melanie drove her black Volkswagen Rabbit to Denise's house, they talked fast. Melanie said, "I'll stay in the car and keep an eye out for Denise. If I see her, I'll tap on the horn."

Tessa nodded. "That sounds good. I'll collect some of the stolen property. We'll drop it off near the police station, then make an anonymous call from a payphone."

"But if Denise is suspicious of Naomi, she'll have hidden the box from her. If Naomi is anything like Amparo, she's going to freeze with fear," Melanie said, shaking her head. "I once overheard her talking to Remedios. Back in Guatemala, they witnessed their father's execution. He was dragged out of bed at night, and then hanged from a tree in their yard."

"Huh." That was too much for Tessa to think about right now. "If Naomi breaks down and cries, I guess I'm going to have to look for the box myself."

Melanie refrained from saying what they were both thinking: "Yes, but where?"

When the car pulled into the driveway of an enormous Tudor-style house, Tessa thought of a tiny needle and a 5,000 square feet haystack. She knocked on the back door. The D.C. heat was making it hard to breathe. On her second knock, a small, dark woman, slightly bent, answered. She had the look of immigration anxiety on her face.

"Hello, Naomi. My name is Teresa Anaya. Amparo sent

me. Please read this," Tessa said, in Spanish, while handing her the note.

❧

For an hour, a sweaty Tessa looked through stacks of boxes in the attic. She then pawed through piles of junk. As she went through an old dresser, it occurred to her that she would not be able to hear Melanie's car horn from up here. A panicked Melanie could have honked and left a while ago.

For all she knew Ms. Denise could be downstairs right now, wondering about the noise coming from the attic. Or maybe she had already called the police. The humiliation of being bailed out of jail by Atticus and his parents made her shudder.

Tessa grabbed Naomi's shoulders and shook. "Naomi, does Ms. Denise have a secret hiding place?"

"I don't know." Naomi's words were barely comprehensible.

Tessa struggled to keep the panic out of her voice as she said, "When I was little, my father built a barbecue pit in the backyard out of bricks. For some reason the coals never stayed lit. Underneath the pit was a place to store the charcoal briquettes. I used to put my favorite dolls in there to hide them from my friend, Dulce." Tessa left out the part about Dulce biting off the doll's heads before lobbing their bodies, like grenades. "Does Ms. Denise have a place like that? A place to hide things?"

Naomi's crying ceased as she listened to the memory. A look of recognition flashed in her eyes. "There is an old radio in the library. She used to hide bottles from her husbands in it." Naomi looked guiltily at Tessa, not comfortable with the betrayal of her employer's confidence.

They tiptoed down the attic stairs and into the hallway, where Tessa snuck a glance out the window. Ms. Denise was not home yet, and Melanie was parked in the same place. The quick relief that passed through Tessa caused her scalp to tingle.

The library was a large white room with busy molding and neglected furnishings. A collection of expensive vintage handbags filled the shelves—no books. By the window was an old wooden radio with "Philco" printed on its art deco face. The two women moved the radio away from the wall, careful not to scuff the floor. It had been gutted and lined with dark blue velvet. "That's it," Naomi said in a voice deadened with fear.

Tessa put on the yellow dishwashing gloves Remedios had leant her. She lifted the lid. They both stared down at the miniature pirate's treasure for a moment. Tessa picked up the surprisingly heavy frame of the twins. In her mind's eye, she watched Denise discover the open box she had neglected to put away. Seeing the broken glass, she realized her maid figured out her dark secret.

"That evil cow!" Tessa said out loud. She selected several engraved items she was sure were reported as stolen: a men's Cartier watch, a brooch with a cluster of pearls, a gold locket with a ruby setting, and a diamond wedding ring set. They pushed the radio back in place before wiping off Naomi's prints.

As they rushed toward the kitchen, Tessa said, "I'll be back this evening. Remember, we've never met."

"Oh, are you having dinner here?" Naomi's face

brightened for the first time.

Tessa stopped. She could not bring herself to tell this kind woman the harsh truth. "Call your sister. She will explain."

Chapter 38

ALEX IS PREGNANT, AGAIN

"I'M PREGNANT," Alex said. She held her breath. Jaime was sitting across the new smoked glass dinette table, eating the romantic dinner that she—actually Quico—had prepared.

Jaime stopped chewing. "Again?"

Alex waited. She never knew how he was going to react to news—good or bad.

Jaime put his fork down and pointed to himself with both thumbs, *"¡Yo soy muy macho! ¡Hijo de la chingada!"* he said, like he just scored the winning goal for Mexico. Leaning forward, he tousled Alex's hair. She hated when he did that. It was the kind of affection you reserve for a dog, not the woman carrying your baby. Masking her annoyance, she smiled as she arranged the curls back into place with her fingers.

"But my sons are not going to grow up above a bar," he said, adding, "No way!" in English. Picking up his fork, he struggled to cut a bite-sized piece of the *pierna de carnero asada* on his plate.

Alex stared at the serrated knife next to his resting hand. She tried to will him to pick it up. "It's not a bar, it's a restaurant. Our family business," she said, a little defensively.

"Yeah, but the bar's right under our apartment."

"I rarely hear anything from the lounge. Do you?" she said, needing to take the sleaze out of his comment.

Jaime held his plate up for seconds of everything, except

the green beans. "Where are you going to put all of our sons, huh? You going to stick the younger ones in drawers at night? Make Junior sleep in the tub when he's older?" Jaime said. Straightening, he looked around. "Where is Junior?"

"Asleep," Alex said, taking his plate. "Maybe you're right. I guess we'll be needing a bigger place, eventually." At the stovetop Alex served Jaime seconds. She stood there a moment taking in her kitchen.

"Why wait? We have the money. This weekend, we are going to buy a house," Jaime said. He pounded the table once with his fist, like a gavel, and court was adjourned.

The Pedrosa family began to look for properties in the Mission, but Jaime did not like anything they saw. That, and he did not want to live around a bunch of *mojados*. They expanded their search to other neighborhoods: Bernal Heights, Portrero Hill, the Haight, Twin Peaks, the Sunset, and the Richmond District. Every time, Jaime shook his head. There was never enough parking or the houses were too small, too close; the neighborhoods too ghetto, gay, or Chinese.

After weeks of driving up and down the coast, they found themselves in San Rafael. Alex was placing a check mark next to the address on her list of open houses as she stepped through the front door. She looked up and out the wide windows with stunning views from three directions, the wrap-around rosewood deck, and then worriedly at her husband. Jaime had a sharp grin on his face, which Alex knew meant that he was impressed.

The four-bedroom, three-bathroom home featured an open floor plan, an office, and a separate entrance off of the private master suite. In the master bedroom, Jaime grunted with approval at the fireplace.

Turning to Alex, Jaime said, "This is it."

༄

Alex reset the car's trip meter before they left. When they got home, she checked it. It's 22 miles from the restaurant. Over a half-hour drive during light traffic, but the Golden Gate Bridge was almost impossible to cross after a major car accident, or a potential bridge jumper. She briefly wondered why people always jumped from the rail facing the city, and never the sea.

That night in bed, Alex confided to her husband that she was terrified of being pulled so far from the Mission. "This is my home. My world. How can I move away from everything and everyone I love?"

Jaime seemed ready for this. "The schools are much better out there, and not just the private ones. Our kids are going to be able to ride bikes without being kidnapped the way your friend from high school was. What was her name?"

Alex absently glanced away. "China."

"Yeah, her. You already know that good parents are supposed to make sacrifices. What have you sacrificed so far? Huh?"

Jaime was right. She was blessed with a wonderful family, her health, and a career she loved. Alex felt there was no choice but to acquiesce.

Chapter 39

TESSA RETURNS TO THE SCENE OF THE CRIME

"WELL, WELL. You're just in time for happy hour," Denise said, greeting Tessa at the door. A stemmed glass filled with clear liquid was in her hand.

It was exactly five o'clock, but Tessa could tell this was not her first drink. "Thanks, but I can't stay long. Melanie is waiting in the car."

"It only takes a second to finish a martini."

As Denise demonstrated, Tessa studied her. She thought back to her first impression of Denise earlier that day. She pegged her as the type of person who never had to deal with the results of her actions. When a conscience is deprived of consequences, it withers, like a plant without water. Prisons and politics are full of people like her.

Naomi was standing silently in the library. She looked like she was about to take a polygraph test she knew she would fail. They made eye contact. Denise took a seat on the couch. With some reluctance, Tessa sat next to her.

"I want you to tell her that I'm on to her and that she's fired. If she thinks that I'm not going to call the authorities, she's crazy."

Denise did not actually accused Naomi of stealing. If she had, the maid could object in Spanish and blurt out the sordid truth. Tessa suddenly understood why she was there. Denise wanted to torture her maid a little before handing her over to the police.

Noting the word "crazy," Tessa figured Denise was expecting to hear *loca* and incorporated the word into the translation. "Naomi. Your embassy has been contacted and we are in the process of attaining political asylum for both you and your sister's families. You will no longer be working for this crazy woman." Naomi stared with surprise at Tessa through melting eyes.

"Wow," Denise said. "Your translation was so much longer than what I said."

Tessa smiled. "When English is translated to Spanish, it expands by 25 percent."

Satisfied with Tessa's explanation and Naomi's reaction, Denise said, "Tell her..." she paused, as though deciding whether to order the chicken or the fish. "I already phoned the police and immigration. I've given them her address. Let her know that she and her family are heading back to Nicaragua."

Again, Tessa took a quick inventory of the words. She wanted to shout, Guatemala, you moron! But said, "This shameless woman has called the police and immigration, but don't worry, it's all been taken care of. I'm saying 'Nicaragua' because she's expecting to hear it. I'll explain later."

❧

The next morning, the police arrived at Denise's house. They had been ringing the doorbell for several minutes when the door swung open. An irate Denise stood in her doorway, wearing a black satin rob and traces of last night's make-up. She was cursing her fired maid for not getting the door.

As the officers pushed passed her, Detective Boyd handed Denise the folded document, explaining the warrant. Her fingerprints were on file for a couple of drunk and disorderly charges that had been dismissed. Denise was dialing the number of her attorney when the box of stolen property was found.

Chapter 40

JOYCE AND BOB'S ANNIVERSARY PARTY

FINALLY, IT WAS THE WEEKEND AGAIN. At Joyce and Bob's lavish anniversary party, most of the conversations were not about how the happy couple had managed to "out-marry" many of their friends, but about the Spring Valley scandal. Standing at Atticus's side, Tessa watched the Senator and his wife grimace whenever Denise's name came up—which was often.

After the party, Atticus and Tessa went straight to their room. As they got ready for bed, Atticus recounted some of the Denise jokes he had heard. "How many Denises does it take to change a light bulb?"

"I have no idea." Tessa was exhausted.

"It only takes one Denise to change *your* light bulb into *her* light bulb."

"Ha," Tessa said, without humor.

"What a party. This evening will live on in infamy," Atticus said, taking off his tie. "Did you manage to have a good time, in spite of everything?"

Tessa nodded. She was leaving in the morning and would never have to see any of these deranged people again. Trying to get out of her funk, she made a weak attempt at humor. "I was especially touched when your mom told the band to play *La Bamba* in my honor," she said, unzipping her emerald green silk dress.

After seeing the plain dress Tessa was planning on wearing, Joyce had insisted on taking her shopping for something "more appropriate." Tessa stared down at the expensive gift, now puddled around her feet. It looked like a swamp.

Atticus became deflated. "I don't get it. My mother has tried to make you feel like part of the family and all you've given her is the cold shoulder. And now you're putting down her efforts."

Given all that had happened, Tessa could not believe that they were about to fight over this. "I'm sorry if that's what you think, but you're way off."

"Am I? OK, fine. Then tell me what's going on with you." When Tessa did not reply, Atticus shook his head. "You've been acting weird since we got here. You're always whispering with one of the Marias. It's like you'd rather hang out with them than us."

Tessa's jaw clenched. "Remedios and Amparo!" she growled.

"Huh?" Atticus said, thinking she was lapsing into Spanish.

"That's their names! The Marias!"

"So?" Atticus said, baffled.

In the silence that followed, Tessa realized that no matter what she said, there was another side and Atticus would choose it. Not to be combative, nor because to a certain degree, logic is cultural. Atticus would take the opposing side because he was a simpleton, just like his father.

For Tessa, the relationship ended when Atticus said, "I know I'm going to get hell for this, but maybe if you didn't act so much like a minority, you wouldn't be treated like one."

Chapter 41

LEAH IS MISTAKEN FOR AN ILLEGAL ALIEN

IT WAS A RAINY SUNDAY in late November and Leah was feeling a little restless without her weekly walk. She was running low on toothpaste and used the excuse to drive into town. On the St. Helena highway, she stared out at the vineyards, now dormant, and let her mind drift. Winter is the season of silent memories.

"Petrichor" was a word she recently learned. It is the smell of the earth after the rain. Leah drew in a cold deep breath. She loved Napa's sterling winter best. Yet, she had thought that about the fall, and the summer before. She was thinking of spring as an unopened gift when she noticed the truck on the side of the road. It could have been the brother of Pepe Le Pew, the hand-me-down truck she was driving. The shell had even been painted with exterior house paint. Only it did not have white stripes.

The hood was propped up and several migrant workers were huddled around the engine. Leah spotted two small children and worried that they would catch pneumonia. She pulled onto the soft shoulder of the road. Rolling down her window, she said in Spanish, "Can I give you a ride?"

Five drenched people nodded and thanked Leah as they piled in the back of the truck, while an elderly man and a little boy hopped into the passenger side. The boy leaned away from her, shivering. His big brown eyes gave him the look of a wet sparrow. Leah turned the heater up.

They had not gone a mile when Leah noticed the flashing red lights in her side mirror. Signaling, she pulled off of the road. She nervously rummaged through her pack for her wallet before rolling down the window.

"Good morning. Did you know your right taillight is out? Can I see your driver's license and registration?" He was the cliché of a country sheriff, potbellied and older. As Leah handed him the information, she read "Stake" on the star pinned to his rain slicker. Leah shuddered.

"Thank you. Now I need to see your permanent resident card." Leah stared blankly at Sheriff Stake. His hat was covered with molded plastic and the brim was acting as a spout and pouring rain water into her truck. "Do you speak English? Do you have proof of citizenship? A green card?" he said, louder, to be better understood.

"No. Do you?" What Leah meant was do people carry some sort of proof of citizenship, something like a license? But the question came out wrong.

"Stay put, smart ass!" The sheriff said. He sloshed back to his car. Leah watched from the side mirror as he radioed the dispatcher. She felt the entire truck pulsating with fear and realized that they were about to be deported. Including her.

A second police car showed up. Leah and the passengers were ushered out of the truck. She made a feeble attempt to clear up the misunderstanding, but the deputy pointed to a spot and said, "Stand there and don't talk and don't move." Leah reluctantly did as she was told.

Standing uncertainly with teeth chattering, Leah thought how the rain on her face felt like cold tears. Headlights turned onto the muddy shoulder of the road. It was not the expected green immigration van, but a black Jeep. A man in a hooded jacket got out. He shook hands with the sheriff. Their conversation quickly escalated to a heated exchange as they approached the deportees.

Leah recognized Jacob a split second before he said, "Leah, what seems to be the problem here?"

The sheriff spoke up before Leah could. "Hold on. This is police business."

Ignoring him, Jacob said, "Why did he pull you over?"

Sheriff Stake's eyes ordered her not to answer.

Jacob caught the look. "It's OK, Leah. You can tell me."

Seconds passed before she whispered, "A broken taillight."

"Roy," Jacob said to the sheriff, "you don't mind if Leah gets in her truck and taps on the brake, do you? I promise she won't flee the scene, will you Leah?"

"Now wait a second, Jacob. If you don't leave right now, I'm going to have to take you in for obstructing justice," the sheriff demanded, only the threat sounded empty.

"I'll leave as soon as she does this one thing. I promise." To Leah, Jacob said, "Would you mind?"

Leah forced herself to ignore the scowling sheriff and got behind the wheel. As Jacob and the lawmen gathered behind the truck, the migrant workers took a few non-threatening steps back for a better view. Leah tapped the brake several times. The rain became a downpour and looked like a filter through the windshield.

Jacob approached the open door, and said, "Thanks, Leah. Would you ask your friends to get back in the truck?"

Confused, Leah waited. The sheriff only grimaced and stared impatiently at the cars on the highway.

Jacob glared at the sheriff. "You pulled her over on a false charge, Roy. There is nothing wrong with the brake lights. If that's not bad enough, you're on the verge of violating Leah's civil rights. Cut them loose, or she's filing a complaint against you, and your department."

Leah softly said that it was OK to get back into the truck. She watched as they wordlessly piled in, taking the same seats as before.

"They all look alike! How am I supposed to tell them apart?" the sheriff said, flapping his arms once for emphasis. "You know you councilmen are too much! Who the hell else are we going to pull over? We're not allowed to pull over drunken tourists. You're the ones worried about the bad publicity."

"So, you admit that you're singling out migrant workers? I'd heard the rumors." Jacob paused. Turning to Leah, he said, "Maybe you should get going."

Leah understood that Jacob was trying to give her a bit of a head start. Her engine rumbled to life.

"I didn't say that. You can't twist my words around." Leah heard Sheriff Stake say as she drove away.

Chapter 42
LEAH BREAKS SEVERAL SCHOOL RULES

THE PROFESSIONAL BAKING FUNDAMENTALS class ended a while ago. Leah stayed behind to clean her station before starting on Eric Peterson's. Eric refused to clean up after himself, complaining to whoever would listen, "When I stay at a hotel, I don't change the sheets before I leave. I've already paid for that service."

Leah watched as Eric's idle logic influenced the more impressionable students. She noticed that after each class, less was cleaned and put away. She was aware that restaurant owners and knife-wielding kitchen employees would never tolerate a lazy chef. The bad habits they were picking up now were bound to die quick and humiliating deaths.

By the time Leah began to wipe down Eric's table with bleach and water-soaked towels, she was the only student left in class. She did not mind the extra cleanup. It was her last class of the day, and a nice way to unwind. She was pretending the galvanized tabletop was a chalkboard that needed to be erased before something new could be written and learned when a voice made her jump.

"There's a basket of homemade macarons on my desk. Do you know anything about that?" Jacob said, leaning in from the doorway.

"Yes. That was me," Leah said. "I wanted to thank you for, well, everything."

"Did everyone get home all right?"

"Yes. I don't know what we would have done without you," Leah said. Her smile was tinged with a kind of sadness.

"You'd probably be calling your sister, collect, from Tijuana about now." Leah laughed. Encouraged, Jacob said, "Listen, I was heading out to get some coffee to go with my delicious French confections. Are you up for a little snack?"

Leah took a self-conscious step back. "I don't think that's a good idea," she said, hearing the word "wife" echo in her head.

"Oh, I see." Jacob removed his toque. Leah did the same. "This is about my wife, isn't it? Leah, I need to explain my situation to you."

"You don't have to explain anything to me."

"Please, just hear me out," Jacob said.

Leah leaned against the metal table as Jacob closed the door. He took a measured breath and squared his shoulders. "I met Yumi in Paris when I was finishing my studies. We were dating for three months when she told me that she was pregnant. A week later, we were married and living together. She had a miscarriage after that. It all happened so fast." The thought seemed to grieve him. "I was apprenticing under a chef that I really admired and was working long hours. I don't know. It seemed easier to stay together than to break up. Finding a decent apartment in Paris can be tougher than New York." Jacob mused, "I can't believe that actually made sense. I know it sounds pathetic, but I was young and really, really stupid."

Jacob leaned against the same table as Leah. "Since then, it's been a marriage of convenience for both of us. It's been convenient for her to live a comfortable life, with all of the privileges of travel and fine dining extended to us. As for me, I've been married to my work. What I'm trying to get across to you is that we move in entirely different circles that never converge. We both prefer it that way."

As he stepped closer to Leah, his voice became soft with contrition. "But when we had lunch, the first time I looked into your eyes, I tripped and fell into them. I love you, Leah. It may not be right, but there it is."

Leah experienced the radiance of joy. Yet, this was happening too fast. Jacob pushed a few stray hairs back and cupped her face. He frowned. "I didn't mean to blurt it out like that. But you already know, don't you? Just like I know you love me."

Leah risked the honest answer. "Yes."

Jacob did not hide his relief. Putting his arms around Leah, he drew her close to him. Anticipating her first kiss, Leah closed her eyes. She smelled cloves on his breath as his lips touched hers. The kiss was slow and lingering, and then became firmer as his body pressed against hers. Like a dream that skips forward, she was suddenly reclining on the steel table. She felt the contrast of cold metal on her backside as the heat from Jacob's body covered her like a blanket.

He was kissing her neck when they heard a group of students' derisive laughter from the hallway. Leah's alarm heightened and she moved to sit up, only Jacob pressed himself into her. Startled, she could almost feel the resolute force of his stare as his knees parted her legs. He pressed his body closer to hers and moved in an instinctual rhythm.

Leah clamped her teeth over her lower lip to keep from making a sound. Jacob watched as Leah's breathing became rapid and her eyelids began to flutter. Jacob felt the tremor pass through her entire body. She suddenly wilted.

The voices in the hallway became fainter as Leah was jarred back from the white mist and heard the shallow bursts of her own breathing. When she opened her eyes, Jacob was gazing down at her. His eyes were filled with wonder and a slight, intimate smile formed on his lips. "Leah," he whispered, kissing her damp forehead.

But humiliation had already welled up in her. She pushed Jacob away and staggered as she stood.

Jacob jumped off the table. "Leah," he pleaded. As his hand reached for her, she shrank back. Her eyes were wild as she ran from the room.

Leah made a quick retreat into the women's restroom. What she was experiencing was not a clean emotion, but a mixture of shame and fear. She splashed cold water onto her face, in an attempt to wash the feel of Jacob's kisses from her skin.

Her hands were trembling as she touched her throbbing lower lip. She must have bitten it when she...Leah turned the faucet back on and began splashing water on her face. She could see Jacob's eyes and how they watched her as she climaxed. Leah began to sob. Her first orgasm on display like that. Plus, she was fully dressed. Was that possible?

She suddenly felt cold under the florescent lights and regretted ducking into the restroom. Pulling out handfuls of paper towels from the dispenser, Leah began to pat herself dry. She wished she could fold herself in half, and then again in half, and keep folding, until she was no bigger than a dust mote.

Checking the hallway Leah glanced to her right, and then to her left. She froze as she looked directly at Eric Peterson. He was leaning against the wall between the men and women's restrooms. Surprised by the drenched Leah, he said, "What happened to you?" His tone curious, but not concerned.

When Leah did not answer, he said, "You didn't think you'd get caught, did you. Well, you of all people should know better than that."

He knows! Leah thought, if Eric knows, everyone will know! When I get back to my room I'll write some goodbye notes and say my prayers. I will then slit my wrists with my paring knife.

Eric gave her a chilly stare. "You are supposed to remove your side towel before going into the restroom."

Leah's hand went straight for the towel by her waist, as if reaching for a holstered gun. Eric recited the school's manual verbatim. "'The side towel must be removed when going to the restroom, when taking out the trash, and when eating meals.'"

Misinterpreting Leah's relief for dejection, Eric felt imperious. "I'm going to have to report this, Leah. The school needs to maintain its high standards of sanitation or my diploma won't be worth shit!" With that, Eric sauntered away.

Chapter 43

ALEX EXPLORES SAN RAFAEL

ALEX SOON DISCOVERED that domestic bliss was not all that it was cracked up to be. The quiet hills of San Rafael felt a little disorienting, like when a car alarm that has been blaring suddenly shuts off. The only Mexicans she saw on her woodsy street were either pointing a leaf blower or trudging up the hill from the bus stop to clean a house.

While window-shopping on Fourth Street, Alex noticed that most of the new mothers were carrying their offspring—newborns to nearly pubescent—in Mayan baby slings. What surprised Alex was that they were paying upwards of forty bucks for a strip of fabric that cost next to nothing to make! Alex made a mental note to look into manufacturing the slings.

She could not help but wonder how these mommies handled minor emergencies like baby barf. Junior's stroller doubled as a U-Haul. It not only held Junior—she could also fit Junior's diaper bag, jacket, toys, extra blanket, her hefty purse, a bag of groceries, and a gallon of milk in it.

She was sitting on a sidewalk bench, licking a double scoop of chunky monkey ice cream, when she noticed a couple of middle-aged new mommies watching her. Alex smiled openly. It would be so nice to make new friends. Smiling as they approached, the woman with the sleeping baby in a hemp sling said, "Hi. Which family are you working for?"

Alex blinked. Before she could answer, the skinny woman

with the twill pouch on her back—filled to capacity with a drooling baby—said, "Do you know of any other nannies looking for work?"

"I'm not his nanny, I'm his mother," she said, fighting the urge to rhyme "nanny" with "mammy."

Noticing her protruding belly, they stared at Alex with somber concern. To them, she was a sad statistic about babies having babies. Their pity made Alex feel inferior.

Without another word the women walked on. Alex watched their backsides and felt her anger flare up. You're the ones that are pathetic, and shortsighted. Haven't you ever heard of the extended family? Have children while you're young, become young grandparents, and pitch in. That way you don't have to hassle total strangers on the street for childcare help!

❧

Alex's due date had come and gone a week ago and her back was bothering her. It was getting late and Jaime still was not home. She was tired and turned in, but once in bed, she could not find a comfortable position.

She heard the hum of the garage door. It was 2:38 am. The restaurant had been closed for over three hours. Knowing Jaime would be angry if he thought she was waiting up, she pretended to be asleep. She pictured him gazing down at his sleeping wife. He would experience a rush of love for her and would kiss her, mindful not to wake her.

Jaime staggered into the bedroom and clumsily undressed for the second time that evening. He dropped onto bed and was asleep almost at once.

Chapter 44
LEAH DISCOVERS A MAP

LEAH STOOD OUTSIDE Basic Skills, willing herself to enter the classroom. Still stinging with shame over her "encounter" with Jacob, she wanted to pack her bags and go home. But Jaime would be there gloating over her failure, while keeping an eye on her flat stomach for the expected bump. She also considered dropping Jacob's class, which she would only have to take again. With finals starting next week, Leah was determined to tough it out.

At the doorway of class, Leah lost her nerve. She turned to leave, when she was swept up by the entering Rainier, Sabine and Enzo. She quickly sank into her seat. For the next three hours, Leah tried to conceal herself by staying perfectly still.

When class was finally over, Leah heaved a sigh of relief. Before dismissing the students, Jacob placed a stack of papers on the counter directly in front of him. "Here are the graded papers from the quiz. Be sure to pick 'em up on your way out."

Leah remained in her seat. She watched her fellow students descend the stairs of the cooking theater, like cattle down a chute. Gathering her books, she caught up with Rainier. "Could you pick my quiz up for me? I—I have to make a phone call," she said, feeling queasy.

"Sure, I'll glide it under your door," Rainier said, with his thick French accent.

"Thank you," she said before slipping out a side door.

Seated on her bed, Leah watched as the paper slid under her door, face down. She picked it up and studied it. Next to the grade, Jacob had scribbled something else in red ink:

12.11

12:11

Leah's brow furrowed. She was tucking the paper into a folder when she noticed strange little bumps, like dried tears on the surface. She held the paper up to the light and saw what appeared to be a watermark. Examining it up close, she caught the scent of lemons.

Remembering Dulce's lemon juice notes from junior high, Leah excitedly rifled through a drawer for a book of matches. Carefully, she waved the flame under the paper until a row of dots appeared. It's a map!

Leah shook the match vigorously, before dropping it into a cup. She struck more matches and followed the dots to a highway. It veered off toward the hills. The flame-licked paper soon had the weathered look of an old treasure map. Leah stared at the X and smiled thoughtfully.

The '12.11' had to be the date and the '12:11' the time. That's tomorrow. Saturday. Leah tingled at the thought of being with Jacob when the words "wife" and "Yumi" ricocheted around her head like a pachinko game.

She sat down and considered the future. If she did not go, Jacob would respect her choice and leave her alone. On the surface, little in her world would change. It was a great life, better than she could ever have hoped for. Folding the map, she stared out the window, seeing nothing of the wet winter day.

❧

Minutes before noon on Saturday, Leah opened the truck door and got behind the wheel. Her hands were shaking as she rifled through her bag for her keys. When she turned the key in the ignition, she was confronted with a dead battery. She tried again and again but the engine only brayed before going silent.

It occurred to her that this might be a sign. She sat back and decided to give the key one more turn. If the truck starts up, I will go to Jacob. If it does not, I will never see him again, outside of class.

Leah closed her eyes and held her breath. As she turned the key, she thought of it as a variation of flipping a coin. When the engine rumbled to life, she almost wept with joy.

As she drove, Leah remembered the first time she had been to the 'X' marked spot. On one of her Sunday hikes, she wandered through a thicket of redwoods leading to an open space as wide as a church. As if turning the page and finding herself in the story she was reading, she was standing in the middle of a perfect circle of redwoods. The towering trees looked like ancient cathedral spires.

Leah visited the library and checked out a book on Sequoia trees. She read that the phenomenon is referred to as a fairy ring. Leah loved the sound of it. Reading on, she learned that sometimes when a redwood dies or is chopped down, a ring of trees sprouts around the site of the original tree. With time, all traces of the felled tree disappear, leaving behind the ring of new trees.

Leah parked and got out of her truck. The chilled air had the lingering scent of wood smoke. Feeling weak with a mixture of dread and hope, she was considering turning back when she spotted a human sundial in the circle of trees. "Jacob," she whispered.

His image was momentarily blurred with tears as she approached. He halved the distance between them, but stopped short. Leah felt a lump in her throat when she swallowed. She took the final step.

They clung to each other until they swayed. Leah nuzzled her cheek against his ear, which felt like a warm peach. Stepping back, Jacob stared into her eyes and said, "Are you sure about us?"

Leah nodded slowly. Jacob kissed her forehead, the exact place he had kissed the last time, as if picking up where he had left off. The smell of his skin, yeasty and warm, was hypnotic. Jacob sipped from Leah's lips. "I have missed you every day of my life," he whispered into her quivering mouth.

He scattered his kisses across her cheek. The tip of his tongue traced a warm wet line down Leah's neck, while his fingers unbuttoned her blouse. Leah felt the chilled air on her bare shoulder, her breast. Her eyes were closed and her head was tilted back. She wanted to say no, not here, but could not find her voice. Her dark nipple shrank and hardened in the cold. As Jacob's warm hand gently squeezed her breast, she felt her labia swell.

Jacob completely undressed Leah. As he rested her bare back onto the earth, she sank into the dead leaves made soft by the season. Jacob was on top of her and heat was radiating from their entwined bodies. For a brief moment, she thought the mud would bake around them and they would be partially embedded, like two stones in a dry riverbed.

As Jacob entered her, she experienced a pinch of pain and

closed her eyes. She felt drops of virgin blood seep into the dark earth. Leah clung harder to him. The pain dissipated and she had the strangest sensation she was entering him. They moved like earthworms until the world disappeared.

After the coupling, the cool mud on their hot skin felt good, but the chill quickly became unpleasant. "We look like two happy pigs," Jacob said, kissing Leah's muddy cheek. A soft rain began to fall. Jacob got up. He helped Leah to her feet.

Feeling shy, Leah slipped on her damp blouse without bothering with the bra. She was suddenly freezing as she picked up and examined her mud-soaked pants. Jacob offered his rain slicker. Leah was grateful that it came down to her knees and covered the mud and the blood between her thighs.

Jacob looked her over. "You can't go back to school like this. Come home with me." Leah's teeth stopped chattering. "Nobody's there. I'm alone until Monday. Your car is safe here. We'll come back for it later."

The rain became a downpour. Leah did not need any more coaxing. They ran to Jacob's Jeep and got in. As Jacob turned the key, the radio came to life, startling Leah. They both laughed as they sped away. Leah stared back at the ring of trees, wanting to memorize everything.

"Are you OK?" Jacob squeezed her hand.

"Yes." Leah stared forward. "I'm OK."

Chapter 45
JACOB TAKES LEAH HOME

JACOB'S NEIGHBORHOOD was on an incline and bore idyllic vistas overlooking Napa Valley. It was a view that Leah had never seen before. As she stared out the window an inky ripple passed through her mind. When they drove onto Jacob's street, Leah said, "I should duck down."

She was slouching and taking on the shape of the bucket seat when Jacob said, "No, we're good." He turned onto a driveway where the garage door was opening, reminding Leah of a shark's mouth. Leah caught a quick glimpse of Jacob's house through the fogged window and the streaks of rain. It was a California bungalow with a sloping gabled roof and a white wicker chair on the front porch.

They both sat motionless in the parked car until the garage door closed, plunging them into total darkness. "I'll be right back," Jacob said. When he opened the Jeep's door, his face briefly became a shifting of shadows and light. In that moment, Leah knew exactly what he would look like if Picasso had painted him.

Jacob stepped through a door leading into the house and left it ajar. Leah stared at the bluish-white outline of the door and listened to the sporadic ticking from the car's engine. The wet dog odor emanating from her wool sweater seemed to wake her. She felt suddenly hyper-aware of what she was doing.

Jacob flipped on a light switch. Leah saw the towel in his hand and drifted back into the dream-like realm. As she got out of the car he held the towel open, turning his head. Smiling shyly, Leah peeled her wet clothes off and quickly rolled her undergarments into her shirt before securing the towel around her. She looked up at Jacob, waiting for guidance.

Taking her hand, he said, "Why don't you shower first?"

Under the warm water from the nozzle, Leah felt cruelly jolted out of the dream again. Staring down at her feet, she thought, This is where Yumi's feet touch. She watched the turbid ribbons of water run from her toes. The drain was hiccupping gulps of tears. Leah felt dizzy.

To steady herself, she tried to focus on the row of hair products on a wire shelf. Jacob's hair smelled of baby shampoo. The Prell must belong to Yumi. She picked up the bottle and squeezed a small amount onto her palm. She sniffed the scent of Yumi's hair. Leah rubbed the shampoo into her scalp and began to sob.

When she finished the mournful shower, she patted herself dry with one of the thirsty towels she imagined Yumi folding into a perfect square. A pink robe was hanging behind the door, but Leah could not bring herself to put it on. Appearing to read her mind, Jacob knocked. He stuck a hand into the bathroom; a dark blue robe was dangling from his fingers. And just like that, Leah felt elated once again. She took the robe, thanked Jacob, and quietly shut the door. She nuzzled the fabric for the reassurance of his scent.

As Jacob showered, Leah wandered through the house.

The living room was decorated with a cozy blend of Sonoma and French country furnishings. Leah went to the oak mantle where flames were licking a stack of crooked wood in the brick fireplace. She searched for photos of Yumi, but saw none.

Jacob was singing an Italian opera as Leah entered the kitchen. She was surprised by how small the cooking area was. She would have expected Jacob to buy a house on the merits of the kitchen alone. Still, he had made the best of the space by aligning the appliances along one of the walls and adding an island with a built-in cutting board.

Dulce always said that you could tell a lot about a person by what's in their refrigerator. Leah timidly pulled the handle and scanned the expected milk, eggs, and vegetables. She paused and stared at an open can of onion dip, a box of Entenmann's Danish twist, a partial Sarah Lee pound cake, and a sliver of pecan pie in a crusty aluminum pan.

Leah could not picture Jacob eating processed food, but thought how everyone has guilty pleasures. Hasn't Mrs. Julia Child admitted to stopping at her favorite fast food chain in Maine from time to time? Closing the doors, she quietly opened drawers.

There were no surprises until she reached a corner cabinet where a hoard of Hostess snacks spilled onto the floor, like the morning's catch. There were apple, lemon, and cherry pies, Twinkies, Ding Dongs, Ho Hos, Donettes, Zingers, and Sno Balls.

Leah experienced an overwhelming urge to see Yumi. She stuffed the snacks back in the cabinet, and then hurried down the hallway. She opened the bedroom door and went straight to the walk-in closet. Unable to find a light switch, Leah bent down and picked up a pair of woman's sandals, size five. Tiny feet, Leah thought.

The shower water ceased. Leah heard the clicking of the shower curtain being drawn open. She quickly rifled through the hanging clothing in the dark, grabbing something with the silky texture of women's apparel. She held the garment out like a newspaper. It was a charcoal pair of silk pants, disproportionate to a short woman's height. Leah could have wrapped the pants around her waist three times.

She rehung the pants and was turning to leave when she noticed a photo on the dresser. It was in a seashell encrusted picture frame. Leah picked it up and stared at Jacob and a heavy-set Japanese woman, whose eyes nearly disappeared in the folds of her smile.

Leah whispered, "Yumi?"

Chapter 46

JACOB TOUCHES ON LEAH'S SECRET DESIRE

"ACCORDING TO LEGEND, Quetzalcoatl, the God of civilization, had just created the human race and was not sure what to feed us when he noticed a red ant carrying a corn kernel out of a mountainside. He turned himself into a black ant, and then went into the mountain and found the hidden corn. Quetzalcoatl took the corn back home where he and the other gods lived. They ate their fill before putting some of the corn into our mouths. And that was our first taste of food. It was the best taste of food, ever."

Leah and Jacob were on a blanket under a cypress tree in Mendocino, overlooking the calm orange-tinted sunset and the tumultuous slate gray sea. It was a rare long weekend away, with Yumi visiting family in New York. As she drew in a deep breath, she took the world the in through all of her senses.

Jacob's head was on Leah's lap. She was hand-feeding him sliced plums from their picnic lunch. His eyes crinkled as he smiled and said, "I never knew that." Leah laughed. Bending forward, she kissed the tip of his nose.

"Have you ever thought about writing a book?" Jacob said. "No, really, Leah, I've been thinking about this for a while. Your head is filled with such a treasure trove of recipes and cooking lore. You should write it down. When you're done, I'm sure my publishing house would be interested. Hell, they'd be giddy to have your book fall into their lap."

Jacob unknowingly was touching on Leah's secret aspiration. The elusive quest of her life was to find one good Mexican cookbook. She had read everything ever written on the subject and wondered why Anglos wrote most, if not all, of the books in existence. Although she appreciated their interest in Mexican cuisine, she often found interpretive errors in the recipes.

"I would not know where to begin," Leah said, dismissively.

"It's surprisingly easy. The school library is an excellent resource at your disposal. I'll show you how to go about getting organized. You could take it from there," Jacob said.

After a long pause, Leah said, "I'll think about it."

That evening, Leah and Jacob ordered Chinese food and stayed in. They ate from containers in front of the fireplace in their suite. Wearing only Jacob's dress shirt, Leah thought how it all felt so silly and great, like she was living someone else's life. With a start, she realized she was. The new sense of freedom emerging was not hers, in the same way that Jacob belonged to someone else.

Leah shook the thought loose. Breaking the fortune cookie in two, she stared numbly at the strip of white paper for a full minute. "Many await your written word."

Jacob read his fortune out loud. "Your soulmate is Leah."

"What?" Leah said, snatching the fortune from his fingers. She gasped as she read, "Your soulmate is Leah."

"Well, I guess that settles that. The cookie never lies," Jacob said, grinning.

"You made these cookies, didn't you?" Leah accused. She

pounced on top of Jacob. Her shirt opened as her hair fell forward, tickling his face. They wrestled awhile. Jacob let Leah win, but only after she agreed to write the cookbook.

On Sunday evening, Leah phoned Quico for their weekly chat. When Quico was getting ready to hang up, she tossed out the cookbook idea, just to see.

"¡Ay mija!" Quico said, sounding surprised, and elated, as if she just took her first step. "You have to do it. I want to help. What can I do?"

Leah reached for a spiral notebook. She flipped to the first page. "I was wondering, what do you think should go in it?"

"Everything." Leah heard Quico smile as he said the one word.

Chapter 47
ALEX DISOWNS LEAH

WHEN ALEX LEARNED that Leah was dating a married man, she severed all family ties with her sister. After Alex gave birth to her second healthy son, it was Tessa, who called with the good news. Leah immediately phoned Alex to congratulate her.

She wanted to sound upbeat, but broke down as soon as she heard her sister's voice. "I am so sorry," Leah wept into the phone.

"So am I," Alex said, flatly, her tone inferring, "I'm sorry that you are a *puta,* too."

❧

During summer break, Leah saw no point in returning to San Francisco. The absence of family in Leah's life had given her a new perspective. Home is not a place; it is a feeling of belonging. Jacob was now her home.

She moved out of the dorms and rented a small cottage off of a quiet country road, heavily scented with jasmine. Using summer school as a ruse to get out of the house, Jacob spent Tuesday and Thursday afternoons at Leah's. The tiny house offered the lovers not only a refuge from the world, but a test kitchen for Leah's recipes.

During the summer months, Leah worked on the cookbook every day from morning to night. After several rough drafts, she developed an outline. It would be the first ever encyclopedia of Mexican cooking, detailing techniques and recipes in addition to passing along folk wisdom.

Letting himself in with his key, Jacob usually found Leah engrossed in some aspect of research. He once walked into the kitchen and discovered her creating an egg chart. Leah explained that an egg from a backyard chicken in Mexico is smaller than the jumbo or standard American eggs. A literal translation of a Mexican recipe could over-egg the dish.

❧

As a rule, Mexican women are generous to a fault with their possessions. As with most rules, there is one exception— Mexican women are stingy with their recipes. If you ask for a recipe they'll gladly write it down for you, minus one key ingredient. The pinch of cumin or the sprigs of *epazote* that transform the dish will always be left out.

Leah decided early on not to skip any ingredients. This was the only point where she and Quico did not agree. "Yes, yes. I've thought about that and maybe we should hold back a little. I mean, the food's going to be better than anything that those *gabachos* have ever tasted. They'll never know the difference," Quico said in Spanish, fanning himself with an index card. They were sitting on Leah's back porch swing, sipping *agua de sandia*. Quico visited often, having fallen in love with Napa, and a waiter at Mustard's.

To Leah, writing the book as accurately as possible scratched some sort of primal itch. She was not going to cheat anyone who had the desire to experience authentic Mexican cooking. She said, "Maybe, but I will."

Chapter 48

LEAH ENCOUNTERS SPRING AND YUMI

LEAH GOT UP EARLY for her Sunday morning hike and to watch as spring awakened. With the longer days came the anticipated longer walks. The winter rains had nourished the Napa soil and unfurled a thriving world of budding greenery. Having experienced all of the seasons nearly three times, she decided that spring was her favorite season.

The past year of research, writing, and school had crystallized Leah's culinary confidence. With a month left until graduation, she already had a firm offer for her first cookbook. It was to be entitled *Sworn Secrets: Confessions from a Mexican Daughter*. Leah did not care for the title, but it was not her place to second-guess her publishers.

By noon, Leah was famished. She headed into town and went straight to her favorite family-run deli. She got into line and studied the specials board. It was a toss-up between the turkey breast, Moroccan carrot and goat cheese with green olive tapenade, or the roasted vegetables with herbs de Provence and curry mayo on whole wheat bread.

"You ugly, ugly woman!" a voice shrilled from behind her. Reflexively, Leah turned before the words registered. The clamoring and good-natured conversations of the deli suddenly ceased. Leah was staring into the angry face of a short, heavy-set Asian woman. Her chubby hands were clenched into dimpled fists at her sides. Leah caught a whiff of

Prell shampoo. Leah wanted to die.

"You leave my husband alone! You whore!" When Yumi said the final word, Leah felt hot spittle or phlegm hit her cheek. She flinched, but did not wipe it off.

Every set of eyes in the deli flipped from the accuser to the accused. Leah was suddenly having trouble breathing. It felt like the air was sucked out of the room. She needed to get to the door, push it open, and break the vacuum seal.

Leah spun around, but could not find the door. Her eyes landed once again on Yumi. Leah could tell she was still yelling by the way her face was contorting, but could not hear her above the roar in her ears. The lack of oxygen was causing Leah's heart to strain. She remembered her childhood goldfish flaying and gulping for air after its bowl had been knocked off of a shelf during an earthquake. She suddenly knew how Ember, the goldfish, had felt.

Leah desperately needed to find the door, before the room faded completely to white. At that moment, a customer mercifully entered from the street. She stumbled toward the blurry light and the sweet, sweet air. Staggering to the alley she bent over and vomited an oily, blackish liquid. Breathing heavy, she stared at the residue from the mortal sin on her soul.

Chapter 49

LEAH HAS A PAINFUL EPIPHIANY

LEAH WAS SITTING on the porch steps of her cottage, still shaking from the confrontation with Yumi earlier that day. She was thinking of how she and Jacob successfully reduced his wife to an obstacle they maneuvered around. The familiar pothole in the road. But Yumi suddenly becoming flesh and bone jarred Leah into a state of conscious remorse.

The thought of making love to Jacob in Yumi's bed filled her with self-loathing and revulsion. What was even more shameful was finding the junk food Yumi was hoarding, seeing her photo, and still not grasping the undercurrent of her situation. Food was this lonely woman's companion, her way of filling the hole her husband had created, and then avoided.

Hearing Jacob's car, she stood up. As he drove up the long driveway, she stared at the potato vine she planted last year. It nearly covered the wood fence bordering the property.

The Jeep abruptly halted and Jacob scrambled out of the car. He appeared tired and disheveled, like he'd been on a long flight. In a way, he had.

"Why did you bring me to your home that first time?"

"Leah, I..." Jacob said. His steps faltered as his words faded away.

"You lied to me, but I let you. I chose to believe you when you said it was a marriage of convenience and equally loveless on both sides. That made it easy for me to be with you."

"It was terrible and wrong, but I did it for the right reasons. Leah, I did it because I love you. It's always been you," Jacob said.

Leah's eyes spilled with tears. "We built a world together on top of her devastation. She loves you, Jacob. She always has."

"I'm sorry I hurt you, hurt her. But, the worst is behind us. I'm going to move out. We can start fresh now. Please, just give us a chance."

The time for words was over. Leah pulled her grandmother's shawl tightly around her shoulders as she turned and walked up the three wooden stairs. For once, the second stair did not creek. She crossed the cottage's porch and opened the screen door. Without looking back at Jacob, she quietly shut both doors behind her.

Chapter 50
LEAH GRADUATES

THE NIGHT BEFORE GRADUATION, Alex phoned Leah to say she was not going to be able to make it. Joaquin, her third son, was teething. "He'll cry through the entire ceremony. I refuse to be the mother with the annoying baby. I've seen too many at the restaurant. Why their parents don't take them outside when they start acting up is beyond me."

Leah sat mute for a moment. It was the first phone call she had received from her sister in nearly three years. She pressed the phone so tightly to her ear the cartilage clicked. "That's a good question," she finally said, expecting Alex to slam the receiver down, now that she delivered her message.

Instead, Alex shifted gears and started complaining about her neighborhood and how everyone corrects her pronunciation of "San Rafael" when they're the ones saying it wrong. She then complained about the house and the huge electric bill. "We're running the air conditioner half of the year. I don't ever remember doing that in San Francisco, do you?"

"We opened windows and created a cross-breeze. Did we even have an air conditioner?" Leah said, trying to keep the conversation going. Alex snorted a laugh that sounded exaggerated. It dawned on Leah that Alex knew about the break-up and this was her way of saying that all was forgiven. On the couch, Leah tucked her feet under her and settled in for the long yearned-for conversation.

❧

During the graduation ceremony, Leah sat nervously in her gold cap and gown, willing herself not to look in Jacob's direction. He, along with the rest of the faculty, was seated on the same stage she was about to cross—in new heels! When her name was called, all she needed to do was walk across the stage without tripping. It felt like too much to ask.

When "Leah Cernuda," rang out from the speakers, Leah jerked. Expecting a smattering of polite applause, Leah was surprised by the rowdy group of people cheering for her. She squinted in their direction. Leah burst into laughter and tears. It was Tessa, who had just graduated from Stanford, along with Tessa's parents and grandparents. Quico was also there with his boyfriend, Matt. They were sitting in a row, attempting to create an audience wave.

Leah wanted to leap off of the stage and into their arms. Once she was back in her seat, she realized that she made it across the stage without thinking of Jacob once.

After the graduation ceremony, Leah's classmates and extended family headed to Mustard's, where they were treated like VIPs since Matt worked there. Several toasts were made to Leah and the other graduates. At some point her classmate Rainier excused himself and secretly paid the check.

Everyone became simultaneously irate and deeply touched when they found out that the check had been taken care of. Rainier pushed money offers away, saying, "I didn't pay, my father did and he's smelly rich."

Everyone laughed. They toasted Rainier's smelly rich dad. Leah's eyes filled with tears as she gazed around the table, cherishing this special moment with these wonderful people.

❧

Leah left Napa early the next morning. A smile from her new collection of favorite memories was lingering on her lips. She was saying goodbye to the passing vineyard when the image on the horizon caught her attention. Jacob's black Jeep was parked on the dirt shoulder. He was leaning against the front grill, but when he recognized her truck, he stood straight.

Leah thought about flashing her turn signal and slowing down, about veering onto the dirt shoulder and getting out of the truck. He would say her name and something inside of her would break. She would fall into his arms, as if he had just returned from war. Later, she would call her former landlord and renew her lease, indefinitely. Once again, she would settle into the life of the lonely affair.

Instead, Leah drove on.

Chapter 51

DULCE'S HOMECOMING

"HELLO?"

"*Órale* Alex, *Wassápenin?*"

"Dulce? Don't tell me you're already here. We're not supposed to pick you up for four hours!"

"I'm in New York, on an airport pay phone. Who's 'we'?"

"Well, it was supposed to be a surprise, but Tessa and Leah are coming with me. And, of course, your three adorable nephews. Wait a second. Why aren't you flying over the Midwest, right now?"

"I missed my connecting flight."

"What did you do this time?"

"Dang. It took all of two seconds for you to think the worst. I didn't do anything. The flight from Amsterdam left late. So we landed late, that's all."

Alex blew out a breath through her nose and they both heard the exhale in the phone. "Call me when you book your ticket, so I know what time to pick you up."

"Nah, don't worry about it. I'll catch a shuttle when I get there."

"Are you sure?"

"*Simón.* I won't be getting in 'til late."

"Well, OK. Me and the boys are spending the night at the apartment with Leah, so we'll see you when you get here."

Alex hung up with her finger. She dialed. When Tessa

answered, she said, "Hey, it's me. Dulce just called from New York. I think she's been busted by security, again."

❧

The next morning, Tessa arrived at the restaurant and found Leah seated in an unlit cocktail booth, folding cloth napkins. "Hi, Leah. Where's Dulce and Alex?" she said, shrugging out of her denim jacket.

"Alex is in her office and Dulce is still asleep," Leah said, moving the folded stacks of linen napkins aside to make room.

"What time did she finally get in?"

"I don't know. I waited up until after midnight and she was still not home."

"Are you sure she's even here? Maybe Alex was right about her being arrested."

"I left a welcome home dinner basket by her door. I checked this morning and it was not there."

"Yeah, and it was the best meal I've had in years," Dulce said, as she ambled toward them from the kitchen. "Here's something they don't mention in travel books—the Mexican food in Europe sucks. You and Alex should start a chain out there. You can call it Caca Alejandra's." Dulce had changed little; her face was thinner, but the gleam of mischief was exactly the same.

"¡Chingona!" Tessa said, holding her arms out wide, and hugging Dulce. Leah was out of the booth and waiting her turn when Dulce grabbed her by the arm and pulled her into their embrace. The three hugged and laughed while jumping up and down. They hugged again, jumped some more, and finally let go.

"Are you jetlagged?" Tessa said.

"Nah, I got up a while ago and took a walk around the Mish," Dulce said, scooting into the booth last. "Nothing's changed around here. I mean it. I was just in the kitchen and Quico is standing exactly where he was the last time I saw him."

"A few things have changed. But I know what you mean," Leah said, wistfully.

🐛

In the office, Alex stared down at her Buddha body. She gained fifty pounds during her first pregnancy and was pregnant again before shedding half of the weight. When she became pregnant a third time, she still carried the weight from a half dozen trimesters. She had given birth to her third son several months ago and people were still asking when she was due. People in the Mission can be so clueless.

Alex heard the reunion going on downstairs. When the peals of laughter reached her, she assumed that she was the object of their ridicule. She worked herself into a state of indignation by considering the choices the others had made.

Why don't they have normal lives, like mine? Dulce's creative, but erratic. Doesn't that combination always end up dead young? Jaime's right. She can't live in the attic or work at the restaurant. If she doesn't get a good dose of tough love, she'll never take life seriously. Still, it's not going to be easy evicting her and not hiring her back, even if it is for her own good. She could stay until the end of the month, but that's it.

Oh, and Tessa is so smart, she's stupid! She claims that it's impossible to maintain a relationship while starting med school. Well then, don't go back to school. She's got a bachelor's degree and can get a good job anywhere. She's pretty enough to take her pick of co-workers. Maybe even nab a CEO.

Alex sighed. Leah, Leah, Leah. She's wasted the best years of her life on a man that used her. She'll never get that time back. I knew he would dump her after graduation. Like I've said before and I'll say again, who wants to look at a pine tree after Christmas?

Alex took a mirror out of her desk and checked her make-up. She had continued with weekly salon visits, adding manicures and pedicures to try to offset the weight gain. Her hair was stiff with product and smelled like an alkaline fruit cup. She used a shampoo with pineapple extract, a coconut conditioner, a papaya leave-in conditioner, a mango mousse, and kiwi-scented hairspray. She shoved the mirror back into her desk before heaving herself out of the chair.

"The prodigal daughter returns," Alex said, flatly, while joining the reunion.

"Hey, Alex!" Dulce said, getting up and putting her arms around her. "Hey, my fingers don't touch!"

Alex felt her face burn hot. "Hardy har, har," she said sarcastically, while pushing Dulce away. "It's baby fat." She was about to scoot into the booth when she hesitated at the narrow opening. When did they get so small?

Dulce pulled up a chair, saying, "You'll probably be called away on official business, so why get too comfortable?"

Alex nodded her thanks as she plopped down on the chair.

"So, how you doing, Alex?" Dulce said, her eyes twinkling.

Alex talked for a while about her three sons and how she

wanted a little girl, so they were going to keep trying, no matter how long it took. She went on about how great Jaime was as a businessman and a father.

She was beginning to repeat herself when Tessa changed the subject. To Dulce, she said, "Did you see China in New York?"

Dulce nodded. "She met me at the airport and we had dinner. Oh yeah, she says hi."

Each of the four friends had her own theory about who sent China's transcripts to the film school in New York. As far-fetched as some of them were, none were stranger than Mother Margaret's part in the cover-up.

"What's she up to?" Alex said.

"Let's see, she's headed to Cuba this summer. She's working on a documentary film about Hemingway."

"Cuba? Can you even go to Cuba? I mean, no airlines fly there from here. Do they?" Alex said, looking around.

"Not from here. They can go through Mexico, but China said that's a bad idea. The Mexican government keeps a record of people with U.S. passports traveling there, then hands the list over to the CIA. China said a friend of hers went through Mexico and when she got back, her phone was tapped. Plus, she's been audited, twice!"

"That's horrible! Is any of it true?" Tessa said.

"Who knows?" Dulce took a sip from a can of soda. "I think they're flying down to the Cayman Islands, and hiring a boat to take them the rest of the way."

There was a sudden loud high-pitch noise. At first, Alex thought it was a broken blender motor. After a few seconds the tone changed, becoming an infant's wail. "Who brought a baby to work?" Alex said, turning her face toward the kitchen.

Dulce slid out of the booth and returned with a baby in her arms. "Who else?" she said, kissing the pale downy head of the infant wrapped in a brown blanket. The baby stopped crying. Bright blue eyes glistened with tears while taking in the lounge.

The three women froze, like a snapshot. "Velvet, meet your *tías*. This is *Tía* Tessa. She's gonna keep you healthy. This is *Tía* Leah. She's going to make you strong with her cooking. And this is *Tía* Alex. She'll be teaching you about guilt. Just kidding. She's gonna teach you how to do math in your head."

Instinct kicked in and the three women reached for the baby.

"*¡Un bebé!*" they all said.

The baby's eyes shifted to the unfamiliar faces. Alex, being the closest, hoisted herself up. She snatched the baby from Dulce before sitting back down heavily. For a second, Dulce pictured a killer whale during feeding time. Velvet's big eyes stared at Alex, who was cooing in Spanish to her.

"Boy or girl?" Tessa said.

"Girl," Dulce said.

"Ah," they said in unison, as if that was the right answer.

Alex rubbed her palm on the tiny head. "Did you shave her head?"

"Nah. She was born that way," Dulce said, chuckling.

"How old is she?" Leah said.

"Eleven weeks. Her birthday's on April Fools' day. No joke!" Dulce boasted.

Tessa noted the sallow skin, cornflower blue eyes, and blond fuzz. It was obvious that there was not a trace of Indian blood in her. She delicately asked, "Is she your baby?"

"Yes," Dulce said, gazing at Velvet. "She's all mine."

It was quiet for a moment before Leah said, "Why didn't you tell us, Dulce?"

"And miss your faces? Yeah, right."

Alex noticed Dulce's naked ring finger and said, "Who's the father?"

Velvet started fussing. Dulce pulled a pacifier from a pocket and put it in the baby's mouth. "I don't know. I never met him. Ah, there are those faces again," Dulce said, shaking a finger at each of them.

Alex quickly became impatient. "What do you mean you never met him?"

Dulce savored Alex's irritation for a moment. "About six months ago, a pregnant girl walked into the bar I was working at and asked if I could spare some change 'cause she was hungry. It was cold outside and I'm not talking a 40-degree *Norte Califas* winter cold, I mean, you stick your hand in the freezer to warm it up, cold. So, I gave her a bowl of hot soup and some bread.

"Just like a stray cat, she was back on my next shift. Jet, that's her name, was a fifteen-year-old runaway from some small town near the Belgium border. I asked her what she was gonna do once the baby was born. She said she was gonna sell it. She'd done it before."

All three women gasped with horror. Alex was passing the baby to Leah. She jerked the infant back to her large bosom.

"She asked me if I knew anyone who wanted to buy a baby. I heard the word 'me' come out of my mouth."

"She sold her child? Just like that? She didn't even know

you!" Alex made a sizzling sound. "Ooh, God's going to punish her good," she said, as she pictured the Lord's vengeful wrath on the little Dutch girl.

Dulce watched Alex with a dull fascination. "Uh, yeah. Anyway, Jet was living in this place. It was kinda like a commune, but not like a Berkeley commune where everybody pitches in. This place looked more like a rat's nest. Jet was sleeping on a dirty mattress on the floor, with a bunch of other rat kids. I took one look around and told her to get her stuff, and we left. I wanted to keep an eye on her and make sure my kid was all right."

Aware that an infant cannot travel internationally without papers, Tessa asked, "How was the adoption handled?"

"The same way it's done in Mexico. I greased a few palms. I made a call to this *abogángster* I knew and he phoned a doctor that worked with us on the adoption. When the baby was born, my name was put on the birth certificate as the mom. Oh, and check this out. I put Willem Brinker as the father. You know, the dean of my school."

"You are so bad," Tessa said, approvingly.

"That must have been so hard for her mother," Leah lamented.

Dulce thought about it. "I don't know. Jet stayed with me for a few days after Vel was born, but once she was strong enough, she asked for her money, and took off."

"How much did she cost?" Alex said, not finding the question the least bit rude.

"One G. And you know what? I could have talked her down to half. But, I didn't, 'cause Velvet's gonna know everything someday."

"Velvet! You named her after a fabric?" Alex said. "Please tell me you named her anything else, even Hortencia, and Velvet is a nickname."

Dulce shook her head. "Nope. 'Velvet' is on her pink slip."

"How did you choose such an unusual name?" Leah said.

Dulce grinned. "It's scratched in the putty of the window in my flat upstairs. You know, the one facing the street. That was the first thing I thought about when I saw her."

"You pictured putty?" Tessa said, incredulous.

"That, and our future in *San Pancho.*"

The three could not begin to process this. The baby began to cry. Alex handed her to Leah. After being startled, Velvet yawned and closed her eyes.

"Have you given any thought to how you plan to support this child?" Alex said, sounding like a parent.

Dulce smiled. "I've been exhibiting every summer and my shows have sold out. So, I've got a little money stashed away. And I've been commissioned to do a couple of pieces. After that, I'll work on a new show."

"Supporting yourself as an artist is one thing, but you are a mother now, Dulce. You have to be responsible for...Velvet. You can't expect to support her by selling images of La Madonna made out of seeds. It's time to put all of your little brushes away and grow up."

"The minute you grow up, you start getting old," Dulce said. She waited for Alex's eruption.

"*¡Ay Dulce!*" Alex slapped the table, waking Velvet and causing her to cry. "It takes two mature people to have an adult conversation. I'm better off talking to the baby." Alex could not restrain her curiosity. "How much money do you have?"

"Almost five grand." They all stared at Dulce. "What can I say? I'm big in Europe." Dulce waited a beat. Smiled. "But you're right. If you hire me back as a bartender, I'll have a job and we'll be covered under your employee health insurance plan."

"Hire you back? Hire you back?" Alex sounded offended as she took the calming baby from Leah. "You were never let go. As long as we own this restaurant, you have a job. Isn't that right, Leah?"

Leah was about to agree when Alex said, "But the baby can't live in an attic. No-sir-ee." Alex's eyes brightened. "I know! You're moving to San Rafael with us. Oh, a baby girl in the house, finally!"

Dulce shot Leah and Tessa a "help me!" look.

"They could move in with me," Leah spoke up.

"Good idea. That way, Dulce can keep the attic for her studio," Tessa said.

Dulce saw Alex's mouth begin to open and said in a rush, "Hey Tessa, what's the difference between 'preventative' and 'preventive'?"

Chapter 52

THE GIRLS GO TO WORK

IT DID NOT TAKE LONG for Dulce to settle into a working and painting routine. Openly disliking Jaime, she was scheduled to tend bar on his nights off. Tessa's parents watched Velvet when she worked. The first time they babysat, they spent hours openly staring into her impossibly blue eyes with fascination.

The transition back to San Francisco and the restaurant was not as easy for Leah. She worked the kitchen line on Dulce's shifts. Still, without Quico, Alex, and most of their former staff, Alejandra's felt like a foreign country.

A week after Dulce returned to work, Alex stopped by to pick up some paperwork. Customers she had not seen in years were seated at the bar, visiting Dulce, and were equally thrilled to see her. The evening was so much fun that Alex started coming in every weekend. She did not realize how much she needed to roll up her sleeves and get flushed with adrenaline. Caught up in the narrowly focused world of raising three sons, she had forgotten how important it was to be part of her own business.

Dashing around the busy restaurant, Alex rapidly shed weight. Within months, she was wearing clothes she had not been able to fit into since her second son was born. Each outfit was a victory. But the weight loss did not last long.

❦

It was close to five on a Sunday and the staff was setting

up for dinner. Leah was inserting the specials page into the stack of menus when Dulce breezed in. "Is Alex upstairs?"

"She's not coming," Leah said.

Dulce paused in mid-step. "Is she sick or dying?"

Leah shook her head. "Jaime's been complaining about never seeing her. He doesn't want her working on his nights off anymore."

"And she bought that?" Dulce said, disgusted. "Jaime doesn't want to get stuck at home babysitting his own kids. I'll bet he's nowhere near Alex or their house right now." Dulce thought a moment. "Hey, why'd they buy a house so far away?"

"I'm not sure," Leah said. She had been wondering the same thing. She considered telling Dulce how Jaime tried to discourage her from moving back to the apartment. He occasionally spent the night upstairs when he was too tired to drive home. As susceptible to *susto* as Leah was, he worried that he might unintentionally startle her and cause a relapse.

The mere thought of being alone with Jaime terrified Leah. She agreed to move out and was apartment hunting when Dulce returned from Amsterdam, with Velvet. Their moving in pushed Jaime out of the apartment for good.

Being the problem solver that she was, Alex bought a roll away bed for Jaime that would be kept in the storage room. When Alex rolled the cot out of the closet, Jaime turned his face toward Leah with a sort of lunge. It was the same look she had seen in the eyes of the transients at Golden Gate Park. A look that said, I am going to enjoy hurting you.

Pedro suddenly yelled from the kitchen, "It's five!"

Straightening the stack of menus, Leah went to the window and flipped the sign from *Cerrado* to *Abierto*.

Outside, a man standing directly in front of her caused Leah to jump back. His face and coat were equally weathered from years of living on the street. He's one of the men from Golden Gate Park! she thought before realizing he was a total stranger. Leah struggled to catch her breath. She saw those three men everywhere.

The homeless man suddenly looked up, as if a plane flying overhead caught his attention. As Leah followed his gaze to the sky, his forehead struck the glass so hard that it rattled the window. He repeatedly slammed his head against the window. From a foot away, Leah watched in horror as his forehead split open and blood splattered onto the smooth, clean glass.

"Ouch! That's gotta hurt," Dulce said as she walked to the phone and called the police. While on hold, she said, "He reminds me of one of those dipping birds. You know, the little plastic bird that looks like it's drinking water."

Dulce spoke briefly into the phone before hanging up. Pulling Leah back, she said, "Don't worry. He's just about to knock himself out."

The man suddenly stopped. He fell onto the sidewalk, as if he had been shoved into a chair. Minutes later, a fire truck pulled up and when the firemen saw the familiar vagrant, they reluctantly approached. Leah stared up at the blood smear on the window. Through her tears it became a red dahlia.

"Will you look at that? I'm not gonna clean that shit up." Dulce yelled toward the kitchen, "Pedro! Bring a bucket and bleach. And bring that squeegee thing!"

Chapter 53

ALEX FINDS A ROLL OF FILM

ALEX'S MONDAY TO DO LIST

Post office. Drop off mail. Get stamps.

Paperwork.

Pick up Jaime's prescription.

Return shirt for Jaime.

Take car for lube job. Lunch at IHOP while I wait!

Go to bank to find out why credit card was declined.

Dry cleaners.

Figure out how to set the time on the VCR.

After picking up the boys from school, Alex stopped at Will's to drop off a couple of bags of old clothes. She was pleased to check off an additional box not on her list.

At home, she pulled into the garage. As she hoisted her three sons from their car seats, she thought, Who says I need to work out? I lift boy barbells every day.

Joaquin managed to become entangled in the car seat's straps. He started fidgeting and let out an ear-piercing shriek.

"It's OK, baby, just stay still."

As she tried to disentangle the straps, Junior chased Andrés around the car. "Stop it, you two! Someone is going to get hurt."

No sooner were the words out of her mouth when she heard Andrés screaming bloody murder. Alex snatched Joaquin from the seat and ran around to the back of the car. Andrés had toppled into an empty box and his feet were dangling in the air.

"*¡Ay, Dios mío!*" Alex yanked him out with her free hand. She looked him over. "Oh, you're fine. No blood," she said, relieved.

Still whimpering, he placed a black film roll container into the palm of her hand. "Where did you get that?"

Junior pointed to the box. Alex popped the lid off and looked at the roll of film. Having taken millions of pictures of the boys, she was not surprised she hadn't noticed the missing roll.

"OK, let's go inside," she said, trying to herd them toward the door to the kitchen. Honestly, she thought, it's like trying to herd cats. "If you don't go inside you won't get a snack."

"Potsicle," Junior–her late-bloomer–said.

Andrés started singing, "Potsicles, potsicles," while Joaquin joined in with "pa, pa, pa..."

"Yes, yes. Wash your hands first. They're filthy."

Before helping Junior up to the sink, Alex dropped the roll of film into a kitchen drawer. The container rolled off the stack of take-out menus. It settled snugly between packets of soy sauce and ketchup.

CAROLYN ELZIG WAS THE DAUGHTER of a commercial financier father and a mother obsessed with her own death. Mr. Douglas Elzig's professional ambition was only matched by his covert desire to impregnate as many women as possible. He achieved his procreation goal by piercing holes through the condoms he used when with the women he targeted. After the baby arrived, he moved out, and then moved on.

This holey condom breeding method had produced five children from five different women—three daughters and two sons. His second child, a girl named Carolyn, had a mother who turned out to be crazy, and often violent. Douglas did not wait around for the baby's birth before deciding to leave.

When Carolyn was four, her mother began to openly discuss her death wish. By seven, Carolyn's horror of losing her mother had dulled. When she arrived home from school, she never knew if she was going to be greeted by happy mommy or the mean impostor. Over chocolate chip cookies or a block of cold butter, Carolyn would listen to the refined suicide plan. She never offered an opinion when asked.

By the time Carolyn was twelve, her mother was dead. Carolyn returned home from school to find her hanging from an exposed beam. She had positioned every lamp in the house on one side of the living room, creating the mass lynching of dozens of shadows on the wall behind her. She had signed the bottom corner of the wall in black brush strokes.

Less than a week later, Douglas Elzig became a practicing father for the first time. Carolyn was sent to New York to live with him and a woman who recently given birth to another ugly baby. After a month, Carolyn and her father moved out. Another girlfriend shortly followed in her place. Carolyn thought of telling the women of their fates, but none were nice to her, and did not deserve a warning.

Attending private schools in Manhattan, Carolyn grew up independent and lonely. After graduating from high school, she moved to Amsterdam where she attended the Institute of Fine Arts. There, she met Dulce.

After Carolyn graduated from art school, she traveled around the world. It was a graduation present from a father who did not want her to return. She ended her sojourn in San Francisco, where she now sat on a barstool at Alejandra's, reading the newspaper.

"Tomorrow's free Tuesday at the museum. Do you want to go?" Carolyn said. She was wearing a blackish shirt and pants. Her brown hair partially covered an ordinary face, which was now buried in the entertainment section of the newspaper.

Dulce nodded. "Sounds good." Feeling philosophical, she said, "You know, after you tend bar for a while, you learn a lot about people. Even though there's something kind of random about customers, most regulars have these strict routines." Dulce rotated the beers in the fridge as she spoke. "Some people want you to top their drink off, so they can keep track of how many they've had by counting the twists or toothpicks. Other customers want a fresh glass and cocktail napkin every time. That way they look like they're on their first drink, no matter how *pedo* they are."

Jaime ducked under the service bar where he dropped a bill by the cash register. Folding his arms, he waited. Dulce ignored it, and him.

"Change this," he demanded.

"Into what? I just opened. I don't have change for a hundred yet," Dulce said, tossing an empty beer box at his feet.

Jaime clenched his jaw. He turned toward the kitchen and said over his shoulder, "Bring a beer to my office. Make sure it's cold this time. En don't forget mi change."

When he was gone, Carolyn said, "So, that must be the infamous Jaime. What's he doing here so early?"

"Trying to get rid of me and Leah," Dulce said, reaching into the cooler for a cold bottle of *Negra Modelo*. "Alex has been so busy changing diapers, she hasn't seen how every time someone quits Jaime hires one of his homeboys. His homeys have been ganging up on the veterans. They're trying to squeeze us out and make room for more of his ass-suckers."

Dulce uncapped the bottle of beer. "Right after me and Leah moved back, Quico told Alex about Jaime's gambling in the bar and hitting on women customers, and how he's always yelling at her employees. Alex told him to quit spreading gossip. She suspended him for the rest of the week, without pay. Her way of warning people to stay out of their personal life, I guess."

Dulce pushed a button and opened the cash register. "It was no skin off of Quico's nose. Leah already gave him half of her book advance. So Quico quit and opened a restaurant with Matt, in Acapulco." Dulce took a small swig from the bottle. "Jaime hired some *pendejo* named Feo to take Quico's place. The food here now sucks." Dulce pulled a bottle of Visine out of a cash register's drawer and held it up for Carolyn to see.

"Is that what I think it is?" Carolyn said.

"A few drops of this stuff will give him the runs." She poured most of the Visine into the bottle.

Carolyn smiled. "I thought that was an old bar myth. Does it really work?"

"I'm not sure, but I've always wanted to know. Let's find out!" Dulce said, as she filled a bank bag with a thick stack of dollar bills and all of the rolled change in the cash register. "I'll be right back."

Chapter 55

LEAH, DULCE, AND VELVET DO LUNCH

LEAH, DULCE, AND VELVET decided to check out a new restaurant in the Castro for lunch. Dulce was driving and Leah stared out the passenger window. She noticed how the dusty shops selling Mexican goods were disappearing from their neighborhood's fringe. The nice weather and lower housing prices were luring *los otros* into the microcosm of Latino life.

Young pallid couples, gay and straight, were buying the old Victorians and restoring them beyond their original splendor. It was easy to spot their homes; the plants on their porches and steps grew out of matching glazed or terra-cotta pots. Also, they painted the old houses in tawdry colors, reminding Leah of elderly women in funereal make-up.

Finding a parking space less than a block from the restaurant, Dulce did a touchdown dance when she got out of Pepe Le Pew. It had rained early that morning and the shaded patches of sidewalk were still wet. Leah noticed that Dulce's left shoe was imprinting "Dulce" on the dry cement. Her right shoe made a mark of two Japanese characters. Dulce explained it was *konton,* the symbol for chaos.

"Yeah, I bought a half dozen pair of these defective shoes at National. See..." Velvet was shifted from Dulce's right hip to her left. "The rubber soles are real thick, so I carved out the bottoms. Kinda like rubber stamps."

"I thought you looked taller," Leah said as they reached

Silk, a bistro serving European-inspired Asian cuisine. They scanned the posted reviews, taking turns reading aloud. "'A highly stylized blend of Asian and Western creations,'" Leah said.

"'Imaginative flavors. California eclecticism at its best,'" Dulce added in an announcer's voice. A thickly accented announcer. They both laughed.

The antique crimson silk kimono hanging like a scarecrow above the host's desk waved in the draft as they entered. The host greeted them by taking his hazel eyes off the reservation book for a fraction of a second. He wore a black suit, with a red silk kerchief peeking out of his pocket.

Leaning toward Leah, Dulce said, "The staff is also a highly stylized blend of Asian and Western creations."

Leah gave the reservation name. The host guided them around a lacquered column, supporting nothing but air. A sexy Thai Buddha sculpture was nestled into the wall behind the bar. On the tabletops, black chopsticks rested on red linen napkins. An indigo polished stone was where the single flowered vase usually rests. No salt or pepper shakers were in sight.

When they sat down, they were not handed menus. Leah explained that it was a pre-set lunch. Dulce studied the clean-lined framed windows. "Good lighting. This ocher wall, right here, is a nice touch. It's facing west, so later when the sun hits it, the reflected light is gonna bounce around and turn the room golden."

Leah smiled serenely as she imagined it.

Velvet considered her surroundings. She amused herself by dropping the chopsticks on the floor. A waiter with pixie features and long black hair arranged in an ornate braid placed two sake cups on the table. He recoiled at the sight of the baby before offering a high chair. Dulce declined.

He began his bored recitation, "This is spring water infused with ginger and seaweed. It will cleanse your palate."

Leah thought back to her first day in Jacob's class, when he had talked about the palate. She felt fatigued.

Dulce gulped back the inch of liquid as Leah took a tiny sip. They both made faces. "Yum," Dulce said, as though "yum" was synonymous with "yuck."

The entrées arrived on square flat plates. Several wrapped morsels of food were carefully arranged on tiny bamboo rungs. A tiger lily carved out of an unrecognizable vegetable filled the corner of the plate.

"What's with the stepladder?" Dulce said.

"It gives the entrée height," Leah said. She sounded tired.

"Why do I need tall food?"

"It's a trend, Dulce," Leah said, glancing around. "It's all getting so out of control. Dishes are being created for shock value. No one cares about taste." This time, her own last word triggered the Jacob jolt, deepening her depression. She stared at her plate and wanted to cry.

"I'll bet it's good." Dulce attempted to appease Leah by biting into the piece from the lowest rung. She stared at the brownish paste in the center. After a few chewy chews, she said, "It doesn't really taste like food, but it's interesting."

Determined to snap Leah out of her misery, Dulce changed the subject. "Hey, I've been thinking about your cookbook. You know what I think? I think a recipe is like a short story. It has a beginning, a middle, and an end."

Leah thought about this. "So, a cookbook is really a compilation of edible short stories?" she said, becoming both skeptical and intrigued.

"Just hear me out, Chef Boyardee. I took a course in creative writing, so, I'm kind of an expert." Dulce shifted the baby a little. "A story needs four components: characters, a plot, setting, and a theme. So, if you were making a jamburger, the main characters would be the ground beef and the bun." Leah tried not to smile at her pronunciation of "hamburger" as Dulce finished off the morsel in her hand. "The setting is where the action takes place, in the kitchen or grill. Are you still with me?"

Leah nodded, slowly. Dulce moved on. "Now, the plot is crucial. There must be conflict, you know, pounding the beef into patties and cutting the cheese. And then, things need to be resolved by bringing all of the ingredients together. Finally, the theme. We ask ourselves, 'What was the point of this?' In the burger's case, to satisfy our hunger." Dulce was now smiling into Leah's eyes. "'Serves four' is like saying, 'Finå, or the end.'"

Amazed, Leah said, "Have you been working on this for long?"

"Nah, I just made it up."

Leah laughed noiselessly. "Is this your way of telling me you want a hamburger?"

Getting the waiter's attention, Dulce asked for the check. Turning back to Leah, she said, "So, what's your story?"

"What do you mean?" Leah was still thinking of the recipe analogy.

"Well, life's a story, too. How does your story go? There

once was a girl named Leah. She worked at Alejandra's and pretended she was invisible."

Leah looked crestfallen. "Don't, Dulce."

"I'm not trying to hurt you. All I'm saying is that maybe the story you're in right now doesn't have such a happy ending for you. Maybe it's time to do some editing."

Leah felt cornered. "And you, Dulce? Are you planning on living here for the rest of your life?"

Velvet became fidgety. Dulce grabbed a bottle from her bag and leaned Velvet back. At first, Velvet sucked greedily. When she slowed, her eyelids grew heavy.

"Sure, why not? I couldn't wait to get back here. Me and Velvet are gonna travel around the world, but the Mission will always be our *tierra*. Let me ask you something. When you graduated, did you want to come back home?"

Leah looked away. "He was my home." She tried not to frown. It was a mistake. Her lower lip began to quiver.

Dulce leaned forward. "Leah. Where do you want your story to go from here?"

PART 3

Chapter 1
FLASHBACK TO WHAT ACTUALLY HAPPENED
TO LEAH AT GOLDEN GATE PARK

IN A SECLUDED PATCH of the park, surrounded by trees and shrubs, three homeless men closed in on the coltish beauty with big Bambi eyes. Letter jacket slowly reached for the hem of Leah's sundress, causing her to flinch. He raised her skirt high enough for the other men to get a good look at her pink cotton underwear.

Leah shifted her eyes away from her humiliation while fighting the urge to push her skirt down. She instinctively knew that any sudden movement would be considered confrontational. If she so much as took a step back, she would trigger their reflex for violence.

Turning to the other two, he asked, "Who ordered dessert?" All three men laughed drunkenly, revealing teeth that reminded Leah of scattered agates.

"I'm gonna lick me some of that Cool Whip before I take the cherry," Letter jacket said. Bending down, he draped Leah's skirt over his head, as if she was a view camera and he was about to take a picture. The hot breath on her thighs caused Leah's legs to go weak and her spine to hum, the way it did when she was too close to a ledge.

"No way, jizzcock! You already called dibs on that," the

bald man said while hooking a thumb toward the unconscious woman. "This one's mine!"

Leah felt the tip of a nose. A cold, wet tongue touched her inner thigh. She started shaking uncontrollably and needed to pee. The bald man pushed letter jacket with the sole of his boot. They watched him fall backwards, almost in slow motion as his entire body curved into the shape of a crescent moon.

Leah stared up at her new threat. The bald man was younger than she first thought. His head was shaven and there was a pattern of scars and round indentations on the sides of his scabby head. She fought the urge to retch.

Letter jacket struggled to his feet. He shoved the bald man with force. They were arguing over who got to fuck her first when the man in the trench coat snatched Leah's bag. He emptied the contents onto the grass. As they stared at the herbal bundle, Leah had the absurd impulse to explain the cuttings.

Letter jacket grabbed Leah by an arm and the bald man did the same. She was throttled by their noxious odors of rancid meat, excrement, and cider. She could feel the calluses on their hands scraping her arms. They were yanking her in opposite directions when she remembered a nature program she once watched. As two hyena pups fought over a chunk of gazelle meat, the announcer said that hyenas are born with teeth. Pups are sometimes killed by siblings while at play.

Leah opened her mouth to scream, but all that came out was a high-pitched squeak. The men stopped the tug-of-war and stared at Leah for a full five seconds. They doubled over with laughter.

"The hell was that! Jeez, is that the best you can do?" the

bald man said. He imitated Leah's weak whine, which generated more laughter from the other two men. All three of the men were now doing Leah impersonations, adding what they perceived as feminine gestures to their dainty squeals. Leah stood thunderstruck.

The sound of twigs snapping in quick rhythm from somewhere to her right caused Leah's eyes to sweep to the bushes. She briefly wondered how much worse this was going to get. A German shepherd and Doberman pinscher lunged over the sage bush with the tight precision of military jets.

The men's playful screams instantly turned into terror-filled shrieks.

Chapter 2

LEAH CONFRONTS HER FEARS

"IF YOU DON'T GO BACK THERE, there will never leave you." Leah thought of Dulce's words often. She chanted this truism as she overcame her agoraphobic tendencies. To get beyond the incident at Golden Gate Park she visited the dreaded place with Quico several days in a row. On their last visit, she felt some of the horror evaporate.

MUNI was the final and least challenging of San Francisco's anxiety hurdles. As Leah sat at the covered bus stop on 16th and Mission, she thought back to the last bus she had taken to Golden Gate Park. Gazing beyond the buildings, she wondered, Who would I be if I had caught a different bus? She startled at the realization that a boyish woman with a really small head was standing over her. "Time!" the woman demanded.

"Uh," Leah glanced at her watch. "It's one-fifteen?" she said.

The boyish woman did not move. Leah worried she had mistakenly answered the wrong question and was considering slipping the Timex off of her wrist and handing it to her. But what if that was not right either?

Tentatively, Leah stood up. She moved out of the way as the boyish woman sat in her vacated seat. Leah stepped forward as she scanned the intersection where every square inch was filled with man-made materials, unnatural colors, and people from every Latin American country. She watched as the pedestrians brimming on the corners waited for the light to change, and thought of a pot about to boil over.

Why. Am. I. Here?

Without warning, the hurried pace of the world suddenly slowed. The shriek of brakes and horns turned Leah's head as a vehicle swerved into view. The big black truck with a side rack carrying sheets of glass wove through traffic, as if it had some exciting news to share with someone.

It cut around a car and through the red light. The truck seemed to spot Leah. The round headlights gave the vehicle an alert expression as it slowly sped toward her.

Someone yelled, *"¡Aguas!"*

Leah watched as people jumped out of her periphery vision, as if she was a drop of water and they, the subsequent splash. The world slowed down even more. The truck was 30 feet away, and then 20. A flash from the shiny grill caused her to think of her father's gold-framed front teeth. In that insane flash, she believed the car was her father, coming to take her away from this frenetic place.

The level of shock built so quickly that Leah was completely numb before the impact; she never heard the crash. The front grill, still grinning, suddenly turn inward, as if punched by a fist. Not a fist but the streetlight a mere three feet in front of where she stood. At the moment of impact, jagged shards of glass broke free from the sheets and were flung from the side of the truck. The glass arrows passed so close one snipped a floating curl close to her ear.

Leah heard screaming behind her. She did not have to look back to know that the boyish woman lay dying. A piece of glass was lodged in her neck. Leah had a bird's-eye view of the scene and the puddle of blood around the woman's head, taking on the shape of a Byzantine halo.

❧

"I don't know," Alex said, rubbing her face. She sat back in the dining room chair and stared across the table at her husband. Leah was diagnosed with post-traumatic shock, or *susto* (depending on one's belief), again. They were arguing over what to do about Leah when Alex felt her resolve weakening.

"We are her family and need to take care of her. If you can think of a better idea, I want to hear it," Jaime said, in Spanish.

"But we have been taking really good care of her. I don't see why we can't keep going the way we have been. She'll snap out of it when she's ready."

"How long do you expect these people to take shifts babysitting her? A month? A year? They all have their own lives. Quico has his own restaurant to run in Mexico. How is he supposed to do that from here?"

"But a psychiatric hospital seems so extreme," Alex said, picturing a hybrid of a lunatic asylum and a prison.

"Leah hasn't said a word in days. *Curanderas* won't see her. They're afraid she'll burn their homes down. If she doesn't get the right treatment now, she's going to end up like that barefoot bag lady with the curly toenails." Jaime reached for Alex's hand. "We'll still be the ones taking care of her through trained people. We also need to take care of her finances."

Alex was staring at the rare sight of her hand in her husband's, and almost missed the last part. "Wait, what about her finances?" Alex blinked several times. "Are you saying you want me to have Leah declared unfit to manage her own affairs?"

Jaime tilted his head to the side. "It's for her own good. You wouldn't give Junior a checkbook, would you?"

Alex sighed. "If Leah isn't better by the weekend, we'll look into mental care facilities. I'll ask Tessa for advice on choosing the best place for her."

"I don't think you should tell her anything. You shouldn't tell Dulce, either. She's crazier than Leah is. Too bad we can't put her away," Jaime snorted, remembering something unpleasant. "No, I think the best thing to do is keep this within our family. See what your lawyer has to say about making Leah crazy, you know, legally."

Chapter 3

TESSA AND DULCE CONSPIRE TO KIDKNAP LEAH

"I THINK WE SHOULD just kidnap her," Dulce said. She and Velvet had returned home and were relieving Tessa from her shift of watching Leah.

"Then what? Hide her in my mom's attic? Buy her a diary?" Tessa said, heatedly. She began to pace back and forth in the living room.

"Can they really do that? Throw anyone in the loony bin?" Dulce said, watching Velvet play with a set of sealed Tupperware she had turned into a bunch of maracas. The dried beans, seashells, bells, and dried rice gave each rattle a unique sound.

"Not exactly, but it only takes two family members to sign the forms that would force Leah to undergo a psychiatric examination. If she is certified as insane, she'll be sent to an asylum," Tessa said, running her hands through her hair. "What I don't get is, why the rush? Leah's reaction is appropriate to the trauma she suffered, the lack of speech and her emotional detachment. What she needs is psychotherapy, not a straightjacket."

Dulce nodded. "Being poked and stared at by a bunch of *gabachos* in lab coats is only gonna make her worse. Hey, you ever heard of the Gaia philosophy?"

Tessa's eyebrow arched at the non sequitur. "You mean, the concept that earth is a single organism, like a cell, and the earth's biosphere is consciously maintaining its own external physical conditions to survive?" She sat on the armrest of the couch. "Where did you hear about the Gaia Hypothesis?"

"Hey, I went to college too," Dulce said. "So, if the world is self-regulating, maybe Leah's in the wrong place. You know, out of her element."

Tessa folded her arms. "Are you saying that Leah, for whatever reason, doesn't fit into the social organism of San Francisco and the environment is trying to purge her; flush her out of its system?"

Dulce smiled. "I couldn't have said it better myself."

"Have you been dropping acid?" Tessa said, sharp-eyed.

"Not for a long time. What I'm saying is Leah belongs somewhere, just not here. We need to figure out where that is and take her there." Velvet farted. Dulce's chin jerked in the baby's direction. "Let me interpret. Velvet just said she thinks Leah should go back to Mexico with Quico."

"If we do anything behind Alex's back, she'll side with Jaime and never talk to us again. She'll only guilt Leah into coming back so they can stick her in a hospital."

Dulce shook her head. "But if we don't do anything, she's gonna end up there anyway."

"What if we contacted Mrs. Cernuda?" Tessa became aware that Dulce did not reply. She glanced up.

A shadow in the hallway moved forward slowly, like an apparition materializing in the lamplight. Leah, dressed in a long white nightgown, was staring at them with melancholy eyes. Both Tessa and Dulce were wondering how long she had been standing there when Leah croaked one word: "Mendocino."

❧

Alex cried when she heard her sister's voice. She became guarded as Leah explained her desperate need to move away from here and to Mendocino. "But you'll be all alone," Alex said, worriedly.

"Yes. I'll be alone," Leah replied, sighing wistfully.

❧

Arrangements were made for a relative to watch Alex's sons, while the Anayas took care of Velvet. The next morning, Tessa, Dulce, Leah, and a skeptical Alex drove to Mendocino. Aside from Leah, none had ever ventured that far north before. During the six-hour drive, they talked about everything and nothing while staring out different windows. They became quiet at the sight of the dramatic coastline.

In the seaside village of Mendocino, they drove past Cape Cod and Victorian structures. Leah explained how the entire town was on the National Register of Historic Places, remembering when Jacob had told her the same thing. They kept going until they reached the high bluffs on the far edge of town.

Getting out of the car, they stood for a long time, watching the wild sea below. Turning back, Alex gazed at the charming village, and then at Leah. She suddenly understood the difference between being native to a place and natural in it. San Francisco must feel to Leah the way San Rafael feels to me, she thought.

"This place. I don't know what to say. It's perfect for you," she said. Leah beamed as Tessa and Dulce nodded thoughtfully.

❧

The four friends spent the next couple of days savoring Mendocino's gourmet restaurants, shopping, and house hunting. Alex multitasked by interviewing the realtors in town. She selected a woman who also had three sons, nicknamed Tiger. Zeroing in on Leah's housing needs—a big kitchen and seclusion—Tiger got busy compiling a listing of properties within Mendocino County.

The second house on the list was a coastal cottage, outside of "the Village," as the locals refer to Mendocino. The four women oohed and awed as they drove up the private gravel road and spotted the yellow house. It was perched on an open grassy lot surrounded by rhododendrons and coastal flora. To the right of the house was a path leading to a secluded beach.

Tiger smiled at their reactions from the porch. She immediately began the tour and her pitch. "The sellers are very motivated..." To Leah, the interior walls of the empty house were the color of old memories. Tiger moved on. "The sellers bought the property as a second home and fought over the renovation. They were about to start on the bathroom but couldn't agree on a commode. Can you believe it escalated into a bitter divorce?"

In the kitchen, Leah marveled at the stone fireplace, the Jenn-Air appliances, the marble-topped island with a second sink, and the huge pantry. Tiger was saying, "All of the electrical and plumbing has been upgraded throughout the house, but the kitchen is the only completely refinished—"

Uncharacteristically, Leah cut Tiger off. "I'll take it!"

Chapter 4

TESSA TALKS ABOUT SCIENCE AND RELIGION

"AND YOU KNOW WHAT really bothers me? When faith gets in the way of teaching children how to think rationally," Tessa said to Dulce. They were sitting in the Monte Carlo, waiting for Mrs. Anaya to finish cleaning a house on Telegraph Hill. Tessa had dropped her mother off at work that morning. She borrowed the car to take Dulce shopping. They went to Costco so Dulce could stock up on diapers, baby wipes, and other bulk items.

"The notion that myths invented back in the Bronze Age by superstitious desert nomads are given exactly the same credence as Darwin and Euclid really bothers me. We should at least leave science class as the one, possibly the only place, where critical thinking and rationality are not suppressed..." Tessa paused. "What was your question?"

Dulce was leaning her head back, breathing through her mouth. "I don't remember. It was a long, long, time ago. But I've got a new question for you. What's taking your mom so long? Go find out."

Tessa checked her watch. They had been waiting for fifteen minutes and she was on her rant for fourteen of them. Turning toward Dulce, she said, "Dulce, I want you to focus. I'll be right back. Do not honk the horn, crank up the radio, talk to anyone, cuss at anyone, or get out of the car."

"Can I play with the emergency brake?"

"I mean it, Dulce. This is my mom's first day working here, and if you do something stupid to get her fired..." Tessa left it at that.

As she got out of the car, two men appeared from the side of the house. They were both in their early thirties, average height, and very attractive. The blond man, dressed in a royal blue velour V-neck sweater, reminded Tessa of Jack from *Three's Company*. His handyman, dark-skinned, high cheek boned, and well built, was wearing a clean T-shirt and stonewashed jeans. They were discussing dimensions and materials when they noticed Tessa standing in the driveway.

"Oh, hi. I'm here to pick up my mother, Maria," Tessa said.

They hesitated, trying to place the name.

"Your housekeeper," Tessa offered, not masking her annoyance.

"Remember, Tessa," Dulce said, from the rolled down car window. "This is your mom's first day working here and if you do something really stupid to get her fired..."

Tessa glowered at Dulce. To the men, she said, "I dropped my mother off here this morning. Is she here or not?" Tessa was beginning to get worried.

"Are you sure you're at the right address?" the man in the stonewashed jeans said. "My housekeeper's name is Ximena."

Tessa shifted her eyes. "Yes. That's her. It's too hard for most people to remember."

He smiled his understanding. "So she goes by Maria to make it easier for everyone," he said, extending a hand. "I'm Gabriel Luna. This is Dwight. He's building a deck in the back."

Tessa felt her cheeks turn crimson as she realized her own prejudicial error. She heard Dulce chuckling.

The front door opened, and Mrs. Anaya stepped out with a bag of garbage in each hand. "Hi, *mija!*" she said, her face brightening. Noticing her employer, she became demure. "I'm almost done. Could you please take the trash out for me?"

Dulce got out of the car to give Tessa a hand as Gabriel wrapped up his business with Dwight. Tessa and Dulce were heading toward the side of the house when Gabriel caught up with them. "Here, let me give you a hand," he said. Dulce held her bag out, but Tessa hesitated. This did not feel right. If her mother found out that he took out his own trash...

"It's this way," Gabriel said, understanding the awkwardness of the sudden reversal, and taking the lead.

Tessa was checking out Gabriel's nice butt when Dulce said, "Hey, Gabriel, when you're done taking out your own trash, our car could use a wash, and wax."

Tessa's head snapped back. "Dulce!" she scolded.

Gabriel laughed. "I'll get Maria to take care of it."

Dulce shot back. "Just make sure she doesn't steal the quarters from the ashtray." This time, all three laughed.

They tossed the trash and walked back to the front where Mrs. Anaya was descending the front porch stairs. "*Señora* Anaya. Please introduce me to your daughters?" Gabriel said, in Spanish.

At first, Mrs. Anaya stammered slightly through the introductions of her daughter, and other daughter. Soon, swelling with maternal pride, she boasted about each of "her girls" while fixing Dulce's hair. She picked a piece of imaginary lint from Tessa's sleeve.

"Are you exhibiting anywhere?" Gabriel said to Dulce.

"This summer, at *Galería de la Raza* in the Mission," Dulce said.

"Well, we'd better get going," Tessa said. She opened the driver's side door.

"Would you send me an invitation to your opening? I recently moved here from Chicago and I'm in dire need of artwork," Gabriel said, pulling out his wallet and handing Dulce a card.

"Just so you know, it's a two-painting minimum for people from Telegraph Hill," she said.

"Nice try," Gabriel said. He caught Tessa's eye while slipping his card between her fingers.

Tessa was curious about this man, but did not want to appear interested. She tucked the card into her pocket and got behind the steering wheel.

Gabriel shut her door. *"Gracias, Señora* Anaya," he said, as he peered passed Tessa. "The house looks great. I'll see you in two weeks?"

Mrs. Anaya smiled and nodded, relieved by the confirmation that the job was permanent. Gabriel fixed his liquid brown eyes on Tessa. His face was close enough for her to kiss. "I'm looking forward to seeing you next month," he said.

Something in his stare was making it difficult for Tessa to breathe. She felt an unwanted blushing heat as she put the car in reverse.

"See you at the opening," Dulce said, from the back seat, her arm resting on the bulk package of Pampers. "And don't forget your checkbook!"

Chapter 5

DULCE FINDS THE ROLL OF FILM

"WHAT IS IT WITH razor blade companies these days?" Alex said, fuming into the phone. "I spent half of the morning looking for a blade to fit Jaime's razor, but every store I went to was out. They sell you the razor, and then never restock the blades, so you have to keep buying new razors. Jaime now owns five razors and no blades. It's a conspiracy, I tell you!"

"Uh huh," Dulce said, distractedly. She was working on a painting. "Did you call me to complain about razors?"

Before Alex could say yes, she remembered why she called. "Thanks for watching the boys last night, but did you forget to feed them dinner? I'm only asking because the tray of enchiladas I left wasn't touched and there were no dirty dishes in the sink. You never do the dishes."

"Your *criaturas* said they were sick of Mexican food and wanted Taco Bell. So, I took them to Taco Bell," Dulce said. "Oh, before I forget, I found a roll of film in the kitchen. I'll drop it off when I go to Gasser's next week."

"Thanks," Alex said, thinking how simultaneously annoying and helpful Dulce was.

"What's on the roll?"

"I'm not sure. It could be anything," Alex said.

"Mystery roll, huh? I love those. I once found a roll of film in an elevator and developed it."

"Anything interesting?"

"Vegetables up some guy's hairy butt."

"Ew! I don't want to hear any more."

"A carrot, a Japanese eggplant, a sweet potato." There was a pause. "At least I think it was a sweet potato."

"Shut up, Dulce!" Alex said, laughing. "It's probably a roll from the holidays that fell out of the car. I've got to go pick up the kids!"

Chapter 6

DULCE GOES TO GASSER'S

"LEAH'S MADE THE LIST AGAIN," Carolyn said, handing Dulce the folded page of the New York Times. Leah's cookbook was number seven on the bestseller list.

"How many weeks is that?" Dulce asked, knowing the answer, but wanting to hear it out loud.

"Eleven weeks," Carolyn said, indulgently.

They were at Gasser's, a regional favorite camera and film store. It was crowded with professional and amateur camera buffs. Dulce had just picked up color slides for her exhibit and several packets of photos.

She scanned the paper while Carolyn opened a packet of prints and started shuffling through the first set. "Who are the nudes?"

Dulce did a perfect double take. "Let me see that." She quickly flipped through the 36 photos, unable to make sense of them. Recognizing an ugly painting in the background—hung way too high, Dulce briefly wondered why people always did that? She realized the pictures were taken in Alex and Jaime's bedroom. It was the mystery roll of film.

"Jaime's busted!" she said, enjoying the Sherlock Holmes moment.

Carolyn made a tsk sound. "Dulce Racelis. Mother, artist, and home wrecker."

"Exactamundo," Dulce said, smiling wolfishly.

The milky glow of a light box was illuminating Carolyn's neck. The light was casting a long shadow on a mole, making it stand out, like the Mount Rushmore noses on a sunny day. Was it her imagination or had the mole changed shape and color?

Chapter 7
DULCE PHONES LEAH

"LET'S SEE. I'll need mint, oregano, carrots, potatoes..." Leah said to the air. She was spending the morning testing recipes for *sopa de albóndigas*. In her follow-up cookbook, she was modifying traditional recipes by placing the emphasis on fresh and healthy ingredients. It was proving to be difficult to stay away from saturated fats, such as lard, without altering the flavor of some of the dishes.

Leah reached for a straw hat hanging on a brass hook. She stepped through the kitchen door and into the backyard. After grabbing gloves, gardening shears, and a faded basket from the potting shed, she stood for a moment taking in her garden.

To the untrained eye, the odd mixture of flowers, herbs, and vegetables might appear to have been planted with no particular pattern. But Jacob would immediately have recognized how the basil, chamomile, chives, rosemary, rue, dill, and mint, growing among the vegetables, were planted to naturally discourage insect infestation.

Jacob had been her intellectual and emotional compass for nearly three years. By bringing her to Mendocino for a long weekend, he unknowingly pointed her in the direction of her future. Every day, she thought about the incredible pain she caused Yumi and recited a prayer.

For all the evil deeds I have done in the past,

Created by my body, speech, and mind,
From beginning-less greed, anger, and delusion,
I now know shame and repent them all.

The dandelions, scattered and clustered like children in a playground, caught Leah's attention. She always had a particular liking for this plant that most gardeners viewed as a menacing weed. But isn't a weed merely an unwanted plant? Not only did this "weed" add a slightly bitter flavor to salads, it was also rich in potassium, calcium, and lecithin, and a stimulant to the kidney and liver.

Leah watched the dandelion's cycle of life with constant astonishment. In its youth, the yellow flower is bright and alert by day. It shuts, like an eye to sleep, at night. During the transition from flower to seed, the pointy petals fall and the plumed seeds turn into a fuzzy ball. The seeds are dispersed in the breeze and, sometimes, between a wish and puff of warm breath.

Leah plucked a fluffy dandelion and was making a wish when she heard her ringing phone. Running back to the house, she answered a little out of breath. "Hello?"

"It's me," Dulce said. "Are you sitting down?"

"I'M HOME!" Tessa yelled, returning from the library.

"Dulce and Leah called!" Mrs. Anaya yelled back, in Spanish. "They both want you to call them, as soon as you get home. Someone else called. I wrote that one down." Mother and daughter often carried on entire conversations from different floors. It drove Mr. Anaya crazy.

Tessa read the pad by the phone, where "Melony Weson" was written in her mother's scratchy hand, followed by a local phone number. It took a moment to decipher the spelling. Tessa went from being thrilled at hearing from her former boyfriend's sister to an icy panic.

"What did she say?" Tessa said, worried that Melanie might have mentioned something about meeting her in Washington, D.C.—a place she had never been to, as far as her parents knew.

"Just that she's in San Francisco and she wants to see you."

The messages from Leah and Dulce slipped Tessa's mind as she returned Melanie's call.

❧

Tessa sat at a table in Alejandra's, a little early for her lunch date with Melanie. Staring through the menu, she relived her final encounter with Atticus's shrew-of-a-mother. When the taxi arrived to take Tessa to the airport, Joyce was waiting for her in the foyer.

"Atticus is sorry he couldn't see you off, but he and the Senator have an important meeting this morning. He asked me to give you this," she said, handing Tessa an unsealed envelope.

An early meeting on a Sunday. Yeah, right! Tessa thought, taking the letter from Joyce. She sensed Joyce had read it and struggled not to care.

"Oh, one more thing, Tess. I know you are the catalyst behind the problems we've had with our domestic help. Before you leave, I just wanted to say how you could save future families from unnecessary stress by dating closer to home."

Even though Tessa was 3,000 miles from home, she understood Joyce was speaking figuratively. Joyce was coolly suggesting that she stick to her own kind. Tessa was not expecting such a blatantly racial parting shot and felt enraged. But going ballistic was exactly what Joyce was hoping for. She would repeat Tessa's final angry words ending with, "you fucking bitch," to her son. She would nod in a way that suggested: You see, your father and I were right about her, all along.

But Tessa had watched Joyce manipulate poor Melanie and had learned a thing or two. "I also got your best friend arrested. Feel free to keep your kleptomaniac pals on your side of the fence." Tessa's voice sounded remarkably unperturbed.

Joyce's eyes narrowed to icy blue slits. "Get out of my house. And get out of my country!"

Tessa felt more exhausted than relieved at leaving. As she carried her luggage to the waiting taxicab, she thought how this final victory was just another ugly victory to add to the longest week of her life. She was relieved she had the foresight to return the emerald green dress for cash instead of store credit. The money would more than cover the unexpected cab fare to the airport.

&

Tessa's eyes came into focus as a smiling Melanie approached the table. She was dressed in an oversized black sweater, a long black skirt, and Doc Marten boots. She looked pleasantly different, but Tessa could not figure out what had changed. They hugged before sitting down.

"I've been so paranoid that I was going to forget to give this to you, so here," Melanie said. She handed Tessa a plastic bag of Mexican wedding cookies. "It's from Remedios."

Tessa smiled warmly. "How is she?"

"Great! After you left, I called a friend who's the director of a private school. I mentioned Remedios to him and how she'd been a high school English teacher in Colombia. His school was in desperate need of bilingual faculty. Since Remedios already had papers, he hired her as a teacher's assistant. The job has great benefits, plus she gets to visit her family during the summer. She's in Colombia now."

"I'm so glad to hear that. How are Amparo and Naomi?"

"They're doing really well. They asked me to give you this," she said, pulling a holy card from a side pocket of her black book bag.

Holy cards are the Catholic equivalent of baseball cards. They're about the same size and are collected and traded. The image on this card was from the painting by Heilige Schutzengel. In it, two kids are crossing a rickety bridge over a tumultuous river, while a guardian angel watches over them. Tessa wondered as she always did, where the hell are their parents?

"Naomi believes it's representative of you three. Amparo said you look just like the angel."

Tessa flipped the card over. "I do not," she said, scrutinizing the floating figure. "Are Amparo and Naomi still working at the convent?" While Joyce was distracted with the final details of the anniversary party, Tessa and Melanie scrambled to secure cleaning positions for the women.

Melanie nodded. "The nuns have helped with their paperwork and secured green cards for them and their families. But the best part for Naomi and Amparo is going to church every day, while getting paid."

Tessa laughed. "Tell them I said hello, and thank you." When she got home, she would place the card in her ballerina box to keep with the rest of her treasured mementos. Tessa tucked the card into her wallet. "I'm sorry I never got in touch with you, Mel. I needed to..."

"I know. You needed to put that trip and my family behind you. I can't say I blame you. My mother is the stuff nightmares are made of."

After they ordered lunch, Melanie told an elated Tessa that she was not visiting San Francisco, but had transferred to the University of California San Francisco's holistic practitioner program. Tessa told an equally surprised Melanie that she had also transferred to UCSF.

"The loans were barely covering my tuition. With the intense workload ahead, there was no way for me to continue working enough hours at Kinko's to cover the extra costs," Tessa said.

"Oh, that's too bad. I'm so sorry," Melanie said,

sympathetically.

Tessa thought how life circles around. Now that she was back at the starting point, she had learned so many things—including the existence of broken people, everywhere. "I'm not. Stanford's nice, but it's not here. I missed my parents and my friends."

"And your parents coin-free washer and dryer," Melanie said.

"Oh yeah. Did I forget to mention the fully stocked refrigerator and free MTV?"

Tessa suddenly realized what was different about Melanie. That look of homesickness she had, ironically while at home, was gone.

"I've been wanting to ask you...where did you learn Spanish?" Tessa said.

Melanie smiled sheepishly. "I've been taking it since middle school and it was my college minor. Most of my friends took French. I don't know. It always seemed more important to be able to communicate with the people taking care of us and our home, rather than trying to impress some snotty acquaintance of my parents."

"Do the Marias know you speak Spanish?"

"Of course."

"I don't get it. Why didn't your mom have you translate for her psycho friends?"

"She probably doesn't know that I speak Spanish. She has no idea who I am." There was a note of pain in Melanie's voice.

Tessa leaned forward and placed a hand on hers. "You are Melanie Weston, superhero. My God, Mel, you have already done more good than your mother has done. Imagine what good you will do in your lifetime?"

As Melanie blushed, Tessa recalled something that had been niggling at her since she left the Weston's home. "Was Atticus named after the character in the novel?"

Melanie shook her head. "That's what he likes to tell people; so does my father. He was named after my mother's confederate ancestor, 'Atticus Andrew Breckinridge.'"

Tessa sat back, thinking how that explained so much about Joyce's "them and us" attitude.

Frances, the only waitress left from the pre-Jaime days, approached the table. "Dulce is looking for you. She's in her studio. Leah's there, too," she said.

"Oh, that's right. Thanks, Frances," Tessa said, remembering the phone messages. Grinning, she said to Melanie, "After lunch, do you have time to see what *my* nightmares are made of?"

Chapter 9

THE CONFERENCE

TESSA AND MELANIE entered Dulce's studio without knocking. Halting, they gaped up at the naked woman in high-heeled shoes. She was lying frozen in an unmade bed with her arms tossed languidly over her head. Her legs, bent at the knees, were spread wide, like a frog prepped with pins for dissection.

Still thinking of the comment about nightmares Tessa had made, Melanie gave her a "you weren't kidding" look.

The enlarged image of the nude woman spanning across the slanted ceiling disappeared. They heard a clickity-clack sound as a gear turned. She was replaced by the image of another woman, also naked, and wearing heels. She was in almost the exact same position as the first.

"*¡Orale pues!* We were just about to put your face on a milk carton," Dulce said to Tessa. She and Carolyn were sitting on the floor. The projector next to them was raised with books to a 45-degree angle.

"Hi, Tessa," Leah said, smiling sadly, as she rose from her seat on the park bench. She gave Tessa a hug.

"Leah," Tessa said. "What are you doing here? Is something wrong?"

"Dulce found some pictures," Leah said, smiling timidly at the stranger next to Tessa. Clearly embarrassed by the hovering nude on the ceiling.

"More like passport pictures. Alex and the boys can catch the next plane out of Jaimeland for good," Dulce said, as she noticed Melanie. "Who's the *ruca?*"

"This is Melanie Weston. Mel, meet Leah Cernuda." Leah and Melanie shook hands as Carolyn got up. "This is Carolyn Elzig." After Carolyn and Melanie shook hands, Tessa continued with the introductions. "And that over there is Dulce Racelis." Dulce gave a quick jerk back of the head in salutation.

"OK, now, start from the beginning," Tessa said.

"Alex found a roll of film in the garage," Leah said.

"I got it developed and that's what was on it," Dulce said, as Leah handed the stack of prints to Tessa.

Tessa flipped through the photos. Melanie watched from over her shoulder. "Oh shit!" slowly seeped from Tessa's mouth. Her face was torn with repulsion and fascination. "Wait a second," she said, staring at something in the corner of a photo.

"Anything look familiar?" Dulce said, holding a pool cue and already knowing the answer.

"I'm not sure. It's too dark," Tessa said.

"That's why Dulce made slides," Carolyn said.

"What have you figured out so far?" Tessa said, as they found seats while staring up at the ceiling.

"They were taken in Alex and Jaime's bedroom," Dulce said, repulsed.

"We just made a list of names. We only recognized eight of the 35 women," Carolyn said.

"Are you telling me there are 35 different women striking that same pose?" Tessa said, unable to grasp it.

"Why 35?" Melanie said. Tessa stared at her blankly. "The roll should have 36 photos. So why are there only 35 prints?"

"Good question." Dulce nodded. "Jaime took a picture of his thumb. He's kind of stupid that way."

"Dulce put the slides in the same order as the negatives and we figured out approximately when they were taken," Carolyn said.

Dulce pulled two of the slides out of the projector. She dropped them in, side by side. "These two slides told us the roll was shot over a year ago. How do we know? This," Dulce said, while clicking, "is fat Juana and she's at the beginning of the roll of film. Natalie's the last shot, before the thumb." Dulce switched slides to a petite white woman with choppy hair, and then back to Juana.

"Juana is not fat," Leah said, to herself, but Dulce heard her.

"She was last year before she drank nothing but those shakes," Dulce clicked again. "Natalie moved here from San Diego. Her hair was that short when she first got here, but she's been growing it out, 'cause her ears get cold."

"Are you sure it's Jaime? It could have been one of his lowlife friends," Tessa said.

"How about a shot of fuck-face himself? Pardon my English," Dulce said to Melanie. She clicked forward a dozen slides, and adjusted the focus. She pointed with the stick to where Jaime had inadvertently caught a sliver of his own reflection in a mirror-framed photo of his three sons. It made Tessa want to throw up.

"But we still don't know why they're all wearing the same pair of shoes," Dulce said, baffled.

"Were all of the photos taken at night?" Tessa said.

Leah nodded, solemnly. "Yes, while Alex was at the restaurant with us," she said, glancing guiltily at Dulce.

"That means the boys would have been at home with them," Tessa said.

"Junior started talking in full sentences last year," Dulce said. "Jaime must have figured he'd say something to Alex. So he made her quit working."

No one spoke as Dulce did a quick click through of all of the images. The motor and fan propeller hummed and whirred as women briefly appeared and then vanished. They were different shapes, sizes, and colors. Some smiled and others appeared impatient, but most had the look of flies caught in a spider's web. They realized, too late, that they had relinquished control to a madman.

Tessa peered at Leah's face, now bathed in blue light. She flinched at each image. Tessa was about to tell Dulce to shut it off when someone shrieked, "My shoes!"

Their heads snapped toward the door, in time to watch Alex faint dead away. The stack of envelopes containing the employees' checks fanned out onto the floor like a dropped card trick.

Chapter 10

ALEX IS AWAKENED BY AN INTRUDER

IT'S STRANGE HOW life can change on such a small thing as a roll of film. And how something lacking a conscience could rip through so many people's lives. A camera is as dangerous as a gun, if you point and shoot without discretion.

Alex was lying in her bed in San Rafael, a different bed than the one in the photos. Her sister and friends had gotten rid of the old bed and purchased this one, along with new pillows and bedding. As depressed as she was, Alex could not help but wonder who picked out such bland sheets?

She wanted to stay all coiled up like a pill bug, until death made the rounds for her. For no reason, she wondered what had happened to all of the roly-polies? She had not seen one since she was a girl. Wait, that's not right. I haven't noticed one since I was young. Alex's forehead wrinkled as she thought about all of the things she failed to notice.

Now that some of the numbness was wearing off and death had apparently skipped her, Alex considered suicide. She followed the veins under the skin of her wrist all the way up her arm. They reminded her of the blue dotted lines around a store coupon, instructing her to 'Cut Here.' Yeah, but who would clean up the mess?

As she contemplated more sanitary ways of ending her life, she stared absently at the dresser. A bottle of Jaime's cologne, Drakkar Noir, caught her eye. Getting out of bed,

Alex grabbed the bottle. She crawled back under the covers. When she unscrewed the lid, the room filled with the smell of her husband.

"Jaime, Jaime, oh Jaime," she moaned, dabbing a little of the cologne behind her ears. Staring at the bottle, she thought, That's it! I'll drink the Drakkar Noir. I'll lie back on my pillow, and die with his name, and scent, on my lips.

Alex's imagination fast-forwarded to Jaime, dressed in his almost Armani suit, placing a single red rose on her white funeral casket. Overcome with grief and remorse, he breaks down right there, in front of everyone. He falls to his knees and looking toward heaven, shouts, "I never deserved you, Alejandra. You were perfect!"

"That'll show him," Alex said, opening the nightstand drawer and reaching for the bottle of sleeping pills, just to be sure. She filled her mouth with the pills and before she allowed herself to think of her sons, she took a big swig of Jaime's cologne.

Alex's gag reflex instantly kicked in, causing her to violently expel the soggy pellets on the plain new duvet cover. She furiously wiped her burning tongue with a bouquet of Kleenex. She then rinsed her mouth in the sink until her tongue cooled. Alex dropped face-first onto her bed.

❧

Alex peered into the office where Jaime was going through some papers. She waited for permission to enter. "What!" he said, not bothering to look up.

Alex was now standing on the very spot her employees stood when they were asking her for something. "Are you still in love with me?" she pleaded, while gingerly touching a glass paperweight on her desk. Noticing it was caked with dust, she gave it a quick swipe with her fingers. She saw the picture of her boys underneath. The glass magnified their sweet faces and made Alex want to start blubbering.

Jaime eased back in the chair and looked away, like it was the stupidest question he had ever heard. In English, he said, "I've never been in love with anyone. 'Specially not you."

Alex woke abruptly, remembering the bad dream as it slipped away. The glance toward the digital clock revealed nothing but a black spot on the nightstand. Turning her head, she realized the nightlight was also off. But it was on a sensor and had a battery. She was about to reach for the lamp when she instinctively knew that she was not alone. Her entire body tensed. "Who's there?"

The curtain in front of the sliding glass door rippled in the breeze. Alex's heart began to race. The shadow was taking a perverse pleasure in increasing her anxiety by not answering.

The figure slowly climbed onto the bed, before climbing on top of her. Alex furtively drew in a breath, preparing to scream. A cold hand covered her mouth. Terror widened her eyes.

"It's me," Jaime whispered into her ear. "Calm down."

Exhaling, Alex's head dropped back onto the pillow. Jaime's hand slackened from her mouth, but he kept it there. "You do not want to wake your friends or the boys. That would not be good for any of them," he said, coldly.

Alex's relief at the sound of her husband's voice was replaced with fear by the unmistakable threat implied to the household's safety. A whimper sounded in her throat. She began to cry. Jaime hurriedly licked the first tear streaking her face, as if it was melting ice cream. Jaime sucked the pools of tears collecting in her tightly shut lids.

Alex felt Jaime harden. His erection sickened her. He lifted her cotton nightgown over her head. He scratched her belly as he yanked her underwear down. Alex's keening was low and dispirited, as she forced herself to eat the dark shame.

Chapter 11
JAIME GETS A HEADACHE

AGAINST ALEX'S WISHES, Dulce reported the rape to the San Rafael Police Department, who, in turn, notified the SFPD. Officer Garcia got the call. At the restaurant, he read Jaime his Miranda rights, in Spanish, while his partner cuffed him. Jaime smirked and joked as they escorted him through the restaurant during lunch rush. He made Feo laugh by putting Pedro, the dishwasher, in charge as he was led through the kitchen door.

Not clear on the distinction between consensual sex and rape, Jaime explained, like he was talking to dull children, that it was impossible for him to commit rape. "'The wife doesn't rule over her own body, her husband does. Go look it up in the fucking Bible!"

"Oh yeah?" Officer Garcia said. He grew up in the Mission and had known the Cernuda, Anaya, and Racelis families all of his life. Although happily married, he had had a secret crush on Dulce since she put him in a half-nelson when they were kids. "Then why did you sneak in through the bedroom?"

"Because those cunts changed the locks, that's why! Hey, I want them arrested for trespassing. You're a cop, how do I do that?"

Ignoring the question, Officer Garcia said, "Why did you unplug all of the lights in the bedroom?"

Jaime laughed, surprised that he knew so much. "I was just

having a little fun."

At the parking lot in the rear of the police station, Officer Garcia helped Jaime out of the backseat. "Watch the hair!" Jaime barked, now taking in the seriousness of his situation. In the blind spot of the parking lot, Officer Garcia accidentally slammed Jaime's head against the cement piling, twice.

Chapter 12

SANCTUARY

THE DAY AFTER Jaime's arrest, a caravan of cars arrived in Mendocino. Leah and a sedated Alex drove up the private road first, followed by Dulce and the three boys in Alex's mini-van. Bringing up the rear were Tessa and Melanie in her Mustang convertible. The grass on the cliffs was now golden and a ghost moon hung low in the afternoon sky.

They took their time settling into the new peace. Leah went to the kitchen and made a spiced tea with cinnamon sticks. She gazed at the well-worn copper pots hanging on shiny hooks, at the smooth round stones of the fireplace and hearth, at the farm table and ladder-back chairs. The setting reminded her of a charming domestic still life. It is so good to be home, she thought.

Tessa was sitting on a wicker chair in the backyard, watching a cloud of gnats languidly swirl like smoke on a windless day. Melanie was standing in Leah's thriving garden, her arms loosely crossed in front of her. Flowers spilling from broken clay pots and trailing vines had her full attention.

Hearing cups rattle, Melanie turned without moving her feet. "Leah, I am in love with this place."

"Thank you," Leah said, setting the tea tray on a low table next to Tessa.

"I was expecting a little garden. This, is a farm. Does it really take all of this produce to make one cookbook?" Melanie said.

Tessa proudly spoke up. "Leah also supplies the local gourmet restaurants with vegetables."

"My produce business was not planned. It just happened," Leah said, as she poured. "Heather, a friend from the academy, is now the chef at a restaurant here in town. She mentioned how it was impossible to find vegetables harvested while the crops were still young and tender. So I planted a little extra."

"Tessa mentioned that you make the same recipe over and over again for your cookbook. What do you do with all of that food?" Melanie said.

"It's taken to the hospice in town. The volunteers do not seem to mind eating variations of the same meal," Leah said.

Dulce came out of the house, grim-faced. "I have to head back, right away. It's Carolyn."

"Is she OK?" Tessa said.

Dulce shook her head. "I need Pepe."

"Of course," Leah said, as they hurried back to the house.

Tessa and Melanie were silent at the somber news. Melanie opened her mouth, but before she could ask, Tessa said, with some reluctance, "Pepe is the truck. We tend to anthropomorphize our cars, pets, plants, appliances, the weather, furniture, food, rocks…pretty much everything."

Chapter 13

DULCE INHERITS CAROLYN

CAROLYN'S ATTORNEY cleared his throat before getting to the last item of her will. "Ms. Racelis, Carolyn bequeathed to you...I don't know how else to say this. She left you her tattoo."

Dulce was momentarily stunned. She felt waves of admiration break through her grief, as she understood. Carolyn had figured out a way to leave a part of herself behind, literally. Dulce nodded with appreciation.

"My daughter did not have any tattoos," Mr. Elzig said. A blond woman Dulce guessed to be the latest girlfriend placed a placating hand on his arm.

There was a torturous silence before the attorney tried again. "Mr. Elzig—Douglas—Carolyn had one tattoo. It covered her entire backside. The back of her head, neck, torso, arms, and legs." He waited for the image to sink in. "Carolyn made all of the arrangements before her death. As the Executor to her will, I carried out her instructions for the extraction and preservation of the tattoo."

The attorney did not go into detail about how the tattoo was surgically removed before the cremation. He chose not to mention how the skin had undergone a similar tanning process as is done with animal hides. Or how the tattoo was sealed in an airtight glass frame.

Mr. Elzig's girlfriend, suddenly a little green, raced out of the room. It was the kind of building where the restroom was shared by all of the commercial tenants on the floor. Dulce wondered what she would do when she realized the restroom key was still in the attorney's desk.

Chapter 14

ALEX EMERGES FROM HER CHRYSALIS

FOR THE PAST FOUR MONTHS, Alex began each day with a nervous breakdown. With all of her romantic notions shattered, she spent the rest of the day feeling raw at the realization that she could not recognize her own life. Burying her face in the pillow, she thought, If I could just stay here for a few years, everything will be all right.

Alex's decision to drop the charges against Jaime upset everyone, but she needed to think about the boys. Jaime is, after all, their father. Before Tessa and Melanie returned to the city, Tessa strong-armed Alex into filing a restraining order against Jaime.

In the weeks that followed her first breakdown, Alex relived every moment of their relationship from a spectator's perspective. She could now see how he had always lived detached from her and the boys. They spent the last six years walking on the same road, only Jaime was on the sidewalk while she had been trudging along on the sand.

One terrible morning, a question Alex never thought to ask suddenly surfaced as she woke. Why the move to San Rafael? She drew in a sharp breath as the answer came to her. She said out loud, "Exile."

Alex watched in her mind's eye as all of the jagged pieces fell into place. What she thought of as a loving marriage, Jaime saw as a coup. Through emotional engineering, he overthrew

Alex from the restaurant. He managed to banish her, Leah, and Quico from their business. Alex's hands covered her ears as she remembered how Quico tried to warn her, and how she punished and pushed him away.

Leah, Alex thought, covering her eyes. I almost sent my sister to the loony bin because of him! But why? Leah was never a threat to anyone! Alex remembered Jaime's insistence at having Leah declared legally unfit to manage her own affairs. She thought of the property their father had left them, and then of Leah's book royalties.

Alex rolled her face onto her pillow and indulged in one more cry, knowing it would be her last. A cold, hard wrath quickly filled the void left by the invisible agony of depression.

Chapter 15
DULCE PREPARES FOR HER FIRST US SHOW

DULCE WAS PACKING for her first U.S. show being held in the Mission District. Since *Galería* was so close to her studio, she did not bother with crates. She was kicking up newspapers to make sure she had not forgotten anything when the phone rang.

"Yeah?"

"Is this Dulce?" a man's voice said.

"Depends," Dulce said.

There was a moment's hesitation. "This is Gabriel Luna."

Dulce knew exactly who he was. They met when she and Tessa picked Mrs. Anaya up after cleaning his house. Still, she could not resist keeping him hanging. Dulce waited a few beats, before she said, "Hey, Gabriel from Telegraph Hill. I'm guessing you got my invitation?"

"Yes, and thanks. I've been expecting it for some time."

"What can I say—art, like fine wine, takes time," Dulce said, without elaborating about Carolyn. Her grief was ebbing, but still close to the surface.

"I'm sure that's true. I just wanted to let you know that I'm planning on being there, with my checkbook."

"Great! I'll let Tessa know you're coming."

Hearing the smile in her voice, Gabriel said, "Am I that easy to read?"

"About as easy as a clock, at noon."

Gabriel laughed. "See you and Tessa on Thursday."

"Ay te huacho," Dulce said before hanging up. She was about to dial Tessa's number when Gordo, a high school student she was mentoring, returned from loading up Pepe. After all this time, Leah's truck was still coming in handy.

"Anything else?" Gordo said.

Dulce caught sight of Carolyn, just hanging there, all by herself. "One more piece."

Chapter 16

ALEX CATCHES UP WITH HER LIFE

ALEX SAT UP and rubbed her neck for a while, and then her arms. She got out of bed and unsteadily shuffled to the shower. She began compiling a to-do list in her head as warm water flattened the waves in her greasy hair. First, I'll make amends with everyone I've hurt, starting with Leah, then Quico. And no more judging Tessa or Dulce, even when they make imbecilic choices. From now on, I'll be as supportive as they are.

Alex took her time washing and conditioning her hair. She shaved under her arms, and then mowed the hair on her legs, while thinking, I'll call my attorney for the name of a good divorce lawyer. I'll put the house in San Rafael on the market. Oh, and I'll bury a statue of St. Joseph in the yard for a speedy sale.

Alex shut off the faucets and was halfway out of the claw foot tub when she realized, with a start, that she had never fired Jaime. How could I have let so much go and still have kept him on? Suddenly worried about the state of the restaurant and her financial affairs, Alex quickly toweled off before dressing.

But something was not right. Her polyester pants were not staying up and her bra was loose. Alex wiped the steamy mirror with her towel in big circles. The thinner Alex staring back caught her off guard. She had been on the heartbreak diet for four months. Alex smiled and her reflection smiled back. What a great way to start the rest of my life!

≈

In the kitchen, Alex could hear cello music playing from unseen speakers. Leah was busy jotting something down in a three-ring binder. Alex scanned the index cards, ingredients, and measuring utensils on the counters and figured she was working on the new cookbook.

"Hi. Where are the boys?" Alex said, crossing her arms.

"Alex, you're up!" Leah said, turning. She wanted to hug her sister, but feared the sudden movement would send her back to bed. "They're at school."

"School. I knew that," Alex said, still foggy. "Can I go with you to pick them up?"

"Of course. They are going to be so happy to see you. But it won't be for a while. I just dropped them off. It's Carla's birthday. She's Junior's best friend, and they're having a party for her after school."

Alex felt deep and profound humility. Leah had whole-heartedly taken over as a full-time parent to her sons. How can I ever thank you for keeping my babies safe, loved, and happy?

"Would you like some coffee?" Leah said. "I'll bring it out to the garden. It's such a beautiful day."

Fighting tears, Alex nodded. She wandered out the back door and into the loud sunlight. Momentarily blinded, she closed her eyes and enjoyed the contrast of the warm sun and the cool breeze on her face. She inhaled air fragrant with basil, mint, and the tangy scent of the sea. So, she thought, this is the world.

Leah joined Alex, handing her a thick ceramic mug. Alex thanked her. She took a sip of coffee. It tasted better than she remembered. "What are those plants over there? They're beautiful," she said, pointing with her chin.

"Those are lily of the Nile, or African lilies. I traded Mrs. Orejon a crumb cake for two plants, one producing purple and one producing white lilies." Leah said, waiting for Alex to choose a chair. "You remember Mrs. Orejon, don't you?"

"Oh yeah," Alex said, sitting down. "She used to make us clap our hands when we walked through her garden. Why was that?"

Leah settled in the seat next to her. "So we could not take clippings of her plants."

Alex's head suddenly felt as heavy as a kettle bell. "I am so sorry for being such a bad sister."

"No, that's not true," Leah protested, lightly touching Alex's arm. "You were my protector. I would never have made it without you."

"Some protector," Alex snorted. She began to cry. Through tears, she confessed her own apathy when Jaime wanted to place her in an asylum. Alex told her of that morning's dark epiphany. When she heard herself say, "He never loved me," it made her heartsick.

Leah thought about Yumi before carefully speaking. "You cannot punish yourself over things that never happened, or what has already taken place. This, right now, is all that matters. We need to appreciate this moment, because this is all there really is."

Alex was impressed. "Is that your secret to happiness?"

Leah nodded, surprised that Alex considered something so obvious a secret.

Remembering Jaime and the restaurant, Alex's face

darkened. "So, what have I missed?" Her lungs tightened in her slightly narrower chest. As scary as the truth might be, she was sure that not knowing was about to kill her.

As if reading her mind, Leah said, "You do not have to worry about Jaime. He's gone. Maybe back to Mexico. He disappeared the day after you dropped the charges."

Alex was having trouble processing this. All she could say was, "Gone?"

"He got into a little trouble, but I really should start from the beginning. When you said that you were going to drop the charges against him, we knew we could not stop you from making the call. You and the boys were safe here, but we needed to protect your finances and the restaurant.

It was all Tessa's idea. Dulce called our attorney, pretending to be you and told him to freeze all of your joint accounts with Jaime. Dulce called our broker, again, pretending to be you and requested that none of your holdings be moved, or transferred without your written approval."

Alex mechanically blinked. "And she got away with that?"

"I had already spoken with them. I told them about the...rape, and mailed a copy of the police report. They were expecting to hear from you, so when Dulce called, she did not have to say much. They did most of the talking." Leah smiled sheepishly. "She's a really good mimic."

"Didn't all of that stuff require my signature?"

Leah nodded. "When you signed the paperwork for the restraining order, you also signed the other papers."

Alex vaguely remembered signing and initialing dozens of papers.

"After Jaime was released from jail, he went straight to the bank and tried to withdraw your savings. When the teller told him they needed your signature, he became really upset, and left. He returned with the forms he tried to fill out and your forged signature. When the manager asked Jaime to leave, Jaime reached through the teller's window and tried to strangle him. Jaime was arrested, and taken to jail."

"No way," was all Alex could say.

Leah's eyes became moist. "Dulce was in San Francisco. Carolyn's cancer came back, only this time it was in her bones. She passed away in April."

Alex rubbed her dry face. "Oh, God. I do remember that." They stared at the sea.

Leah searched Alex's face, to make sure it was OK to continue. "Dulce heard about Jaime's arrest, and she called us, here. I gave her the combination to the safe in your office. She was emptying it when she heard Jaime, downstairs. We found out later that Feo had bailed him out of jail.

Dulce made it out of your office and called the police from our apartment. When she heard Jaime screaming, she knew he was at the empty safe. She grabbed Velvet and snuck out of the building through the outside stairs, where she heard glass breaking inside. When the police arrived, Jaime was trying to set the bar on fire.

Gilbert, I mean, Officer Garcia and Officer Yuen put out the fire, but Jaime got away. There was very little damage, mostly broken liquor bottles." Alex's face was as white as salt. "I guess that's enough for now."

"No!" Alex said, wanting to go back to bed and burrow under layers of blankets. Leaning her head back on the wicker mesh, she waved a limp hand. "Go on."

Chapter 17
DULCE'S EXHIBIT

"IT LOOKS LIKE a really good turnout," Philip, *Galería De La Raza's* director, said to Dulce, Tessa, and Melanie. They glanced around the crowded room with appreciation. Their eyes followed the spillover crowd to the sidewalk. "We've already sold 15 of the 17 larger pieces and several more offers have been made for Carolyn," he said, pinching his lips together.

Dulce knew Philip wanted her to ask him for how much? She did not bite. "Like I already said, Carolyn is not for sale. I'll tell you what, put a 'sold' card under her, but don't put a price." Philip left to do her bidding.

Glancing at the watch on Tessa's wrist, Dulce said, "The film's about to start."

"What film?" Melanie said.

"I got a reel of Disney's *Sleeping Beauty* and me and some *Galería* people dubbed a new soundtrack over the original. I wrote the script myself. It's called *Huevona*." Philip was back. "I need to borrow her," he said, leading Dulce by the elbow to a group of people with expectant faces.

Seeing Melanie's quizzical gaze, Tessa said, *"Huevona* is a derogatory term for 'lazy.'"

"I guess that explains why it wasn't in my textbooks," Melanie said, processing the new word. "So, Princess Aurora was not actually cursed, but lazy?"

Tessa cringed. "I'm almost afraid to watch it."

Looking over at "Carolyn," Melanie said, "I think it's sweet, how she's refusing to sell that strange painting she did of Carolyn."

"It's not a painting, exactly," Tessa said. She had never mentioned the tattoo to Melanie, and was surprised to see it here. Mel's family already thought Mexicans were a bunch of savages. Why prove them right?

The piece did not look like Dulce's paintings on black velvet, or any of the other eclectic works. It was more rudimentary, like a chalk outline of a body. On the canvas was a richly colored octopus with tentacles stretching the length of the appendages.

"An ink drawing?" Melanie guessed.

"Sort of," Tessa said. "Actually, it's Carolyn's tattoo."

Melanie stared at Tessa with blank astonishment. Her head whipped back to the tattoo. "You're kidding?"

Tessa shook her head. "I wish I was. She bequeathed it to Dulce."

Melanie's features shift a thousand times as it sank in. "I'll meet you in the screening room," she murmured.

Tessa watched as she walked zombie-like into the cluster of people in front of "Carolyn."

During the opening credits of *Huevona*, the dark and windowless room filled up like a crowded elevator. For Tessa, it was surreal to watch this childhood favorite while listening to the dubbed voices. In Dulce's version, the three good fairies, or *comadres*, were complaining, with thick accents, about how the king and queen did not want to baptize their baby.

"Your friend is a very disturbed person," someone said

into Tessa's right ear.

The warm breath made Tessa's spine tingle. "Isn't she, though?" she said, sounding like a proud parent.

"I think she is going to do well in the art world. In fact, I bought two of her paintings," Gabriel said, now standing next to her.

"She'll be happy to hear that you honored the two-painting minimum," Tessa said, staring into his handsome face.

"Is your mom here? I'd like to say hello and meet your father."

"No, they couldn't make it. They're babysitting Velvet, Dulce's daughter."

They watched the film for a while, in silence. Tessa was hyperaware that she was standing next to the man she had thought about every day since they met. The edges of his business card were fuzzy, like fabric, from being handled so much. She had even tried calling him a couple of times, but chickened out when the receptionist answered.

Recently, Tessa had convinced herself that she built him up, romantically. They had only spent a few minutes together, several months back. How could she possibly feel anything real for him?

In the film, the mere touch of an appliance, a spinning wheel, wears *Huevona* out. She, and her lazy parents, take a really long siesta. With no paycheck, the gardeners take off and the landscaping around the castle *se va al carajo*.

Tessa laughed. She caught Gabriel staring at her from under his fringe of thick black lashes. She expected him to look away; instead, their eyes locked. In that moment, they were the only two people in the room.

❧

Philip pulled Dulce away from Tessa and Melanie to introduce her to the press. A lanky reporter from a local newspaper asked Dulce to elaborate on the piece called "Carolyn." Raising her snapping brown eyes to his, Dulce said, "People aren't just good subjects *in* art; they make good materials *for* art."

Chapter 18

DULCE BECOMES INSPIRED

EVERYONE WHO READ about "Carolyn" in the newspapers, or saw the story on the news, had a strong opinion about the artist. One critic referred to Dulce as "barbaric" and her work as "an abomination against art reminiscent of the Nazi exploitation of Jews."

As a rebuttal, an article by a Chicano professor at the University of California, Berkeley, stated that Dulce's art medium was culturally innate. "The Aztec high priests were known to peel off the skins of the sacrificial victims. They would roll the skins onto their own bodies and over their heads. Dulce Racelis may be genetically predisposed to this ritual and has tapped into her acute indigenous instincts." Dulce had to laugh at that one.

Within days, stacks of mail addressed to Dulce were arriving at *Galería*. Mixed in with the love and hate mail, a letter with "Huntsville Prison" stamped in red ink caught her attention. It was from a death row inmate in Texas, asking her to take his tattoos. He was scheduled to die by lethal injection.

Dulce wrote him back, asking him why he wanted to leave her his tattoos. Two weeks later, he replied.

Dear Dulce,

You don't know how good it is to get mail. I don't need stamps or anything, but thanks for asking.

I guess I should start from the beginning. My wife, Sonia, had a job and I didn't. I felt real bad I couldn't take care of her and our three kids (Isabel is five, Richard and Robert are my twin boys—they are both four). I mean I was the man of the house.

It wasn't like I wasn't trying to find work. I filled out applications everywhere. But no one called me back.

I went to this grocery store, that looks like a warehouse and the manager asked me if I speak Spanish. I said I could. We talked for a long time in English and Spanish. He tells me they're hiring and the job has benefits and when can I start. I say I can start right now.

He tells me to fill out an application, then he got called away. I sat in his office all excited and I started filling out the application. There were math problems on the second page. I did the first few multiplication problems, but they got harder and then there was division. I don't know long division, so I couldn't finish it. That piece of paper couldn't of hurt me more if it had fists. I shoved the application into my pocket and left.

I ran into a friend named Jesse from the old days. He wanted to know if I was up for a party with chips and parents, his funny way of saying he had some PCP. I got into my old ways and started using again. Sonia knew something wasn't right, but she was scared to even think about what I was doing, and she never said nothing.

Everything went bad real fast. I had already spent the grocery money on dust and there was no food in the house. I told Sonia that I would go shopping tomorrow. So now I was trapped. No groceries, and no money to buy groceries.

I knew Jesse had money (some was mine) and dust at his house. I was going to go over there and take both. Jesse and his wife wouldn't be home because they work, and his mother babysat.

I put my kids in the car and took them over to Jesse's house. I started thinking about how good Jesse had it. I was no better than an old lady watching kids and I started getting real mad.

When I got to his house, I told my kids to play in the front yard. Jesse's mom opened the door and I said I left my jacket there. I went into Jesse's room to look for his stash and couldn't find it. If I'd just kept cool everything would have turned out so different.

But I started tearing the place apart. I flipped the mattress and I could hear things breaking. I remember seeing Jesse's mom come in. She was carrying the baby and the little girl was holding on to her skirt. Her face was all scared and the kids were crying. I said, "Where is it?" She handed me one of Jesse's jackets. I grabbed it out of her hand and threw it. I said, "Where is it?" She did it again, this time with a different jacket.

The next thing I know, I'm looking out the window and breathing hard. I could see my kids playing some game they just made up. I looked down and saw Jesse's mom staring at me. Only she was dead. Jesse's baby boy wasn't moving either. He was on the rug, next to her and looked just like a doll. I looked around for Jesse's daughter, and I started crying. The dresser was on top of her and all I could see were her little legs. I was too scared to see if she was alive, so I left her under there.

I wish I had pulled the dresser off of her 'cause she comes and visits me every night in my dreams. She doesn't have a face.

I was covered in blood. I tried to wash the blood off of me in the sink, but there was too much. I took a shower and put on Jesse's clothes.

I kept looking for the money and his stash, but never found it. I took the money in Jesse's mom's purse, and then I went into the kitchen and filled a couple of grocery bags with their food. Sonia said to be sure to get milk and eggs, but they were out of eggs too. I went outside, got my kids and left. Dulce, I killed two innocent babies and a nice *abuelita* for six dollars, bus change, and two bags of groceries.

I'm not making excuses for what I did, but none of it was real. It was like I was watching everything on an old black and white TV that skips. I mean, if I had seen what I did on a movie, I would feel something, right? I would say, "Dang! That dude's all messed up!"

The police found the application in the pocket of the pants I left at Jesse's house. When I was arrested I wanted to plead guilty, but my lawyer talked me out of it. He said, with all of the dope in my system, I would get life. I was found guilty in less than an hour and they sentenced me to death. It goes to show you that lawyers don't know nothing.

Well, that's my story. I try to make my peace with God every day. I am scheduled for execution in two months. I don't know where I'm going, but I'm in hell right now. Most people don't know this, but hell is not being able to hug and smell my kids. Hell is not sleeping next to my wife. Hell is knowing that I've made their lives so much harder than they already were.

So, here's why I want to give you my tattoos. I need to tag the world when I go. I want you to take the tattoos and hang them in your show, so people I'm never going to meet will know that I was here. If one of them is walking down the same road, I want to warn him. I want him to look at the names of my kids that used to be over my heart. I want him to see the spider-web that used to be on my elbow and I want to say, "No matter how bad it is, you still have a chance!"

Thanks Dulce and may God bless you, and keep you safe from people like me.

Paz,

Robert (Sneeker) Vargas

Dulce wrote him back, agreeing to take the tattoos. She called Carolyn's attorney to make the arrangements.

Chapter 19
FLASHBACK TO ALEX'S 18TH BIRTHDAY

ALEX TOOK HER PLACE at the head of the horseshoe-shaped table, in between her mother and sister. The overhead lights were dimmed as two busboys trundled in the cake, their faces serious with concentration.

Dulce turned back to Tessa. "Unless Alex has a blow dryer back there, she's not gonna be able to put out that towering inferno with just one breath."

Alex lit up as if by footlights, smiled as the guests sang "Happy Birthday" in a chorus of accents. Closing her eyes, she fervently made the same three-fold wish, for popularity, beauty, and a boyfriend, that never came true. Only this time, she replaced "boyfriend" with "husband."

Alex focused like a swimmer getting ready to compete. She drew in a deep breath and began to blow a fine stream of air mere inches from the lower glinting flames. Her head banked back and easily blew past the second tier. As she reached the final tier, a dead candle, right smack in the middle of the cake, flickered back to life.

As Alex blew out the final mocking flame, Tessa was surprised to see Dulce smiling. "Why are you so happy?" she said, tersely. Tessa was starting college at Stanford in the fall, as pre-med. Her wish for a full scholarship had just gone up in smoke.

"Because, I made a counter-wish, that's why."

Tessa stared at her a moment, as though she was translating the words. She said, *"¿Qué?"*

"I wished for the opposite of what I wanted. When Alex missed that candle, like I knew she would, my wish didn't come true. So, what I don't want to happen isn't gonna happen." Dulce was heading to Jakarta the day after graduation and was going to backpack through Southeast Asia. She had wished for a boring trip.

Tessa crossed her arms and glared. "You're saying that the opposite of what I wished for is going to come true?" She shook her head. "Do me a favor. Leave your brain to science. I have got to see what's in there."

Dulce's eyes sparkled. "Ooh, make that your wish for next year!"

Alex's *Tío Chúy* pushed himself heavily away from the table. His forgotten napkin fell from his lap when he stood up and announced, "It's time for the birthday girl to open her presents."

"What did you get her?" Dulce said to Tessa.

"I made a scrapbook of her first year at the restaurant, starting with the press release I wrote to the food critics."

"Are the flyers I made in there?"

Tessa nodded. "Of course, and all of the reviews, before and after pictures of the restaurant and the staff. Other mementos too, like matchbooks and cocktail napkins."

"That's nice too." Cupping her hand around her mouth, Dulce yelled, "Open mine first! It's the really big one!"

Dulce's present was the size of a plank and was wrapped in the Sunday comics, with *"Vieja"* written in thick Magic Marker strokes. Leah and her mother stood up and quickly cleared the dishes to make room.

Normally, Alex was really careful about not damaging the wrapping paper, but seeing how Dulce was too cheap to fork out money for a store-bought roll, she tore it to shreds. At the same moment, everyone read, "Alejandra's Restaurante" elegantly carved in curvy letters.

Dulce had signed up for a wood shop course offered by the city to make the gift for Alex. She had gone to some pains to match the wood with the bar's inlaid details and in choosing a warm stain that would stand out a little. Tilting her head, Dulce nodded slowly, satisfied with the way the letters had turned out.

It was suddenly quiet in the banquet room. *Tío Chúy* deliberately cleared his throat. "In memory of your father, my brother Ernesto, you cannot change the restaurant's name."

Mrs. Cernuda's eyes gazed up to heaven before resting on her brother-in-law. She gave an almost imperceptible nod for him to continue, but he did not catch it. Her second nod, better timed, was as abrupt as a hoe striking hard dirt.

"Oh. If you change the name of the restaurant, you will be erasing your father from this place, his place. He left you everything; can't you leave him this little?"

Alex, red-faced, stared at her uncle.

"Cacahuates is not an appetizing name," Leah said. No one in the room so much as coughed. Suddenly the center of so much unwanted attention, she felt forced to explain. "The name was fine when the business was a *taqueria* on a dirt lot, but it does not fit with what Alex has created here. Caca—"

"Can we talk about this later? *Tenemos* company," their mother interrupted.

Dulce's jaw dropped as her widening eyes turned to Tessa. "That's the most words I've ever heard Leah say!"

Tessa watched as the guests took sides and argued with the ardor reserved for orphan causes. This, right here, was exactly what she was not going to miss at college. She was ready to disassociate herself from these people and their notions—old-fashioned to insane.

Tessa shook the thought free as she remembered the sign. If Dulce had just carved "Cacahuates," like a normal person would have done, no one would have thought twice about changing the name. Her anger dissolved as she worked it through. If Dulce had not forced the issue right now, in front of everyone, Alex would never have dared to even hope to change the name. What Dulce had given her was more than the sign; she had given Alex the opportunity to make the change, without appearing selfish or disrespectful.

Tessa's thoughts were broken off as Dulce poured a melted margarita from a pitcher into a glass. As several of the voices filled with fury, Dulce grinned. She mouthed, "Some party, huh?"

Chapter 20
ALEX'S 25TH BIRTHDAY

Alex decided to celebrate turning 25 in Mendocino with the girls. It would be their first time together on her birthday in six years. To commemorate the occasion, and her weight loss, she bought herself a bathing suit. It was a black one-piece with an attached floral skirt.

She was looking forward to the simple pleasure of feeling the sun on the back of her thighs. Having shed a big chunk of her 'baby fat,' she wanted to show off her new body, which was looking a lot like her old body. Who would have thought that the journey back to average would be so arduous?

As planned, Tessa, Dulce, and Melanie arrived at Leah's minutes before Alex and the boys. On the drive up the coast, Tessa casually mentioned to Melanie their strange tradition of making wishes on Alex's birthday cake, without going into any detail. Now huddled around the coffee table, Melanie could see that they were serious.

"Alex missed a candle by accident when she turned 18," Dulce was saying. "Whatever she wished for must of come true, 'cause she did it on purpose when she turned 19."

Tessa studied Dulce. "What did you wish for?" she said.

"Huh?" Dulce said, feigning ignorance.

"The boring trip wish was when Alex turned 18. What did you wish for when she turned 19?"

Leah stared at Dulce with interest.

Dulce did something that was so rare it may have been a first. She blushed. As if on cue, Velvet plopped down onto Dulce's lap—her personal folding chair. Dulce fingered the scar on the palm of her left hand. "I wished I would never be a parent," she said. She kissed the top of her daughter's head.

They heard Alex's horn blaring outside. "So, what's Alex gonna do?" Dulce said, as they stood up.

"She's going to skip a candle. We need to wish for the opposite of what we want," Tessa said.

As Leah opened the front door and waved, Melanie said, "May I make a counter-wish too?"

❧

"God. Where was the fire?" Alex said, miffed by the other's race at the final stretch.

Leah's house suddenly seemed to come to life with the arrival of Alex and the boys. Once the noisy brood settled in, the women gathered in the kitchen to make tamales for Alex's birthday dinner. Leah had already prepared the pork filling and made the *masa* in her industrial mixer. All that was left were the fun parts: sipping fruity sangria while assembling the tamales.

Alex sat at one end of the old kitchen table, spooning *masa* from a large bowl onto two overlapping husks. She alternately handed them off to Tessa or Melanie, who spooned in spiced pork before topping each one with a black olive. They in turn handed the tamales to Dulce and Leah to tie the ends closed with shredded pieces of wet husk. Velvet and Joaquin, Alex's youngest son, oversaw the process from their high chairs, while stuffing themselves with broken olives.

Dulce was explaining how she had just received her fourth

tattoo when Alex interrupted. "I think that is the sickest thing I've ever heard." She broke her vow never to judge Dulce or Tessa days after she made it.

"Hey, they're the ones that came to me," Dulce said, enjoying Alex's ire. It felt like old times.

"First, you hang your girlfriend's backside, naked, on a hook for people to just gawk at. Now you're collecting tattoos like some deranged grim reaper? Have you no respect for the dead?"

"Oh come on, Alex," Tessa said. "Carolyn was an artist, remember? She knew Dulce would exhibit her. And she really would have loved her debut."

"Who has contacted you?" Melanie said.

"So far, I've gotten letters from prisoners, a business man, a biker, sick people, oh, and a Holocaust survivor!" Dulce was clearly excited about her new pen pals.

Alex made a face. "Just when I think you've reached the bottom, you go and find a lower level. Don't you know that the Jews are the Mexicans of Europe?"

Trying not to laugh, Tessa said, "I thought that was the Irish."

"No. They're the Mexicans of the British Isles," Alex corrected with something of the schoolmarm in her tone.

"Oh yeah? Who are the Mexicans to the Mexicans?" Dulce said, expecting Alex to see the joke at her expense.

"Indians," Alex said, like the answer was obvious. The conversation ended abruptly when two muddy boys raced in from the backyard, depositing birthday mud pies on their mother's lap.

❦

That evening, the women watched the sunset from the beach at the end of the sandy trail near Leah's house, while the children played. Although they were seated close together, each woman was alone with her thoughts. The kids scanned the ebbing tide for bubbles in the sand before digging for crabs. They squealed with delight when they felt the crawlers tickling their small palms. Theirs were the only footprints on the swept beach.

After the sun had dropped behind the sea and the sky was the color of the California poppies in Leah's yard, they made their way back to the house. Greeted by the aroma of steaming tamales, all were instantly famished. The mood was jovial as they carried platters of food out to the table under the grape arbor lit up by twinkling lights and Japanese paper lanterns.

They spoke of food while feasting on avocados stuffed with crabmeat, tamales, spicy plantains, street corn on the cob, and drank *agua de fresa*. Like most people recovering from an addiction, Alex made a show of serving herself only one *tamal*.

After the quiet lull that follows a good meal, Leah got up and stacked a few dishes. The motion set off chatter and busy hands as all of the women began to clear the table for the birthday cake. Alex had requested a cake with the fewest calories possible, so Leah made an angel food cake with strawberries from her garden, and low-fat whipped cream.

As Leah brought out the birthday cake, sets of eyes darted around in quick and silent conversations. Tessa was going to wish she would not win the lottery, especially not get five of the six numbers. All she did not want was enough money to pay off the rest of her education. Dulce was going to wish for a dull and uneventful life for herself and Velvet. Melanie decided to wish that she never found love. She glanced sideways at Dulce.

Aware that the wishes held no power and never had, Leah wished for absolutely nothing.

Alex had given a lot of thought to the wish she made six years ago. At some point in time, it occurred to her that she should have wished for what she really needed, instead of what she thought she wanted. She planned on getting it right this time.

Standing over the cake, she closed her eyes. I wish Jaime needed me as much as I need him. Opening her eyes, she stared at the ring of flames. As she drew in a deep breath, Junior and Andrés leaned in, puckering. They blew hot air and spittle all over the cake.

Startled, the women looked up.

Dulce said, "Alex gets a do-over!" But it was already too late. Pretending to be Godzilla and Rodan, the boys knocked over the dead candles they said were telephone poles before clawing the cake.

❧

Dulce, Tessa, and Leah carried what was left of dessert back into the kitchen. When out of earshot, Dulce whispered vehemently, "What does it mean?"

"I'm not sure," Tessa said. It was quiet as she and Dulce pondered similar questions: Alex blew out none of the candles, so does that mean all of the wishes are null and void? All of the candles were blown out, so does that mean the wishes are still on? And, since all of the candles were blown out by the boys, will the counter-, or actual, wishes come true?

Under the grapevine arbor, Melanie and Alex chatted.

Melanie watched, with amazement, as the sugar in the boys' systems was immediately converted into mischievous energy. Snatching Andrés' party hat, Junior made a mad dash toward the beach trail. Alex scooped up Joaquin and ran after them. Melanie hoisted Velvet onto her hip and followed.

Tessa and Dulce were debating the finer points of possible outcomes when the phone rang. Leah answered, hoping it was her mother calling to wish Alex a happy birthday. Leah's face seemed to fall. She made feeble attempts to interrupt the caller.

Grabbing the phone from her, Dulce said into the receiver, "This better not be you!"

"Get Alex!" Jaime demanded.

"Get fucked!" Dulce shot back. She slammed the phone down.

"What did he say to you?" Tessa said, to Leah.

"He said we can't watch the boys all of the time."

"That's a threat," Tessa said, picking up the phone to call the police. She quickly covered the mouthpiece. "His phone's off the hook," she mouthed.

As Tessa listened intently, she noticed Leah's phone had a built-in answering machine. She pushed the record button. They watched as the cassette tape silently turned. After a minute, Tessa hung up. She hit the rewind button. "I hope this works," she said, pushing play.

"...sit down and have another drink. Let the lawyers handle it," a voice slurred in Spanish from the answering machine.

"That's Feo," Leah said, putting her hand close to her throat.

"I can't do that. Her lawyers are going to say that her

stupid little sister owns have of everything. Can you believe that? And they will try to give me something like..." There was a pause. "...much less than half of everything. Hey, I've earned more than that. I mean, look at that *torta!*" There was laughter, then, "No, I'm taking my boys back to Chiapas. If Alex wants them, she's going to have to really pay."

"Wait until they're in San Francisco. We'll help you get them back."

"No! I want them now!" Jaime whined, drunkenly. "Where are my keys?" There were muffled voices. Someone must have noticed that the phone was off the hook. They heard a rattling sound, before the other end went silent.

"I'm calling the police," Tessa said.

"Why?" Dulce said. "What's he gonna do? Show up in Mendocino at three in the morning and start knocking on doors?"

"A drunk motorcyclist is about to get on the road. I need to notify the police," Tessa said.

As she dialed 911, Dulce rolled her eyes to Leah. "Jaime the criminal mastermind is gonna kidnap the three boys and make a clean getaway on his motorcycle."

It was a long day for the driver of the Chevy truck. He and his girlfriend had been to a wedding in Manteca. They would have spent the night at a motel, but could not justify the cost, since they were only 70 miles from home.

When they reached the fog on the Golden Gate Bridge, both sighed with relief. "I can't wait to get out of this dress," she said.

He watched as she hiked up her skirt. She pulled her

nylons off. He smiled as her panties rolled off with them. "Ooh," he said, "let me see."

At that moment, a single headlight from oncoming traffic veered toward them, snapping the driver's attention back to the road. They saw a flash of flannel, right before feeling the impact of rubber, metal, and then flesh hit the windshield.

Chapter 21
CHINA RECEIVES A TITLE

THE PHONE RANG early the next morning with the news of Jaime's accident. Moments after the call, the women and sleepy children piled into three cars. The silent caravan drove back to San Francisco.

❧

Nearing the Mission district, Leah felt her pulse speed up. She had stayed clear of the City since the incident with the attack car and had never planned on returning. Yet, she knew something beyond her control would eventually pull her back. As she reached the edge of the Mission she worried that it was too soon for her to be there.

At a red light, she watched an electric bus go by, reminding her of a sniffing dog on a tight leash. After several buses passed, she noticed the new mural on the side of a corner store. She stopped breathing altogether.

The mural must have been done by Dulce. It was of a young woman in a simple white slip dress, looking beatifically toward heaven. Her hands were folded in prayer. The pink ribbon stenciled under her read:

In Memory of Our Loving Daughter
Christina "China" Nieves
Pray for us

❧

"No! That can't be right!" Dulce said, shaking her head vigorously. She, Tessa, Leah, and Melanie were sitting in the waiting room at San Francisco General while Alex visited Jaime in ICU. "Are you saying that you saved that *tapado's* life?"

Tessa nodded, gloomily. "The police were alerted of the drunk motorcyclist and spotted Jaime as he drove onto the bridge. They were in pursuit when he swerved and took a header into oncoming traffic. They administered CPR until the ambulance arrived."

Dulce leaned back in her chair. "You see, that just proves God's a man."

"Cheer up, Dulce. He has a spinal injury. He'll be paralyzed for the rest of his life," Tessa said, sardonically.

"That's something, I guess," Dulce said, mildly consoled.

After a long silence, Leah's curiosity got the best of her. "Has anyone seen the mural of China?"

Dulce and Tessa both smiled widely. "Didn't I tell you about that?" Dulce said, thinking back. "China's parents commissioned it. They paid me with a bag of crumbled *feria* from her shrine."

Tessa said, "They're on the campaign trail to sainthood and thought the exposure would be good. But they don't just want to make her a saint. China's parents want her to be the patron saint of kidnapped victims, and hostages." Dulce, Tessa, and even Leah began to laugh.

A look of consternation filled Melanie's face. "Who's China?"

"She's a friend of ours from the neighborhood," Tessa said.

"How did she die?" Melanie said.

Tessa sighed, thinking, oh boy. "China's not dead."

Melanie's eyebrows furrowed, "Wait, I thought a person had to be dead to be considered for sainthood?"

Tessa was about to explain when Dulce said, "Let me field this one." Turning to Melanie, she said, "China's parents disowned her for moving to New York. She graduated from film school out there. Anyway, after she left the Mish, her father told someone that she had disappeared."

"Why did he say that?" Melanie said.

"'Cause he's stupid and ignorant. When people started saying she was kidnapped and murdered, the church got all involved. When China heard that she was going to become a saint, she sent a documentary film crew to gather footage." Dulce grinned. "The way China put it, if they're gonna turn her life and death into a Fellini film, she's gonna film it and turn it into a documentary."

"How are China's parents dealing with the documentary and all of the public exposure?" Melanie said.

"I think they believe their own lie 'cause they've been working with the film crew. Mrs. Nieves even gave them a tour of their home. She cried when she showed them China's room. They got footage of all of it," Dulce said.

"Where are they staying?" Leah said.

"In the attic above our apartment," Dulce said.

"Is China here?" Leah said, hopefully.

Dulce swigged from her can of Pepsi. "She's gonna be here next week for the special mass in her honor."

Tessa chuckled. "The Roman Catholic Church just gave her the title of being 'Venerable.' It's the first step in becoming a saint."

Dulce smirked like the devil. "The crew even got footage of Padre Lucas pointing to the last spot China was seen in church when she was praying for the hostages in Iran. There's a white smudge there."

All four were smiling mischievously as Alex returned from seeing Jaime.

❧

In the hospital parking lot, Tessa, Dulce, and Melanie accompanied Leah and a mildly sedated Alex to Pepe. With a wave, they watched as the two drove off. Turning to Dulce, Tessa said, "Gabriel's on his way to pick us up. We'll go to my house and get Velvet, and then drop you two off at your place."

"Or I can give her a ride," Melanie offered.

Dulce stared thoughtfully at Melanie. She nodded. "Sounds good."

A few minutes later, Gabriel pulled up. They were walking Tessa to his car when Tessa said to Melanie, "Call, if she gets out of control."

Smiling, Melanie said, "I think I can handle her."

"Oh yeah? We'll see," Dulce said.

Dulce and Melanie waved as Gabriel's BMW drove away. Remembering Melanie drove a convertible, Dulce said, "Can we put the top down?"

"Sure."

"You know what would be good right now? Food. You hungry? How about we go and get Velvet, then cruise to North Beach for some serious Italian food?"

Chapter 22
ALEX'S THIRD WISH COMES TRUE

WHEN ALEX WISHED that Jaime needed her, she did not expect anything this drastic. All the same, she was fine with the outcome. Alex reasoned that the result of the birthday wish was no more severe than it needed to be to ensure its outcome. So, in a way, it was Jaime's own doing.

While Jaime slowly recovered in the hospital, Alex sold the house in San Rafael and bought a fixer-upper in the Mission. She hired a construction crew to build a ramp and provide adequate maneuvering space within the house. A sliding door was installed in the bathroom, and the bathtub was replaced with a roll-in shower.

After being released from the hospital, Alex took Jaime to his new home. She pushed the wheelchair up the ramp behind the house, explaining their new schedules. It was beginning to dawn on him that the added role of nurse gave Alex total control over him. As she rolled the wheelchair through the back door, Jaime felt like he was about to be shoved off of a steep cliff.

Alex was not a stupid woman. She knew this was barely about love; it was about possession. She shrugged. While closing the back door, she thought, That works for me!

Serves four

or

Finå

Mexican Spanish y Slang Glossary

Abierto – Open

Abogángster – A corrupt lawyer; the word derives from abogado (lawyer) and gangster

Albóndigas – Meatballs; a traditional Mexican meatball soup; Spanish history traces the soup back to the Moors from the Arab invasion in 711 AD. Some food historians believe that albóndigas are of ancient Roman descent.

Abuelita – Granny; literally means 'little grandmother'

Agua de sandia – Watermelon water

Agua de fresa – Strawberry water

¡Aguas! – Watch out; head's up; what Latinos say when cops are spotted; literally means waters; historically, women in Mexico would holler the word before tossing dirty water from their window to warn passing people.

Amá – Mom; used mostly in rural areas of Mexico

Ándale pues – OK then; go on

Apúrate – Hurry up; hustle

¡Ay, Dios mío! – Oh my God!

¡Ay qué bella! – Oh, how beautiful!

Ay te huacho/ay te watcho – See you later

Babosa – Slug; dribbler; fool; simpleton

Barrida – Sweeping; a ritual cleansing for purification. An object (egg, rosemary brush, lemon, crucifix, etc.) is used to sweep away negative energies.

Bebé – The most common word for baby. Always masculine, even when referring to a girl.

Birria – A spicy Mexican meat stew usually made with goat, lamb or mutton

Bote, el – Literally means can; jail

Caca – Poop; a term meaning fecal matter used by Latina mothers to deter their kids from touching something

Cacahuates – Peanuts; an expletive kids use when grownups are within earshot, and vice versa; the loophole that turns crude profanity into benign food, like saying, son-of-a-biscuit, or kiss my ass-paragus

Caliente – Hot, sexy

Cantinflas – Mario Moreno Reyes (1911 - 1993) Actor; Charlie Chaplin of Mexico; Cantinflas made 49 films, but is best known for his role as Passepartout in the 1956 film *Around the World in 80 Days*.

Causa, la – The cause

Cerrado – Closed

Chale – From échale, means throw it out; no way

Chanclas – House slippers; flip flops worn typically by Latina mothers and can be easily removed to be thrown; the deadliest weapon known to Latino kids

China/os – Slang for person with curly hair; Asian; trousers

Chistes – Jokes

Chonies – Spanish slang for underwear; derived from the Spanish word for calzones

Chota, La – Police, the

Claro que sí – Of course

Comida – A meal, the principal meal taken in the mid or late afternoon

Criaturas – Kids; a cognate of 'creature,' is sometimes used as an affectionate term. Criatura is always feminine, even if it refers to a boy.

Crudo – Raw; Hungover

Cuco Sanchez – Singer, songwriter, guitarist, and actor; composer of nearly 200 songs, including songs for some of the movies he acted in.

Culo – Ass; booty; buttocks

Curandera – A woman who practices folk medicine; healer; a person who cures by using medicinal plants, charms, massage, and faith healing.

Día de Nuestra Señora de Guadalupe – The patron and symbol of Mexico; The Virgin of Guadalupe appeared to Juan Diego on Tepeyac Hill, bridging the worlds of the Aztec and that of the Spanish conquerors.

Doña – Mrs; used as a courtesy title before the name of a woman

¿Entiendes? – Do you understand?

Espanto – Terror; a more severe and potentially fatal form of susto

Exactamundo – Catch phrase of Fonzie from *Happy Days*. It is also the way some Anglos pronounce the Spanish word 'exactamente,' which means 'Exactly.'

Feria – Money; literally a fair or festival

Fútbol – Soccer; A highly respected sport in all countries except for the US

Gabacha/o – Pejorative term for an Anglo person

Guácala – Ewe! Yuck!

Guacamole – Derives from the Nahautl word 'ahuacamolli,' which translates to 'testicle sauce.'

Güera – Blonde; a term used for Latinas who have a fairer complexion and lighter hair/eyes.

Güey – Dude; bastard; fool; demeaning but used often with affection; from the term for a castrated bull

Hijo/a – Son or daughter.

Hijo de la chingada – Son of a bitch

Híjole – Jeez; a general expression of surprise, annoyance or exasperation

Huaraches – Leather sandals

Huevón/a – An extremely lazy male/female; someone with large huevos (eggs/ testicles)

Ja, ja – Ha, ha

Jamburger – Hamburger

Jamón – Ham; the bacon

Jefa – Mother or wife; chief

La señora que hace los cakes – The cake lady; usually hired because she is less expensive than the bakery, and for her relation to a community.

Limpia – Ritual cleansing; a cleansing of the body, emotions, mind and soul from negative energies. Traditionally, it is used to get rid of blockages. Some people believe that it removes witchcraft, curses and hexes.

Malinche – Literally means the captain's woman. Before she was Malinche, she was Malinali and was sold into slavery by her mother. The indigenous woman accompanied Hernán Cortés and played an active role in the Spanish conquest of Mexico. Seen by some as the traitor of the race; others see La Malinche as the founding figure of the Mexican race.

Mantilla – Lace veil

Mija – Term of affection; short from 'mi hija' meaning my daughter

Mojado – Spanish for wet; a racial slur for an illegal Mexican immigrant who crossed the US/Mexican border by swimming across the Rio Grande.

Naranjas – Literally means oranges; nope

¡No mames! – Derives from the word mamar meaning

'suck'; a vulgar or informal way to say you're kidding; stop messing around; no way

Novia, La – Bride; girlfriend

Ojalá que sí – I hope so; one of the most well-known words to come from the Arabic expression: 'ma sha Allah' which means 'should God will it.'

Orale – A greeting; right on; expression used to encourage someone to do a certain thing.

Otra vaga – Another loose one; another vagabond

Otros, los – The others; a derogatory way of referring to all non-Latinos

Papaya – Slang for pussy

Pedo – Literally means fart; intoxicated; problem; ¿Que pedo? also means, what's up?

Pendejas/os – Pubic hair, or anal hair; asshole; carries an extra implication of rank and willful incompetence

Pinche – An adjective to describe something as insignificant, lousy, miserable or worthless; literally means tight, stingy, ungenerous

Puta – Whore

Quetzalcoatl – Feathered Snake. One of the major deities of the Aztec, Toltecs, and other Middle American peoples. He is the creator of the sky; creator of the original cosmos and participated in the creation and destruction of various world periods.

¿Qué? – What?

¿Qué noticia? – What news?

¿Qué onda? – What's happening?

Quihubo /quihúbole – Greeting; What was there? How's it going?

Rajas – Roasted chile strips with cream, onions and

seasonings

Recuerdo – Memento, memory

Remedios – Remedies, cure; woman's name

Rosario – Wake; woman's name

Ruca – Literally means old woman; girlfriend

San Pancho – San Francisco

Sebeneleben – 7-Eleven

Se va al carajo – Goes to hell; going down the drain

Simón – Yeah! (from Sí)

Sinvergüenzo – A shameless person

Suave – Smoothly agreeable; pleasant

Suavitel – Cheap fabric softener marketed by Colgate-Palmolive

Suéter – Sweater

Susto – Scare; a loss of the soul due to a sudden frightening experience such as an accident, a fall, or witnessing any other potentially dangerous event.

Tapado – Covered; constipated; uptight

Tenemos company – We have company

Tía/o – Aunt; uncle

Tierra – Earth; home

Tin-Tan – Germán Valdés (1915 - 1973) Mexican actor, singer and comedian

Tonta – Dumb; foolish, silly

Torta – Literally means cake; derogatory slang for a fat female

Trampa – Tramp

Vato – Dude, pal, or brother; can also be used to refer to a fellow gang member

Vieja – Literally means old woman; girlfriend, wife

Yerbera – Herbalist

Acknowledgments

I am deeply indebted to the following people for reading the manuscript and making suggestions for its improvement: Wayne Dunn, Marilyn Bryan, Woody Minor, Melanie Rogers, Miriam Wolf, Martha Alicia Sandoval, Mia Sandoval, France Sandoval-Shima, Karen Thompson, Mark Shroeder, Louise Oram, Tyler Sack, Mira Kennedy, Jorge Carrerra, Bronwyn Harris, Cyndi Sutter and Andrea Montejo.

More books from
Harvard Square Editions

People and Peppers, Kelvin Christopher James

Gates of Eden, Charles Degelman

Love's Affliction, Fidelis Mkparu

Transoceanic Lights, S. Li

Close, Erika Raskin

Anomie, Jeff Lockwood

Living Treasures, Yang Huang

Leaving Kent State, Sabrina Fedel

Dark Lady of Hollywood, Diane Haithman

How Fast Can You Run, Harriet Levin Millan

A Cat Came Back, Simone Martel

Nature's Confession, J.L. Morin

No Worse Sin, Kyla Bennett

Stained, Abda Khan

Reader, I would love to hear your thoughts
on my book. If you enjoyed this book,
please leave a review!

CPSIA information can be obtained
at www.ICGtesting.com
Printed in the USA
LVHW031724070319
609858LV00003B/501/P